SMOKE, VAMPIRES, & MIRRORS

SASHA URBAN SERIES: BOOK 7

DIMA ZALES

♠ MOZAIKA PUBLICATIONS ♠

Published by Mozaika Publications, an imprint of Mozaika LLC.
www.mozaikallc.com

Cover by Orina Kafe
www.orinakafe-art.com

ISBN-13: 978-1-63142-515-8
Print ISBN-13: 978-1-63142-516-5

CHAPTER ONE

"NERO," I whisper loudly. Wriggling out of his embrace, I shake him. "Wake up."

His eyes snap open, then narrow in on my face as he jackknifes to a sitting position.

He must've noticed my panic.

"Did you have another nightmare?" he demands.

I blink, momentarily distracted. "*Another* nightmare? When did I have the first one?"

"You don't recall?" Lifting his hand, he rubs the back of my head as if I were a cat. "You were making whimpering noises and soft cries in the middle of the night. Woke me up twice."

Seriously, nightmares? How come I don't recall any?

Could I have dreamed about the upcoming apocalypse before I had my awake vision? But no. Dream-based visions went away when I gained conscious control. They must be run-of-the-mill nightmares—and they probably pale in comparison to grim reality.

Nero lowers his hand. "So what's wrong, then?"

I take in a breath, fighting the urge to put his hand back where it was. "I just had two nightmarish visions."

"Visions?" He frowns. "What visions?"

I draw in another breath and rattle out that Tartarus—the extremely powerful Cognizant who can feed on whole worlds—is coming to Earth for an all-he-can-eat buffet.

"I saw both of my parents as dried husks," I say, my chin trembling. "Everyone you and I have ever known will die."

Nero stares at me, then reaches out and pulls me against his powerful chest, his arms wrapping around me securely. Though soothing, his touch doesn't calm me—especially when I realize that he's not actually saying anything in reply to my story.

I was hoping for a "let's run to Earth and save everyone this very moment" kind of response.

Stroking my back, he kisses my temple. "You sure this wasn't a nightmare?" he murmurs, continuing to pet me as if I were a chinchilla.

I jerk away. "Of course I'm sure."

He studies me, then nods. "Okay. Given the circumstances, I had to ask."

"I was wide awake and stone-cold sober," I grit out. "And it was two visions in a row. I'm sure this Armageddon is the real deal." Jumping to my feet, I grab my clothes and furiously pull them on, then stuff the gate sword into the back of my pants.

"Fair enough." Nero stands up, unconcerned with his nudity. Not that he has any clothes—he flew here in his dragon form. Stepping toward me, he says, "I want you to tell me exactly what happened after I left Earth. Specifically, how you ended up becoming a vampire. You mentioned it briefly at the castle, but I want—"

"What?" My nostrils flare. "I tell you Earth is about to get destroyed, and you want me to tell you a campfire story?"

His jaw tightens. "I need to consider every variable."

"And I need to know what our plan of action is," I say sharply.

"So let me get this straight." Nero leans in. "You *don't* find it suspicious that Tartarus shows up so soon after Lilith and Nostradamus—two people who are obsessed with him?"

I stare at him. "I didn't get a chance to think about that."

Nero raises his eyebrows, waiting coolly, and I give in with a sigh. I tell him everything, starting with how the chorts attacked Felix and how they would've killed Mom and Dad if I hadn't turned myself in. When I get to the part where they tortured me, Nero's face looks so frightening I get the feeling the chorts are lucky they're already dead. I then tell him about Nostradamus's memories and his quest to avenge his family—who were killed by Tartarus—and how he prophesied to Lilith that Tartarus will be her doom.

"Then Felix used his power to get me Lilith's phone conversations, and I found out about the setup," I say toward the end. "She was the one who sicced the chorts on me, and I'm a vampire as a result of that. Can we act now? We need to—"

"Think before we 'act,'" Nero says. Switching to Russian, he adds, "Measure seven times, cut once."

"Assuming there's anything to cut after all the measuring," I grumble, recognizing the proverb from one of the textbooks I recently studied.

"You want to be proactive? How about you ask your seer powers what needs to be done."

"How about I what?" I gape at him.

"When I consult seers, I tell them my goal, and they look at the future to find a course of action that can bring about the goal in question."

"Oh." I bite my lip. "I've never tried something so direct."

"Do so now," Nero orders, his gaze falling to my lips.

"Fine." I close my eyes and do my best to calm down enough to jump into Headspace.

It takes me a few seconds to reach the necessary state of focus, but as soon as I do, I find myself floating, surrounded by vision shapes.

Shapes that don't seem to be interesting, as the tune they emit is reminiscent of elevator Muzak.

There's no way these bland visions have anything to do with Tartarus. If I had to guess, they probably foretell Fluffster talking about our yearly paper towel budget, or Felix prattling on about why he loves his favorite computer algorithm.

But if these are not what I need, how do I do what Nero said? How do I "tell" my powers I want to see a vision of something that will prevent Tartarus's arrival on Earth?

Well, since everything else in Headspace often involves the essence of concepts and people, why don't I try that?

Somehow.

I float there and do my best to get at the essence of the problem. I channel the grief I felt at seeing my parents' empty husks. For good measure, I also add in my annoyance at Nero for not instantly jumping into action, and my awe at the enormity of the task at hand.

Even though I'm not sure what I'm doing, it seems to work. New shapes show up around me, and they're as unsettling as the others were boring. The music they emit makes me wonder if I'm about to see a future where I personally skin every fluffy kitten on Earth in a ritual to make Tartarus go away.

Or make soup out of Fluffster and Lucifur.

Leave it to fate to turn something good—like preventing apocalypse—into something bad.

Metaphorically shivering, I float for a bit, unsure if I dare to touch the shapes in question.

Well, there's no helping it.

I must know.

Gathering my courage, I reach for the nearest shape and ready myself for the worst.

CHAPTER TWO

I WAKE up to the sound of familiar voices.

"*Batman v Superman* should still have a higher score on the movie review sites," Ariel says from somewhere. "Even the last *Matrix* movie—your own least favorite—has higher ratings."

"Why do you always have to bring *The Matrix* into it?" Felix grumbles. "Is it because you're still jealous that the first *Matrix* has better scores than any *Batman* ever?"

"I'm not going there again," Ariel says, and I can almost see her eyeroll. "You must at least agree that *Armageddon*—a movie that also stars Ben Affleck—shouldn't have a higher score than *Batman v Superman*."

The word Armageddon sends a jolt of adrenaline through my system, dispelling the remnants of my grogginess.

Sitting up, I rub my eyes.

Felix and Ariel are both looking at me with worried

expressions on their faces. Speaking in unison, they say, "How are you feeling?"

"I've had better days," I say, trying to figure out where we are.

The bland room doesn't have any furniture besides my bed, and there are no windows. It also smells vaguely of medicine—so maybe it's a nurse's office or a hospital room?

With a loud bang, the gray door behind my friends breaks into shards.

Hovering a few inches from the ground is Lilith—my biological mother and, on one of the Otherlands, an evil goddess.

Eyes turned into mirrors, she flies inside.

Ariel turns.

"Stand there, and don't move," Lilith orders in a honey-laced voice.

Ariel's body tenses as the glamour turns her into a mannequin.

"You too," Lilith croons to Felix, who instantly turns into a statue.

"Good job," she says to my friends before her eyes turn back to normal and she faces me. "Sasha, dear, how are you feeling?"

"What are you doing here?" I jump off the bed, staring her down.

"I'm here to check on you." Her beatific smile shows off her fangs. "Your well-being is very important to me."

"Yeah, right. Which is why you called the chorts and

told them to ask me about Rasputin. Are you going to pretend you didn't expect them to kill me?"

Her smile disappears without a trace. "I was working with a seer, which means I knew you'd turn. Every mother wants her children to reach their true potential. You should be thanking me for this."

"Uh-huh, sure. Thank you so very much. Getting tortured was a blast."

Frowning, Lilith floats down until her feet touch the gray linoleum floor. "If you're going to be an ungrateful brat, I'm going to stop playing nice mommy with you."

I stare at her uncomprehendingly. All the people she brutally killed in front of me, all attempts to get me to finish off the injured chorts—that was the *nice* version of her?

"It's a lot to take in," I lie, deciding I don't want her to turn off the charm.

But it's too late. She narrows her eyes and says, "Since you seem to hate me for no reason, how about I give you one—and make you that much stronger in the process." She looks at Ariel, then at Felix and says, "Eeny, meeny, miny, moe."

A horrible feeling grows in the pit of my stomach as her gaze lands on Felix.

"It's settled then," she says with a predatory smile. "I want you to kill *this* one."

I stare at her, dumbfounded, but she just stands there expectantly—like she really thinks there's a universe where I'd kill my friend just because a psycho asked me to.

"Listen," I say, putting more acting into it. "I'm not ungrateful, I just—"

"Did I not say it clearly enough?" She rubs her chin. "How about this? I *command* you to rip out his heart."

The word *"command"* slams into my brain like a truck, and I feel like I'm falling.

Except I'm not really falling. It's my free will and the core of my consciousness that are being banished somewhere deep down.

A millisecond after the strange sensation comes over me, I feel as though I'm locked in some secret underground bunker inside my own brain—and my body begins to move with a zombie-like determination.

"There you go," Lilith croons. "I know this can be tricky in the beginning."

From deep in my exile, I want my mouth to scream in horror, but nothing passes my lips.

Desperately, I will my body to halt, but that doesn't work either.

Before I can process what's happening, my right hand lifts in a marionette-like movement, then plunges into Felix's chest with a speed and strength I didn't know I was capable of.

Despite being under the influence of glamour, Felix screams in pain—but only for a second. Then he slumps around my hand, unconscious.

What am I doing? What is my body doing? How can this be happening?

"No. Please stop!" is what I would be shouting if my mouth worked.

Oblivious to my will, my body grabs Felix's no longer-beating heart, rips it out, and tosses it at Lilith's feet.

What remains of Felix collapses into a bleeding heap of meat on the floor.

In the depths of my mind, I'm howling in horror and grief—but my body just stands there, calm as a stone.

"Very good," Lilith says. "Now as your reward, you can drink that one." She nods at Ariel.

This is one of the nightmares Nero mentioned. It has to be. There's just no way—

My body leaps toward Ariel.

I struggle to snap out of it, but my fangs enter Ariel's throat and her blood floods my system with unwelcome, unholy pleasure.

"Finish your food," Lilith commands—and to my horror, my body keeps drinking until Ariel has no more blood to give.

"Ready to go?" Lilith grins at me as Ariel's dead body collapses on the floor next to Felix's.

Turning, she heads to the door, and my treacherous body follows.

CHAPTER THREE

I'M BACK in the dragon world, standing inside the crater Nero and I made last night at the edge of the forest meadow. I'm wheezing—which means I'm in full control of my body again.

"What happened?" Nero grabs my arms. "Are you okay?"

"It was a vision," I gasp out. "A horrible, horrible vision."

"What did you see?" Nero's gaze drills into me. "What needs to happen to stop Tartarus?"

Stop Tartarus.

I was so overwhelmed by the horror I just witnessed, I forgot that the vision was supposed to tell me how to prevent an apocalypse.

But how could the death of my friends possibly help with—

"Sasha." Nero's gaze darkens. "Speak to me."

My heart racing like a gerbil in a wheel, I raggedly tell Nero what I just foresaw.

As I go on, Nero's limbal rings grow out of control. "When you mentioned Lilith at the castle, I was worried about this very scenario," he grimly says when I'm done. "She gave you her blood to create a sire bond when you turned."

A sire bond.

Of course.

How did I not think of this sooner?

Lucretia drank Gaius's blood, and when she turned into a vampire, he was able to make her do his bidding —until we killed him, that is.

I should've thought about the sire thing as soon as I turned, but I was too busy saving Nero's life and then enjoying my reward.

Numbly, I rub the back of my neck. "So Lilith has power over me. I have to do her bidding."

"Yes, but she needs to actually speak to you in order to utilize that power," Nero says menacingly—and I can almost picture him ripping out Lilith's tongue to make sure that doesn't happen.

Except he wouldn't necessarily succeed. With all the power Lilith has acquired by being worshipped on her world, she could kill him if he tried to intercede on my behalf.

As if reading my mind, Nero growls, "Stop thinking about it. What you foresaw will not happen. I won't let her near you. I'd sooner see Earth die."

Earth.

I almost forgot about that.

When I asked my seer powers how to save everyone, they replied with "become Lilith's slave."

But why?

How could that help?

Maybe I didn't focus on the question properly?

This warrants a second opinion. And third, if need be. And fourth.

I strain to go back into Headspace, but the focus doesn't come. I must be too stressed.

With huge effort, I inhale a deep breath and focus again. Then again.

By the fifth attempt, I admit defeat. It's not stress. I'm out of seer juice because I just had two visions of the targeted timeframe variety—and those are extra costly. But—

Before I can finish the thought, Nero steps back, shines with energy, and turns into his dragon form.

Wow.

Gently reaching out with his claw, he grabs me and deposits me on his giant back. Then, without so much as a "buckle your seatbelt" roar, he leaps into the sky and whooshes toward the castle.

If I were prone to heart attacks, I'd have one here and now. Dragon-back riding is stressful on a calm day, and given how freaked out I already am, my heart feels like it might jump out of my ribcage and punch me in the face.

In a blink, we pass the battlefield—which has been

cleaned up, especially closer to the castle entrance where Nero lands.

Pozoj—the hawked-nosed dragon from the other day—is there to greet us. Calmly, he watches as Nero deposits me next to him and turns back into his naked self.

It's a sign of my extreme anxiety that the sight evokes only a mild tingle of heat in me.

"This is Sasha," Nero growls at the other dragon. "Watch her. I need to go power up." And in a blur of motion, he disappears into the castle.

"It's nice to meet you, Sasha," Pozoj says. "Claudia was just telling me about you."

"She was?" I even out my breathing. "Good things, I hope."

"I was telling him how impressed I was," Claudia says as she steps out of the castle, a megaton smile on her face. "I was also telling him how happy I am to know that my brother has been in good hands all this time."

"Oh, um… he wasn't in my hands." I shuffle from foot to foot. "Speaking of your brother, do you know where he just went? There's something we need to discuss and—"

"To enjoy his new hoard of treasure, I'd imagine," Pozoj says with a note of wistfulness. "You heard him. He said he needs to power up."

"Power up?" I look at Claudia, then back at Pozoj. "What does that mean?"

"How much do you know about dragons?" Claudia

asks, and I can't help but notice how close she's standing to Pozoj, and how they both look like they're itching to touch one another's hand. Clearly, Claudia has been socializing in double time while Nero and I were away.

"I know Nero can heal major injuries by lying on top of his treasure on Earth," I say. "And that he'd have more energy and need less sleep after doing that."

"Right, but powering up is much more than that," Claudia says. "Everything that makes us what we are is enhanced. Speed of movement, reaction time, stamina—"

"I really need to talk to him," I say, but I can already guess where this is going.

"You don't want to disturb a dragon on top of his hoard," Pozoj says matter-of-factly, confirming my concern.

"Give my brother at least a few hours," Claudia says. "Then I'll take you to him myself."

"But I'm in a rush," I say. "I'm a seer and—"

"A seer and a vampire?" Claudia says as both she and Pozoj look at me with renewed interest.

"Yes," I say, wondering how upset they'd be if I grabbed them by their collars and gave them a shake to impart my sense of urgency. "Can you take me to Nero now?"

"I'm sorry," Claudia says. "I don't want to upset him after just reuniting."

I look at Pozoj.

"I don't know where the imperial trove is," he says. "And, more importantly, I'm not suicidal."

"Fine," I snap. "Can you at least take me to the Cognizant from Earth?"

"Gladly," Claudia says and finally grabs Pozoj by the hand. "Follow us."

She prances into the castle, dragging the male dragon behind her, and I hurry to keep up.

As we walk, Claudia begins flirting with Pozoj, and I learn that he's from the richest, noblest dragon family on this world—which is probably why Nero gave him a safer post in yesterday's conflict. After a while, I tune out their banter in another attempt to enter Headspace.

No luck.

Well, I don't need a vision to predict the near future. I can do so based on past events.

For starters, to keep me safe, Nero is probably going to want to lock me up and throw away the key. And maybe it's a rare case when I should let him do so. After all, if I don't go to Earth, I can't kill Felix and Ariel.

Assuming I killed them on Earth, that is.

Of course, there are other, much better ways to prevent that vision from happening. For example, I can avoid hospitals and other medical facilities—and that is exactly what I'm going to do.

I can't *not* go to Earth. Though my seer powers are depleted, a powerful intuition tells me that if I don't try to deal with the Tartarus problem personally, my parents are as good as dead.

Now the million-dollar question is: will Nero help me prevent the upcoming apocalypse in the first place?

He did say he'd sooner see Earth die than let Lilith have me.

Is it possible he'll be content to rule here, on his dragon world, and let the denizens of Earth deal with the threat on their own?

"There they are," Claudia says as we enter a large dining hall that is noisier than a night club.

At a humongous table in the middle sits almost everyone Nero had brought to help him fight those big battles. Only the giants—Colton excluded—and the centaurs are not present.

Everyone is feasting on varied delicacies except for Vlad, who is sipping a liquid that looks suspiciously like blood.

"Sasha," Kit exclaims excitedly, turning into me. In my voice, she says, "I was wondering if Nero caught up with you." She wiggles her/my eyebrows suggestively, and I fight two urges: to blush and to smother Kit.

"No time for gossip," I say, imbuing my tone with as much urgency as I can. "I have information that everyone from Earth needs to be aware of."

Vlad, Kit, Colton, Albina, the big werewolf guy, the lady who can control animals, and the maybe-elf look at me with varying degrees of curiosity.

"It's Tartarus," I say loudly. "He's coming to Earth."

The room goes dead quiet.

Now that I have everyone's attention, I tell them what I foresaw, and—coming up with an evil idea on the fly—I end with, "Nero owes you a favor for your help here on the dragon world. If you care what happens to your home, call in that favor today and demand that he help you save it."

There. Even if Nero didn't plan to help before, he's going to find it hard not to do so now.

Everyone starts asking questions at the same time, and I attempt to answer what I can, which isn't much.

"Listen," I say after what feels like an hour of back-and-forth. "Every minute we spend here talking is a minute less for Earth."

Everyone falls silent, clearly waiting for me to tell them what the next step should be, and I have no clue.

"You should've told me your conversation with Nero is literally world-changing." Claudia grabs my elbow. "Let's go to the trove—to hell with his grumpiness."

"Great," I mutter. "Let's go."

Vlad, Kit, and the rest get up to join, but Claudia shakes her head. "He shouldn't harm me or Sasha, but anyone else would be taking too much of a risk," she explains.

The other Cognizant sit back down and start talking amongst themselves.

"Are you *sure* Nero holds me in the same 'do not harm' group as you?" I ask Claudia as we rush through a corridor and reach a spiral staircase leading down.

"I saw the way he looks at you." Claudia runs down the stairs so fast I have trouble keeping up at my vampire best. "I'm pretty sure he wouldn't harm you.

Much. Probably." A floor later, she adds, "Maybe let me do the talking just in case."

"Great idea," I say, my stomach squeezing with a bad feeling.

"Oh, and you should know the trove is outside the castle wards," she says a few more floors later. "Which means he's going to be in his dragon form."

"Perfect," I mumble. "Angry Nero in dragon form. What could possibly go wrong?"

CHAPTER FOUR

THE STAIRCASE GOES DOWN and down and down, seemingly to the center of the planet. At first, the walls around us are the signature silver-tinted obsidian of the castle, then they turn to rock strata.

The noise begins when the strata goes from brown to black. It sounds like a distant dragon roar.

As we descend farther, I realize the roar isn't a roar, but the dragon version of snoring.

Before I can ask Claudia about it, she speeds up, leaping five to six stairs in each jump until we reach a musty and cold cave-like opening that leads to another, much bigger space.

"Wow," I say.

"Yeah," Claudia replies. "It's been a while since I've seen this place."

Diamonds, gold, platinum, priceless works of art—the place is brimming with so much wealth and bling it hurts my eyes.

Nero's Earth treasure trove is but a tiny imposter compared to this vastness. Converted into cash, this treasure might exceed ten years of GDP for a mid-sized nation.

On top of all the loot lies Nero in his dragon form—except he seems bigger than usual, and more majestic.

The roar-snore is coming from him, and at this distance, it's nearly deafening.

"Earth is on the brink of destruction and you take a nap?" I say loudly. "Seriously?"

Nero keeps on snoring.

Taking off her clothing, Claudia walks over a million dollars' worth of gold and turns into a dragon herself.

Nero doesn't show any sign of being aware of her.

Claudia roars.

Nero keeps on sleeping.

With a flash, she turns back and gets dressed.

"Healing sleep that deep is rare," she shouts in my ear over the snoring. "It only happens after grievous wounds or extremely strenuous activity." She looks thoughtful. "I didn't think the fight with Yudo took *this* much out of him."

"So what do we do?" I ask, hoping Claudia doesn't see my blush. I can think of another strenuous activity Nero partook in recently, one that resulted in a crater in the ground and felled trees. Also, relatedly, how much blood did I drink from him last night? Could it have been an amount that equates to a "grievous wound?"

"There's nothing we can do," she says. "We go back up and wait."

"But—"

"It's for the best." She puts a hand on my shoulder. "As I was trying to explain before, when a dragon is awoken from this state, he can be crankier than an army of hibernating wool-beasts."

"Fine," I say. "Lead me back."

We go up and into the giant dining hall where we left everyone—and we find them on their feet, getting ready to leave.

Vlad approaches with a concerned expression. "Where is Nero?"

I roll my eyes. "Getting his beauty sleep."

"He might need a few hours in the best case, a day at the worst," Claudia says. "He'll be of more help to you when he's done."

"In that case, the others and I will head back to Earth and discuss your vision with the rest of the Council," Vlad says to me. "Tell Nero that we indeed would like to call in the favors he owes us in order to save Earth."

"Will do," I say solemnly.

"How about that drink?" Kit winks at me, then turns into Nero and shows me his/her neck.

"I'm still good," I say. "Besides, you wouldn't want to delay your fellow Council members, would you?"

Kit's pout looks comically foreign on Nero's face. Then she turns back into herself and joins everyone as they stride out.

"So," Claudia says when they're gone. "It's just us."

"Yeah," I grumble. "Are you sure there's no way to rouse your lazy brother somehow?"

"Not that I know of," she says.

"What if we go back down and smack him?" I start pacing the room, but the vampire stamina makes it hard to burn off anxious energy in this way.

She cringes. "Even if such a violent approach worked, we'd risk dying in the aftermath—especially you, since you're not as sturdy as a dragon."

"What if I give him a kiss?" I say half-jokingly. "That works on sleeping princesses, so maybe it can also work on a sleeping king, or emperor, or whatever he is now."

She grins. "This might be that one rare case where kissing my brother might not get you what you want."

"Hey." I stop my pacing. "What are you trying to say?"

"Nothing." She walks over to the table and takes a seat. "Come join me. If you keep on walking around like that, you'll give me a headache."

Dragons get headaches?

Grudgingly, I walk over to the table and plop into a wooden chair opposite hers.

"Now," she says. "Since we have privacy and time to kill, can you please tell the story of how you and Nero met?"

I take in a deep breath and exhale noisily. "We didn't have a charming first encounter, if that's what you're after. I have no idea when he first saw me, but I imagine I was inappropriately young at the time."

Claudia's eyes bulge.

"Yeah," I say. "And the first time I saw *him*, it was at a job interview—so, given the way jobs work on our world, romance was the last thing on my mind."

Despite being clearly disappointed, Nero's sister drills me for more info. Soon, the interrogation pivots, and I end up telling her all about my recent adventures.

"The Council forbade you from indulging in your greatest passion?" she says disapprovingly when I get to the part where they told me not to perform magic ever again or else.

"Yeah," I say, frowning at the memory. "They don't want humans to learn about the existence of the Cognizant, and though my illusions are not utilizing my powers, I can still grow more powerful if the humans worship me just so."

"I'm glad our humans know who and what we are and that we don't have those stupid Councils." She grabs a nearby goblet with wine. "I'm surprised Nero put up with all that nonsense."

"I'd say he adjusted to Earth well," I say. "He's one of the wealthiest and most powerful beings on Earth— and you know what that means for dragon powers."

"Still." She sips her wine. "I don't think I will like Earth."

I raise my eyebrows. "You say that as though you're going to go there."

"Of course I'm going to go," she says. "It's not just Nero who owes everyone a favor. If it weren't for you and the others from Earth, I'd still be in that cage." Her expression momentarily darkens, but turns sunny just as quickly. "Besides"—she grins—"this fight sounds like it will be a lot of fun."

"Fun for a dragon, maybe," I say. Then, choosing my words carefully, I ask, "What was it like, to be a prisoner for so many years?"

The dark expression is back with a vengeance, and I immediately feel guilty for prying.

"I wouldn't wish it on my worst enemy," Claudia says after a beat, her voice strained. "If it weren't for books and revenge fantasies, I would've lost my mind."

The door creaks, and Pozoj walks in.

"There you are," Claudia says, her gloom gone without a trace. "Sasha was just telling me about her skills as a conjuror."

"A what?" he asks, joining us at the table.

"How about I show you?" I say, deciding to cheer up Claudia with my favorite pastime. "Do you have this here?" I take out my deck of cards and spread them on the table.

"That looks like a Tarot deck," Pozoj says. "Only they're all wrong."

"I'll have to show you something where card values don't matter," I say and shuffle the deck. "How about this?" I split the cards in half, turning one half face up as I keep the other half face down.

I then shuffle the cards in this tipsy-turvy fashion, so that the interlaced cards are a mix of face-up and face-down at random.

"Now how long do you think it would take to sort out this mess I just made?" I ask as I do some secret moves that are made that much easier with my newfound vampire dexterity.

"Three minutes," Claudia says.

"Two," Pozoj adds.

I wave my hand over the cards, then spread them ceremoniously.

As if by magic, every card is now facing the correct way.

"That can't be," Pozoj exclaims. "Are you an illusionist on top of seer and vampire?"

"I'm not," I say. "At least not *that* kind of illusionist."

"Do something else," Claudia says greedily.

I strain my brain to recall more effects that don't require much knowledge of the card values and proceed with a mini show that makes me realize how much I've missed performing like this.

Their reactions are outstanding—in part due to the fact that there are no sleight-of-hand magicians on this world, but also because these guys don't have TV or computers, so their attention spans are way longer and standards for entertainment are way lower.

Maybe I can stay here with Nero and become his court magician à la Merlin? That would be almost as cool as my own TV show—maybe even cooler in some ways.

Wait, what am I thinking? Earth is in danger, and I'm already looking for a new world to settle on?

My keen vampire hearing informs me that someone new has stepped into the room. Then I hear Nero ask, "Where is everyone?"

I guiltily hide the cards and turn to face him.

That nap did his body some serious good. He looks radiantly healthy.

And as a side effect, sexy as hell.

"They've gone ahead to Earth," Claudia says, standing up. "I will go get ready for our journey."

"You what?" Nero narrows his eyes at his sister, then looks accusingly at me.

"I'm joining Sasha's quest to save Earth," Claudia says in a tone that seems to imply, "And I dare *anyone* to try to stop me."

"This sounds like a family matter," Pozoj says, backing up. "I'm going to go."

"No," Claudia says imperiously. "You're coming with me."

"Sounds like I am." Pozoj rubs his chin.

"Let's go." Claudia grabs his hand and drags him out at a speed that would dislocate the shoulder of a non-dragon.

Nero watches them leave with an unreadable expression on his face, and I can't help feeling like I'm in big trouble—for no reason.

"I'm also going to Earth," I say firmly when he turns to face me. "Don't even think about locking me up somewhere for 'my protection.'"

There.

I said it—and will defend my stance with everything I've got.

CHAPTER FIVE

NERO NODS. "OKAY."

"It should be up to me to put myself in danger or not as I wish. You can't just—wait." I look at him like he's sprouted horns. "Did you just say 'okay?'"

"Yes." He comes toward me. "Since you always find trouble despite whatever guards I place on you, I decided it would be best to keep you at my side at all times."

"Right." I lift my chin. "Just know that I'll be at your side only if I *want* to be at your side."

"And you do." A dark smile touches the corners of his eyes as he stops in front of me. "You know you do."

"And we're going to Earth," I say, ignoring the swarm of butterflies his proximity stirs up in my stomach. "The members of the Council asked me to tell you that the favor you owe them is going to be your help with Tartarus."

His face hardens. "Did you really think I was going

to let Lucretia and my other employees die? And your parents and all my allies on the Council? That I boosted my power just for laughs?"

Deciding it wouldn't be wise to remind him about the "let Earth die" comment he made earlier, I quickly put on my magician hat and rattle out, "You should thank me. Now you get to save Earth—as you would have anyway—but also owe fewer favors to people when you're done."

"And how should I thank you?" He leans in, his limbal rings expanding.

I swallow. "I don't know. I can't think of anything that wouldn't turn this nice castle to rubble."

"Oh, don't worry," he murmurs, gazing down at me. "Thanks to the wards, things would be different if I thanked you here."

Oh, that's right.

The castle prevents dragons from turning—the turning being, presumably, why our last encounter got so damaging to our surroundings.

I gulp in air audibly as my gaze flits between his lips and his neck.

Nero's lips curve, and he dips his head until those lips touch my ear. "No blood this time," he whispers. "I want you to be aware of every moment. Every touch. Every thrust."

Wow.

I think I just had a heat flash.

I've never been this turned on by words before. But

we can't do what I'm dying to do. Earth is running out of time.

"Time," is all I manage to say to Nero when he raises his head. "Have to hurry."

"If we go to Earth by wing, we'll get there before Vlad and the others," he says logically—and even this, somehow, sounds seductive.

Before my blood pressure can spike at the idea of traveling 'by wing,' he bends his head again and captures my lips with his.

Double wow.

Our kiss is more mindful this time, like we're savoring each other, trying to memorize every movement and sensation. At the same time, we start ridding each other of pesky clothing. With each piece of material that comes off, the heat inside me grows, every stroke of his palms over my skin further stoking my need.

Feeling like I'm burning, I sweep glasses and plates off the table onto the floor with a wide arc of my hand, and Nero grabs me by the waist and sits me onto the freed-up space, still kissing me.

Damn, this is good. Even better than I recall—not that I recall much of our last encounter. But I do remember us kissing when I was human, and this is infinitely hotter.

Could it be my vampire senses heightening everything? Or his power nap?

Then again, maybe it's my feelings toward him that are changing and coloring my perceptions.

Before I can delve into that further, Nero moves his lips to my neck, then down, down, down, and my brain scrambles like eggs on a frying pan as he starts feasting on me. My whole body shudders with orgasm after orgasm that arrive as if to the beats of the *Candy Shop* song. And then things escalate as I return the favor and we proceed to the home run.

It's official.

This is the best sex I could imagine.

Mind-blowing doesn't even start to describe it.

When it's over, and I lie sprawled on the table on top of Nero, I feel glad he didn't let me drink his blood —or do anything else that would mess with my memory.

I *want* to remember this.

If we fail and Tartarus kills me along with all the people on Earth, I will still die a relatively happy woman. Especially if Tartarus lets me do what I just did with Nero one more time.

Or two. Or three.

"We should get ready," Nero murmurs, but he doesn't let me go.

"Yeah, we should," I say, but I don't extricate myself from his hold.

"I made arrangements for you to see someone about those nightmares," he tells me softly. "I also want you to have a session with Lucretia when—"

"You what?" I pull away, more confused than angry.

"I spoke to Bailey Spade," he says, sitting up. "She can see you as soon as we get to Earth."

Bailey Spade. Why does that name sound familiar? "The dream walker?" I exclaim, remembering him talking to her during our helicopter ride. "How did you speak to her? Is she here?" I look around as though this mystery person is about to jump out from under the table.

"To power up, I slept," Nero says matter-of-factly.

"Great," I say sarcastically. "That explains everything. Thanks."

"Once she establishes a connection with a client, Bailey can visit their dreams regardless of what Otherland she's on," Nero explains. "Only the first session needs to be in person. She has to touch you when you're asleep—which is why I asked her to meet us on Earth."

No longer feeling the post-coital bliss, I jump off the table and start to dress. "Why do I have to do this? I don't even need to sleep anymore, so no nightmares. Problem solved."

"Nightmares are just a way for your subconscious to let you know something is wrong," Nero says, pulling on his own clothes. "And you don't *have* to do this. It would just make me feel better if you did."

Is this Nero asking nicely?

It's so sudden I swallow my snide remarks and consider it—and quickly decide that no harm could come from some therapy. Provided I'm alive to enjoy the healed mind, that is.

"I'll definitely talk to Lucretia," I tell Nero. "And I'll think about the dream stuff as well."

"Good," he says. "Now let's go."

————

AS IF POSSESSING some sixth sense, Nero locates Claudia in the labyrinth that is the castle, and we all go outside where Pozoj is waiting by the door, holding a rucksack.

"I want you to look after things until we get back," Nero tells Pozoj as he undresses once more and sticks his clothing into the rucksack.

"Must he?" Claudia says with a pout. "I wanted him with us."

"I need someone trustworthy here," Nero says, and Claudia concedes with a sigh.

Pozoj starts to say something, but Claudia begins to undress and he turns into a mute—probably not trusting himself to speak with all that drooling.

Those two definitely have something going on.

Swaying her hips, Claudia walks up so close to Pozoj that he'd be able to give her a breast screening if he wished. In the most seductive way possible, she stuffs her dress into the rucksack, then grabs the bag from Pozoj's unsteady hands and hands it to me.

This is when I stop gloating over Pozoj's discomfort and recall what the plan is.

Yep, sure enough.

Nero and Claudia are turning into dragons.

"Going by wing" is exactly what I feared—me on dragon back again.

Confirming my guess, Nero grabs me with his claw and has me mount him.

Again.

"Good luck," Pozoj finally manages to say, and Claudia roars back something that sounds like "thanks" and zooms into the air.

Nero launches up too, and I grab onto him for dear life. When we flew before, he clearly wasn't in as much of a rush as he is now.

Five or six underwear-soiling minutes later, we're already by the gates, and I get a reprieve as the siblings take on their human shapes and we enter the gates on foot, with me doing my best to ignore both of their naked bodies.

Well, actually, I ogle Nero's but politely avert my eyes from his sister.

We walk this way through a few Otherlands, and during our trip, Claudia asks Nero a million questions about his life back on Earth. I listen intently but don't learn anything I didn't already know.

"This is a world that Tartarus already destroyed," I tell Claudia when we get to the JFK airport clone and exit the underground corridors to the sight of all the husks.

She looks around, wide-eyed. "How awful. I think I might've been here as a child once, long before this happened."

Stepping over corpses, we head toward the exit.

"So, Nero," I say as we walk. "I've been meaning to

share with you an idea I had. A way to prevent that vision with Ariel and Felix."

"Yes?" he says without stopping. "Aside from sitting this out, of course."

"Well, that's kind of it. I want *them* to sit this out." I step outside. "And, in case it needs to be said, I'd like you to assign guards to watch them to make sure they can't end up in that room with me."

Nero looks at me with a raised eyebrow. "Do you understand the irony of what you're asking?"

"This is different from when you kept locking *me* up for my protection," I say.

"Sure," Nero says. "Tell yourself that."

"I'll ask them nicely first," I say defensively.

"Sasha." Nero stops and gently clasps my chin, forcing me to look up at him. His eyes are almost puppy-asking-for-bacon pleading. "Can you please sit this one out? It would mean a lot to me if you would. Pretty please?"

"No," I say, outraged. "I already told you—"

"See." He lets me go, the pleading expression replaced with a smug one. "That's what asking nicely accomplishes."

I grit my teeth. "Will you help me or not? I don't care if this makes me a hypocrite."

"Consider it done," he says. Then he steps away and turns into a dragon.

"Mr. Grouchy wins again." Claudia winks at me, then also assumes her dragon form.

I sigh as Nero places me on his back, and the flying

commences once more. This time, it's more interesting than scary because I'm getting used to this mode of transportation and because the world below me is so much like Earth.

When we reach this place's equivalent of Manhattan, I'm tempted to snap a few selfies, but I don't, in case that breaks some Cognizant rule I'm not aware of.

"This is so cool," I yell to Nero and pat his scaly neck. "Helicopter tours have nothing on dragon-back flights."

Nero replies with an amused-sounding roar, then dives for the Statue of Liberty to give me a good look at it. This version of the monument is holding a sword instead of a torch for some reason—but otherwise looks the same.

Claudia catches up with us, and we speed up as we turn toward New Jersey.

Before long, we land.

"I didn't see Vlad or the others," I tell Nero when he turns back into his mouthwateringly naked self.

"They might've taken the boat," he says and, to my disappointment, grabs the clothes from the rucksack I've been carrying. "I'm sure they're not far behind," he adds as he gets dressed.

"Fine," I say and take the lead, walking toward the next set of gates. Nero and Claudia follow, resuming their earlier chat.

"The next world is Gomorrah," I say to Claudia

when we stop before the gate leading there. "After that, Earth."

"This is so exciting," she says. "I last visited Gomorrah when I was little. It was magical."

Nodding, I step into the gate—and nearly collide with Ariel, Felix, and Rasputin when I exit on the other side.

CHAPTER SIX

"WHAT ARE YOU DOING HERE?" I exclaim as Claudia and Nero step out of the gate after me.

"I foresaw that you'd come out of this gate," Rasputin explains in Russian, and Felix translates my biological father's words for Ariel. "So we decided to greet you."

Oh yeah.

I did see a vision where Rasputin told Ariel and Felix that he foresaw my arrival on Gomorrah. He even knew I'd be a vampire, and told my friends about it.

That conversation must've happened recently, and might explain why Ariel is looking at me so strangely.

"This is Claudia," I say. "She's Nero's sister."

Everyone examines Claudia with poorly concealed curiosity. Then they look at Nero, likely to determine a resemblance—which is quite obviously there.

"How about I tell you the story of her rescue as we walk to Nero's club?" I say and begin walking.

Everyone follows me, and I launch into the story of Nero's war on the usurper. By the time we're mid-way through the lobby of the skyscraper, I've finished telling them how rescuing Claudia had gone down—with Felix translating for Ariel since I was speaking Russian throughout.

Clearly bored, Claudia interrupts my story mid-way to ask me for my deck of cards. I hand it to her, and she begins examining them, as if she might find hidden leprechauns that help me with my "magic."

I resume the story and conclude with, "After that, I saw a vision of you guys talking in Rasputin's room. So, Felix, thank you for the research on Lilith. Because of that, we know she used the chorts to arrange my death and my transformation into a vampire."

A vampire sire-bonded to her—but I don't mention that to them yet. Nor do I say anything about the looming threat of Tartarus.

The last thing I want is for them to panic and rush to Earth.

"This seer stuff really hurts my head sometimes." Felix's unibrow seesaws across his forehead. "You know what I did from a vision—but in that vision, Rasputin knew you'd thank me, also from a vision."

"Speaking of that." I tug at Rasputin's elbow. "Do you know why we came here?"

"No," he says. "My vision ended before you got a chance to explain, and I didn't dig deeper because I'm trying to preserve my seer powers, just in case."

"That makes sense," I say as we cross the street to

Nero's club, with Claudia gawking at the Gomorrah sights next to me. "Then I'll explain shortly. First, though, I have a big favor I want to ask of Felix and Ariel."

The noise of the music inside the club doesn't let anyone reply to my announcement, but when we get inside the elevator, Felix asks, "What's the favor, and why do I have a bad feeling about it?"

"I saw a very bad vision involving the two of you," I say. "So I wanted to ask you to take a vacation here on Gomorrah—basically, to stay away from Earth for a few days. Also, I want you to stay out of hospital rooms —even on this world, just in case. And, most importantly, you need to stay away from me."

Ariel clears her throat. "Are you going to tell us why?"

"I'd rather not." I glance at my shoes.

"Does it have anything to do with your new state of being?" She sounds concerned.

"It does, but you don't break your sobriety, if that's what you're worried about," I say.

Ariel visibly relaxes, but Felix's jaw juts out. "If this is about being able to stand up for myself, I'm working on something with Itzel that might—"

"This isn't a fight that can be won by force," I say. "Staying away is the only option." The elevator opens, and I exit after Claudia, who rushes down the corridor, clearly excited to explore even the most boring parts of her brother's club. "I know I'm asking a lot."

"I'll do it." Ariel takes out her vape pen and takes a

puff. "But I can't stay here for long. It's better if I'm at rehab."

Of course. Is it hard for her being around me now that I'm a vampire? Or is it just Nero's club that poses a problem?

"You can be wherever you want," Nero replies before I can say anything. "My guards can watch over you there just as well."

"I'm not staying here if you're going to be facing danger," Felix says. "I'm coming with you."

I look at Nero, who raises a questioning eyebrow. I can tell the bastard is enjoying this.

"Felix, please," I say, using my strongest version of the puppy eyes. "I don't ask you for much. Can't you just give me this one thing?"

He snorts. "Yeah, right. You ask me for stuff all the time. Remember the research you thanked me for a minute ago? What if you need my skills *again*?"

"I'll have to make do without," I say. "I can't risk what I foresaw."

"Tell me what the risk is, and I'll decide," Felix says.

"Fine." I stop and take in a deep breath. "In my vision, I kill you."

Ariel backs away, nearly stumbling over Rasputin.

For some reason, that hurts me. Does she think that because I'm a vampire, I'm capable of such an atrocity?

"You'd never do that," Felix says confidently, which makes me feel a tiny bit better.

"I wouldn't if it were up to me," I say.

"Unfortunately, in this vision, I have no choice in the matter."

Felix looks thoughtful for a moment, then smacks his forehead. "Of course. It's the sire bond. How did I not think about that?"

Damn, he's quick. I might as well fess up.

"You're right," I say. "My monster of a mother would've made me do it."

Felix frowns. "But that means you need us more than ever."

"Sasha has *me*," Nero states. "I'll make *sure* she's okay."

Felix blinks at Nero as if he forgot the dragon was there. "What happens if I refuse? Or is that why you brought us to this club? To do to us what Nero likes to do to you?"

Nero gives me a meaningful look.

"Please, Felix, don't refuse," I say.

"Why even bother with this charade?" he grumbles. "You can always glamour me again to do whatever you wish."

"I'm sorry about the other day," I say. "I promise I'll make it up to you. And I'll owe you one for this."

"Fine," Felix says. "But I don't want to be stuck in this club for however long this will take."

"I can spare a few bouncers to walk around Gomorrah with you," Nero says. "But, if you were to leave their company, I'd be disappointed. You wouldn't want to disappoint me, would you, Felix?"

My friend audibly gulps. "No, sir. I need to work

with Itzel on our project anyway. This might be for the best."

"What's the project?" I ask, eager to change the topic.

"Golem version two," Felix answers excitedly. "Body armor edition."

"Oh?" I ask, genuinely curious now.

"Remember the robot I lost when we fought Baba Yaga?" Felix says. "And remember the power boost in movement Itzel built into the spacesuits we used to save him?" He nods at Rasputin.

"Sure," I say, already getting an inkling of where he's going with this.

"I decided I want something I can use in case there's another fight, so we're blending the two projects." Grievances forgotten, Felix beams with excitement.

"They're ripping off Batman's suit from *Batman v Superman*," Ariel says, and for a moment, she sounds like her normal self again.

"If anything, we'd be ripping off *Iron Man*," Felix says and launches into a comparison of the movies—but I'm no longer listening.

Their banter reminds me too much of what they were talking about before Lilith made me kill them, and the dread wipes away any remnants of guilt I felt for asking them to sit out this fight.

Now I just need to tackle one issue that's bugging me, and we can go.

"Hey, guys," I say. "Can you go ahead to Rasputin's quarters while Ariel and I have a quick chat?"

Nero nods, then herds everyone until they catch up with Claudia and enter the rooms he'd allocated to my father.

I turn to Ariel, examining her perfect features. "Hey," I say softly.

"Hey yourself." Ariel takes another puff of her vape pen and exhales a cannabis-scented cloud.

"I just wanted to say that I would never, under any circumstances, let you drink my blood," I say, figuring I need to just come out with it. "So if *that's* what's bothering you, please don't—"

"That's not—" She starts to say, then stops. "In any case, I don't think you mean what you just said. Wouldn't you give me your blood to, say, save my life?"

"Fine. Maybe I should never say never, but I swear that if I had to, I'd use only the tiniest amount of my blood to save you—which seems to be safe. Just look at Felix—he didn't get addicted to Lilith in the least. And I'd look for alternatives first, I promise."

She takes another drag of her pen without saying anything.

"All right, let me put this another way. I'm the same Sasha you've always known, and I wouldn't do anything to jeopardize your sobriety."

She puts the vape pen away and takes in a deep breath. "I know that. Rationally, I know you're the same person as before—but when I look at you now, all I see is your new nature. I'm sorry. It's hard for me to explain. I'll do my best to get over it, but please be patient with me."

"Of course," I say, keeping the hurt from my voice. "Don't even worry about it."

"Thanks," Ariel says and follows the others down the corridor.

Oh, well. There's a decent chance this will all resolve itself soon—by me perishing at the hands of Lilith or Tartarus.

I enter Rasputin's quarters a few steps behind Ariel.

If the museum of modern art collaborated with IKEA to create the sleekest, most minimalist-looking studio they could, this might be the result.

Felix, Rasputin, and Nero are sitting on the uber-modern mesh chairs in the posh kitchen I saw in my vision and through a spy camera in Nero's office, while Claudia is walking around the whole place, admiring the Cubist paintings someone hung on the walls.

"I've made the arrangements." Nero stands up from his chair and walks toward me. "Those of us going to Earth should do so now, while the others will wait for my guards to arrive."

At her brother's words, Claudia peels her eyes away from a painting and heads for the door. Rasputin follows after her.

"Where are you going?" I ask him with a frown.

"To Earth," Rasputin says. "I'm not letting you deal with that monster on your own."

To my relief, Nero steps in his way. "No. The St. Petersburg Council still considers you persona non grata."

Rasputin looks as though he wants to shove Nero

aside, but he doesn't dare do so. "Woland and the chorts are dead," he says tightly. "I'm sure he was the main driver behind their grievance with me."

"True, but the official ruling against you was never overturned," Nero says. "If they wanted to, the St. Petersburg Council could send something nastier than the chorts after you. Then we'd have to deal with it, and we have enough problems on our hands."

Rasputin turns to me, and I nod, grateful to Nero for having my back on this. "He's right. Your presence there could be a hindrance. Besides, as a seer, you might be more useful to us here."

"This isn't right." Rasputin rounds on Nero. "A father should—"

"Think about what's best for his daughter," Nero says in a hard tone. "And you staying here *is* what's best."

Before Rasputin can argue more, a loud knock shakes the door.

Nero walks over to open it. Outside are two beefy bouncers who stand rod still when they see him.

"These gentlemen will take you wherever you need to go," Nero says to Ariel and Felix.

"And I'll be able to send you messages via Headspace through my father," I tell them as they look at me pleadingly. "Thank you again for putting up with my crazy."

"Sure," Felix mutters, and getting up, he trudges to the door, with Ariel on his heels.

With one last look, both of my roommates leave with their escorts.

Sighing, I walk over to the table and plop down.

Nero, Claudia, and Rasputin join me there, with Claudia looking through my card deck again.

"Go ahead, call me a hypocrite." I look at Nero with narrowed eyes. "I know I didn't tell them their loved ones are in peril. But if I had, they would've gone to Earth immediately. You know that."

"I do," he says softly. Reaching over, he covers my hand with his. "Don't worry. In a few days, I'll have my guards ask both Felix and Ariel to put together a list of people they want evacuated. And you should put together such a list yourself, just in case."

"Right, of course." I swallow. "Except my parents, being human, wouldn't be able to go through the gates."

"I know, but we'll figure something out. I promise you." He squeezes my hand reassuringly.

Rasputin is frowning at both of us now. "What are you talking about? What peril?"

"It relates to what I wanted your help with," I say and tell him about my vision of the upcoming apocalypse, ending with how my powers served me the vision of Ariel and Felix dying as a solution to the Tartarus problem.

"Tartarus." Rasputin spits it out like a curse. Launching to his feet, he walks over to his fridge, grabs a frost-covered bottle of vodka from the freezer, and takes a swig straight from the bottle.

I look at Nero, but he just shrugs. Claudia looks clueless as well.

Coming back to the table, Rasputin sets the bottle down within his reach and says grimly, "All my pain is ultimately that monster's fault." He takes another swallow of vodka. "All of it."

I stare at him blankly. "What do you mean?"

"I didn't get a chance to tell you this before, but, in a strange way, you owe your very existence to Tartarus," Rasputin says and avoids eye contact when I gape at him in shock.

I turn to Nero again and see him frowning in confusion. Whatever this is, he's not in the loop—which might be the first time ever.

"How do I owe my existence to Tartarus?" I ask, my voice unsteady. "I thought I owe it to you and Lilith."

Rasputin unbuttons the top of his shirt. "As you know, Nostradamus's only purpose in life is revenge on Tartarus."

I nod.

"Something that should also not be a surprise is that Lilith is obsessed with her immortality," he continues as Claudia reaches for his bottle and takes a cautious sip.

Choking, she begins coughing, and Rasputin draws in a steadying breath. "Right," he says after she's done. "What you probably don't know is that long ago, Nostradamus foretold that Lilith would die at the hands of Tartarus—unless her daughter killed him first." He finally meets my gaze.

"Yes, that's right," he says as I stare at him in disbelief. "A daughter born of a powerful Russian seer." He takes the bottle from Claudia and gulps down another mouthful—to Claudia's wincing dismay. "That damned prophecy of his is why Lilith seduced me," Rasputin continues, "and why she planned to turn you, our daughter, into an unflinching killing machine that could be preemptively unleashed on Tartarus. That's the fate I prevented by—"

"Leaving me at the airport," I finish numbly as the implications explode in my head.

There's seer manipulation, and then there's having me be born just so I could be a tool for revenge.

Also, how was I ever supposed to defeat Tartarus when he's a threat to someone as powerful as Lilith?

Well, I guess if Rasputin hadn't taken me away from her, Lilith could've made me an evil god on her world —just like Mommy but with seer powers. And by now, I'd be as powerful as she is. Except that didn't happen, so I doubt Nostradamus's prophecy will come true.

At least the part where I defeat Tartarus and save Lilith. Pretty sure my biological mother is doomed— though this does explain why she's made me a vampire.

She must still be holding out some hope.

"I'm sorry I had to give you up," Rasputin says, looking away again. "It was the only way you could grow up without Lilith's toxic influence."

Right.

It all fits, and I probably should be thanking him— except now it might cost Earth its existence.

In the silence that follows, Claudia stands up and walks over to the refrigerator. Moving dragon fast, she takes out the pastry I saw in my vision—one that looks like a cross between pizza and a Cinnabon—and brings it over to the table, along with plates for everyone.

"How do you know about Nostradamus's prophecies?" Nero asks Rasputin, his voice dangerously low. "And why didn't you tell me about this before?"

"I only learned Sasha's fate when Lilith captured me." Rasputin picks at his snack without much appetite. "She let slip Nostradamus's name, so I stockpiled some power and challenged him in Headspace. When we joined, I saw a memory of him talking with Lilith. Then he admitted the rest of it to me, saying that he never intended for Sasha to suffer, and that his visions—like all predictions—are not guaranteed, especially when the people involved become aware of their possible fates."

"Did you look at the future yourself?" Nero demands. "How do you know Nostradamus was telling the truth? How is Sasha supposed to defeat Tartarus?"

"He couldn't have faked his memories, but as to what he said, I don't know if he was telling the truth. And I have no idea how, and if, Sasha can defeat Tartarus. I couldn't foresee any of it," Rasputin says. "A vision of this magnitude requires a large stockpile of power, and after that encounter with Nostradamus, he'd been making sure I can't get it by regularly attacking me in Headspace and draining my powers.

And what little I would recover, I needed to survive Lilith's tortures."

Nero's hand tightens on the table. "I think I need to have a chat with Nostradamus, see if I can loosen his tongue a bit."

"Get in line," I say, then look at Rasputin. "What do you mean by 'stockpiling?' I didn't know you could do that with seer power."

"It's something only the most powerful seers can do," Rasputin says. "Do you know how you can run out of your power and use no more until the next day?"

I nod.

"Well, what happens if you don't use the power for that day?" he asks.

I shrug. "You have more the next day? I hadn't noticed any difference, to be honest, and neither Darian nor the bannik—my main sources of seer information—mentioned this to me."

"Most seers, like Darian and the bannik for example, wouldn't have more power the next day," he says. "But some of us—the most powerful—*can* learn how to stockpile our unused power for bigger expenditures. It requires you to go into Headspace every day but leave without activating any visions. After that, the next day, you'll have more power than just a day's worth—and if you keep doing it, you stockpile enough for some major visions."

"Wow," I say. "That would've been useful information. Assuming I'm powerful enough to do this, of course."

"I think you are," Rasputin says. "You'll have to test it when you get the chance."

"What I don't understand is how Nostradamus was able to drain *your* power," Nero says, looking at him. "Aren't you the more powerful seer?"

Rasputin shrugs. "All else being equal, I might be more powerful. But he had stockpiled his power for decades, maybe even centuries, while I had used up mine at the wrong time."

Nero narrows his eyes. "If it's about my request, you should've told me all this before you drained your power reserves on my rescue project." He glances at Claudia, who's still munching on her pastry.

"Oh, at that point, I didn't have much power anyway," Rasputin says. "The real hit to those reserves was that hundred-year prophecy I made for you about Earth's history—but that was worth it, because it convinced you to look after Sasha."

Nero's jaw tightens at the jab, but he doesn't say anything. We all know he wouldn't have helped Rasputin if it weren't for the hundred-year prediction that made him so rich—and thus more powerful as a dragon—over the years.

After all, as a baby, I didn't have my current charms. Such as they are.

"The good news is, I do have enough power now to look a few months into the future—or to have many short-term visions," Rasputin says. "Tell me how to best help you. I can, for example, verify that Ariel and Felix will be safe."

"In that case, can you check to see if Sasha will fall under Lilith's sire bond?" Nero asks. "And if so, how to prevent it?"

"Yes," Rasputin says. "I'll get on that."

He closes his eyes and evens his breathing.

I check if my own powers have recovered and, to my huge relief, find myself in Headspace.

There, I face a cloud of shapes playing a deadly tune.

Great.

There goes any hope of ever using the stockpiling trick I just learned about. To do so would mean ignoring these visions of doom, and I can't do that.

Metaphysically sighing, I reach for one deadly vision and prepare to see what new problems the universe will throw at me.

CHAPTER SEVEN

I'M in a hotel bathroom vigorously attacking my teeth with a toothbrush.

This attempt at personal hygiene is long overdue. Turns out, without the routine of daily sleeping, it's hard to remember to do such things with any regularity.

Maybe I should set a timer on my phone to remind me to brush in the future?

Then again, do I even need fluoride anymore?

I'll have to ask someone how they find my breath, but something tells me vampires don't get gingivitis or halitosis. And I bet our teeth don't yellow over time either.

I know one thing for sure. With an all-liquid diet, I'm never going to floss again.

Suddenly, my vampire super-hearing picks up a noise that sounds like someone opening the door and creeping into the room.

My seer sense—and common sense—rings an alarm.

Without bothering to spit, I toss the toothbrush into the sink and zoom out of the bathroom—smack into a giant intruder.

Stumbling back, I take in his appearance and gulp nervously, swallowing the minty grossness in my mouth.

This guy is what a growth hormone molecule would look like if a magic fairy turned it into a man.

Even his earlobes look like they have muscles.

Weirdly, his hair is long and permed—and has enough hair spray on it to have opened a hole in the ozone layer, à la the style favored in the eighties.

Maybe he's a rock star?

The outfit doesn't exactly match. Instead of glittery spandex or whatever, he's wearing a circa-eighties bomber jacket, tight jeans, and clunky white sneakers.

In his beefy hand, he's holding another anachronism—a polaroid photo.

I back up some more, examining my crappy options for escape.

There are none.

He's blocking the path to the door with his massive body, and going out the window involves figuring out how to fly.

Fine.

Time to use what little vampire powers I'm good at. I will my eyes to go into glamour mode, and when they're nice and mirror-y, I catch his gaze.

"Leave. Now," I order in a honey-laced voice.

He doesn't.

Instead, he looks at his photo, then at me, then grunts and shines with energy.

I stare openmouthed.

His clothes rip into shreds, and the man is replaced by a giant wolf-like thing standing on all fours.

Oh, great. He's a werewolf.

I back away again, my heart hammering in my chest with the primal fear inherited from ancient survivors of saber-toothed tigers.

Even before this change, the guy seemed big and scary. Now, he's an obscene bundle of muscles, teeth, and claws—and bigger than I thought a werewolf could get. Even bigger than the beast who was helping Nero during the battles on the dragon world, and that guy was monstrous.

Growling, the intruder bares his dagger-like teeth and advances on me.

My fangs extending automatically, I dodge a swipe of his massive paw—so instead of my stomach, his claws disembowel the corner of the bed.

There goes that security deposit.

He swipes at me with his other paw—but I twist to the side with supernatural speed, and the dresser gets decimated instead of my face.

Desperate, I viciously kick him in the ribcage.

At least I mean to. But before my foot connects, the guy dodges the strike. Then, moving faster than something this size should be able to, he clamps his teeth on my thigh.

Crying out in pain, I lose my balance and smack my head on the corner of a nightstand. Stars explode in my vision, and when I recover, I realize the beast is dragging me by my leg through the room.

Flailing, I hit his giant head as hard as I can.

His teeth clamp on me tighter. Growling low in his throat, he jerks his head, throwing me into the air like a dog would a chew toy.

There's a moment of weightlessness, and then my back hits the window.

Glass explodes around me, lacerating my skin as I grapple for the window frame—only to get my palms sliced to shreds with the sharp edges of the glass as the momentum carries me out.

I drop like a stone, and as the air whooshes past my ears, I catch a glimpse of the ground below me.

Far below me.

Like twenty stories below me.

Even with vampire healing, there's no way I will survive.

CHAPTER EIGHT

BACK IN RASPUTIN'S APARTMENT, I stare at Nero, Claudia, and Rasputin in shock.

Who was that guy? Why will he try to kill me?

Also—perhaps less important—why the hell was he dressed like that? And what was up with that hair?

I know some of the eighties' fashion is back, but not to *this* degree.

And why was he holding a paper photograph? Is he the last person on Earth without a smartphone?

Before I can voice any of this, Rasputin's face goes from contemplative to furious.

Opening his eyes, he jackknifes to his feet and smacks the table with his palm, all while muttering Russian expletives under his breath.

"What's wrong with him?" Claudia asks, staring at him wide-eyed.

"Maybe he saw the same thing I just did?" I say. "Or

maybe he didn't see a way for me to escape falling under Lilith's sire bond?"

"Worse," Rasputin growls. "It's Nostradamus. He attacked me in Headspace. I'm without power again."

"That bastard." I jump to my feet. "I wonder if he was also behind what I just foresaw? I mean, he already hangs out with one werewolf, so maybe—"

"Wait," Nero says. "What are you talking about?"

As I tell them, Rasputin sits down in a defeated slump, and Nero's face darkens.

"You sure you've never seen that guy before?" Nero asks sternly when I finish.

"Of course, I'm sure." I cross my arms over my chest. "I'd remember him. Trust me."

Nero drums his fingers on the table. "And you're also sure he was bigger than Eduardo?"

I frown. "Who's Eduardo?"

"He helped me the other day," Nero says. "He's the leader of his pack and a Councilor. I didn't think his kind could get bigger than he is."

"I think my attacker was bigger," I say. "But then he was right in front of me, so maybe he just *seemed* bigger thanks to all that adrenaline?"

Nero's jaw tightens. "And where was I in your vision?"

"I have no idea," I say.

His eyes narrow. "Why were you by yourself? Which hotel was it?"

"No clue."

His hands start to curl into fists. Noticing it, he

takes a deep breath and uncurls them. "Fine. Now that I know what's coming, we're going to be attached at the hip. And you're going to stay away from *all* hotels from now on."

"Yes, boss," I say. "Anything else?"

"You will go back into Headspace and try to learn more about this attack," he says.

"Sure," I say. "I was going to suggest the same thing."

"Good," Nero says. "What are you waiting for?"

He and everyone else stare at me expectantly.

I close my eyes to lessen the impact of all that pressure, then even out my breath and focus.

I end up in Headspace right away, surrounded by shapes that look identical to the werewolf attack vision.

Score.

I don't even have to do anything.

My subconscious—or whatever—got me the shapes I need.

Before I get a chance to reach out to them, a new shape shows up between me and my target.

It's an entity that radiates power and regret.

A familiar entity.

I've seen it—him—in Headspace recently, when I summoned him to ask for help from the chorts.

It's Nostradamus.

And thanks to Rasputin's experience, I can guess why he's here.

He wants my powers.

Well, he's not going to get them.

I begin backing away, figuring if I metaphysically touch myself, he can't snare me into a Headspace battle.

Only it's too late.

He's already grabbing onto me with multiple ethereal wisps, like a hungry octopus latching onto a crayfish.

I strain to get free.

He sprouts more and more wisps, and his hold strengthens.

I resist for as long as I can, but then something gives and Nostradamus reels me into the joining.

CHAPTER NINE

I FIND myself in Nostradamus's memory once more.

I/he is bound in chains and in considerable pain, but what's interesting is that he still has eyes to see with—which is how I know we're in some sort of dank dungeon cell.

What's even more interesting is whom he's looking at.

It's Tartarus himself and one of his children—except I only know this because that's what Nostradamus thinks as he looks up.

To me, neither Tartarus nor the so-called child look the way I'd expect.

The "child" is a grown man with wild eyes and a permanent-seeming smirk on his face, while Tartarus looks like a kind and wise old *woman*.

As if to answer my confusion, Nostradamus thinks, "Tartarus is not Cassandra. She died ages ago. Everyone sees someone sacred to them when gazing upon this monster. That is all there is to it. He isn't Cassandra. He's not worthy of wearing her face."

Interesting.

I thought Tartarus just sucks energy out of humans—but I guess he also looks different to everyone.

I wonder who he'd look like to me?

"It's unfortunate your wife and son died," Tartarus says, and his voice also sounds like that of Cassandra. "I've long wanted to have a seer among my children. And now, instead of three seers to breed, I only have you."

Breed a seer?

Wow.

That's just like Baba Yaga—and she was the worst person I've ever met.

Nostradamus is also triggered by that phrase, but in his case, a bunch of disturbing memories flit through his mind, and I, being in his head right now, can unfortunately glimpse them.

All are based on visions he foresaw once it was too late, when he was already in Tartarus's clutches.

Visions in which his family survived Tartarus's invasion.

In those unlikely futures, his wife would've been raped and forced to have child after child. And if that weren't horrific enough, when the offspring failed to have either Tartarus's powers or seer powers, they would've been killed.

His son's fate wouldn't have been as dire. The boy would've been more willing to sire children with one of Tartarus's daughters—the one with succubus powers. Here again, though, no powers in his offspring would've meant death for them.

When it came to himself, Nostradamus did not see a single future where he cooperated with the breeding program.

Instead, he found one where he could escape.

The price would be his eyes, but the benefits are that Tartarus will not have a seer in his army in any foreseeable future. More importantly, by surviving, Nostradamus will be able to stockpile power until he has enough to get his revenge.

"I think he's ignoring you, sire," the wild-eyed one says to Tartarus mockingly.

"He's probably wondering why he didn't foresee his capture," Tartarus says to the guy, then looks down at Nostradamus. "It was all thanks to Lug here." He nods at his "child." "He's the bane of your kind's existence—a probability manipulator—and I had him shield me from you."

I/Nostradamus narrows his eyes at Lug and mentally adds him to the list of people he'll subject to his vengeance.

Seeing the look, Lug walks over, grins like a maniac, and savagely kicks me/Nostradamus in the head, ending the memory.

———

ANOTHER MEMORY STARTS.

In this one, Nostradamus has already lost his sight.

I/He is standing somewhere, touching something on the wall.

Ah. His fingers are reading French Braille on a card that states: *Plan Ultime.*

Nodding, he focuses in a way familiar to us both, then leaps into Headspace.

Fascinated, I witness as Nostradamus does something I haven't done before: instead of focusing on the essence of a person, he dwells on the essence of the room he's in. I didn't even think a room can have an essence. Additionally, he's targeting a time period of a millisecond into the future—but this I already knew how to do.

A cloud of safe-seeming shapes appear in front of him, and he activates one.

In the vision that starts, he's in a large empty room with corkboards covering every wall.

This is the place he was just in, the essence of which he was thinking about.

Marius—Nostradamus's guide dog/werewolf—is here as well, slurping water from a five-gallon bowl on the floor.

This is when it hits me.

In this vision, Nostradamus can actually see.

He mentioned seer abilities still work for him, but this memory puts it in perspective.

By glimpsing such near future, he can actually experience vision again—which brings up interesting questions about seer powers that I don't have time for.

Ignoring Marius, Nostradamus stares at the nearest board, which has hundreds of cards pinned to it, most of which are connected by colored string.

Each card has writing in Braille and regular cursive French, and the one that says *Plan Ultime* is the center piece.

What catches my attention is a set of cards to the side—cards that have my name on them.

Beatrice, says one of the cards connected by a red string to my name. Below her name is a drawing of a woman with black eyes and a heart-shaped face. Her Cognizant power is listed—necromancer—and the date and time she's going to come to Earth and entangle with me.

A red string connects this card with another. This one has the date and time when Ariel and I battled Beatrice at the *Bodies* exhibit in Vegas.

Wow.

Nostradamus knew about my misadventures before they happened.

There's also a card and a drawing of the pretty face of the dreamy-eyed Harper—which lists her as a succubus and Beatrice's lover—and there's a card for when she tried to kill Felix and me.

And the pattern keeps going.

There's a card for Baba Yaga, and a bunch of cards summarizing my encounters with the witch.

A card for the deathly thin Koschei—Baba Yaga's hard-to-kill minion.

A card for Gaius—Baba Yaga's Enforcer ally and the person who got Ariel addicted to vampire blood.

There's even a card for Darian—the seer who got me into my misadventures, with a note that states that Darian will be mistaken when he thinks he has a future with me. According to Nostradamus's note, Darian has no future.

Wow.

How far into the future does this go?

Is what will happen to me later today on this wall?

I will Nostradamus's head to turn more to the right, but he doesn't. And before I can see how much more he predicted, the memory terminates.

CHAPTER TEN

THE MEMORY PART of the joining is over, as I'm in that telltale emptiness that is the joining environment, and there's a synapse-hologram of Nostradamus floating in front of me. As per usual, he's attached to that uncanny shape-entity that is his Headspace representation.

"You." My anger makes me drop a few feet. "You're here to drain my powers, aren't you?"

"I'm sorry," he says. "This is the only way to make sure you don't ruin everything."

"Your *Plan Ultime,* you mean? I saw your memories. I know about that."

He floats down, a worried grimace twisting his face. "All the more reason you have to be neutralized. This is the last I will say to you. I'm going to meditate, and I suggest you do the same."

To punctuate his words, he folds himself into a lotus position and just floats there, a Buddha-like expression on his face.

"You've got to be kidding me," I shout and float toward him. "You're not just going to ignore me."

He doesn't react.

I shout obscenities at him.

His expression doesn't change.

I fly toward him, reaching to strangle him, but my hands go right through his neck.

I resume yelling and cursing—all of which he ignores.

Eventually, I get tired and just float there. Instead of wasting time on venting, I might as well use this downtime to think of my next move.

Focusing inwardly, I relax.

With my mind calmer, I get an idea of how I can thwart Nostradamus—but I instantly banish it, in case he can somehow read my thoughts in this strange place.

Grudgingly, I attempt meditating as he suggested.

It's surprisingly easy to do here, thanks to feeling weightless and having no external distractions.

Despite earlier anger, I actually feel serene in no time.

This goes on for a while, but then, after what feels like a weekend meditation retreat, the Headspace battle finally terminates.

CHAPTER ELEVEN

I'M BACK in the kitchen.

Nero, Claudia, and Rasputin stare at me questioningly.

"The bastard did it to me too," I say. "Showed up and forced me into a Headspace battle."

Rasputin smacks the table again, and Nero's hands curl into fists.

Just to be sure things are as bad as they seem, I attempt going into Headspace.

Nope.

I can't.

"No power left," I confirm. "But at least I saw some of Nostradamus's memories."

Everyone looks intrigued, so I tell them about the encounter with Tartarus and what I glimpsed on the corkboard.

"The memories I experienced were not as useful," Rasputin says. "In one, I saw how that trickster—Lug—

blinded Nostradamus, which, ironically, opened a small window of opportunity for him to escape."

"What about that corkboard?" I ask. "Did you see it?"

"No," Rasputin says. "All the other memories I saw were older, mostly of happy times when his family was alive."

"I saw one like that too, another time," I say, feeling a pang of empathy that the manipulative bastard doesn't deserve. "He was with his son."

"How much do you know about this Cassandra, the woman Nostradamus saw Tartarus as?" Nero asks. "Is that a lead?"

"According to Nostradamus, she's dead," I say. "So I doubt she can help."

Grabbing the vodka bottle, Rasputin takes a healthy gulp. "Cassandra was Nostradamus's Mentor," he says when he stops grimacing from the burn. "He must've looked up to her—which is why Nostradamus saw what he saw. Rumor is, when you look at Tartarus, you see someone you respect and revere."

"Right," I say. "Nostradamus was thinking something along those lines. He thought he saw Cassandra because Tartarus makes people see someone sacred to them."

"I thought that was just a myth," Nero says. "They say humans see him as a god or some famous prophet —which is how he gets the worship on each world so easily, especially on worlds with mass media technology, like TV."

"Wow," I say. "So on Earth, people would see him as something like the Buddha or Jesus?"

"Probably," Nero says. "And children might see Santa Claus." He looks at Rasputin. "Or in Russia, Grandfather Frost."

"Would that power work through TV?" I ask. "Would every single person looking at a TV screen see someone different?"

"It's likely," Nero says.

"So odd," I say. "I mean, if everyone sees something different, it's not shapeshifting, like with Kit."

"He's not a shapeshifter." Rasputin looks at the vodka bottle, but doesn't drink. "His power is more like extremely strong glamour."

"Crazy," I mutter as I picture the pandemonium that will result from his arrival on Earth. He'll go on TV, and videos of the Second Coming—or whatever the media will call it—will go viral in a heartbeat.

He'll be worshipped in no time.

"Even rumors never mentioned his children," Nero says, bringing my attention back to our discussion. "Based on Sasha's vision, it seems like he doesn't take over worlds by himself, as everyone said."

"It makes sense, though," Rasputin says. "How can a single being, no matter how powerful, take over a whole world?"

"Lilith did," Nero says.

Rasputin nods. "True. But she took over a more primitive world, one without technology. Humans on a world like Earth have weapons that can kill anything."

"Good point." I massage my chin. "These children of his—especially ones like that trickster, Lug—will severely complicate plans for defense of Earth."

"Save the defense talk for when we talk this over with the Council," Nero says. "Speaking of which, Claudia and I better go."

I narrow my eyes. "You mean Sasha, Claudia, and I better go."

Nero regards me with an unreadable expression. "Even with your seer powers drained, you insist on joining?"

"Hells yeah." Anticipating another argument, I say, "Think about it for a second. In my vision, I was alone when that werewolf attacked me. Us staying together is the best way to prevent that future from happening."

"Fine." Nero stands up. "*We* better go."

"Just one moment," I say. "I had an idea before. I think I know how to stockpile power rather quickly."

Nero sits back down, and everyone looks at me with rapt attention.

I turn to Rasputin. "Remember how you said you can save some power every day for stockpiling?"

Rasputin nods.

"What if you had more days?" I ask eagerly.

Nero nods approvingly. He must've guessed where I'm going with this.

"There's a world called Atlantis," I say. "Time there runs so fast that the boys Vlad was training in one of my visions turned to grown men almost overnight. If

Nostradamus is on Earth and you go to Atlantis, you'll have a major advantage when it comes to stockpiling."

Rasputin's face lights up. "You're right. Now that you mention it, this is how Nostradamus bested me in the first place. I was stuck on Lilith's world, where time runs slow, while he was somewhere where it's fast. Now I get to turn the tables on him."

"Good," Nero says, getting up again. "I'll find someone to take you. Let's go."

Turning on his heel, he strides out of the apartment.

We follow Nero all the way to the elevator. When we get downstairs, he talks to a few bouncers and points at Rasputin.

"So this is another goodbye," Rasputin says, blinking as he stares at me.

"For now," I say, faking cheerfulness. "Once I have my powers back, I will look for you in Headspace."

"Be careful," he says and reaches over to hug me.

"I will do my best," I say, hugging him back. "You be careful too—*Papa*."

As I pull away, I can see that the little endearment did its job. Rasputin's face glows like a Christmas tree.

On my end, I almost meant the sentiment this time. I do wish he could come to Earth, so we could spend more time together. If I survive the werewolf's attack *and* Tartarus—which is a big "if"—I'll have to figure out a way to get the St. Petersburg Council off my father's back.

Somehow.

"Let's go," Nero orders over his shoulder and pushes his way through the gyrating dancers to the club's exit.

Claudia and I rush to follow him, sprinting all the way to the elevator in the hub skyscraper.

The ride up is quick, and once on the roof, we jog to the Earth gate.

When we exit on the opposite side, we bump into a disheveled Eric—the teleporter guard whom Nero left to watch over me.

He must've recovered from the tranquilizer nappy-nap I put him in.

"Eric," I say. "Fancy meeting you here."

He gives me a barely perceptible frown, then cringes under Nero's glare.

"I know I messed up," he says. "She—"

"Save it," Nero growls. "Take us to Sasha's apartment. Now."

"Sure," Eric says and walks up to Claudia. "Her first?"

"Whatever," Nero says. Then he tells Claudia, "He's going to touch you in order to teleport you somewhere. Don't kill him."

Claudia rolls her eyes as Eric puts a hand on her shoulder, and they wink out of existence.

"Who needs a limo with Eric around?" I mumble. Then the teleporter reappears alone and puts a hand on my shoulder.

Poof, and I'm standing by the door of my apartment next to grinning Claudia.

"I've never teleported before," she says giddily. "That was amazing."

I grin at her. "I know, right? I'd give my left fang to be able to do that. The illusions I'd be able to perform would blow the minds of every magician in the world. Even Copperfield."

Eric reappears with Nero.

"Come back in an hour, or when I text you," Nero tells the teleporter. "Whichever comes first."

"Deal," Eric says, and blips out of existence again.

I reach into my pocket to get the key. "It's not a castle," I say. "But I call it home."

Holding the door wide, I let the motley crew inside.

"Sasha!" Fluffster shouts in my head, then dashes over to greet us, his little furry paws skidding on the floor. "You're back." He looks at me sternly. "I was worried."

Seeing my domovoi's chinchilla form, Claudia literally squeals with delight. "What is that? Please don't tell me you'd eat such a marvel."

"Eat him?" I look at Fluffster, then at Claudia. "Where did you get that idea?"

Fluffster backs away—he no doubt remembers the horror-movie-like documentary we saw about the poachers who kill chinchillas. According to it, they don't let the meat go to waste—and it's supposed to be fatty, like a duck.

"Who is she?" Fluffster asks. "She seems powerful, like Nero."

Lucifur—the cat I've inherited from Rose—saunters

over to check what the fuss is about. She looks unimpressed with all of us. The expression on her flat face seems to say, "If anyone is going to eat that fluffy morsel, it would be Our Majesty, provided someone sticks him into a can of Fancy Feast. Now scram, before you pay for your insolence with your lives."

"Wow," Claudia says, gaping at Lucifur. "That creature is even cuter. Is it common to keep a veritable zoo in your home here on Earth?"

"Hey," I say. "Fluffster is cuter—and, more importantly, unlike the cat's, his feelings can be hurt."

"I apologize," Claudia says, looking at Lucifur.

"That's not Fluffster," I say and point at the domovoi. "*That* is Fluffster."

I grab my heavenly-furred friend and hold him so Claudia can have a closer look. "This is Nero's sister, Claudia," I tell him. "Claudia, *this* is Fluffster. He's a domovoi—a type of Cognizant."

"A domovoi?" She looks at Fluffster a lot more respectfully. "I didn't realize. They usually look like humans on our world."

"The locals keep animals as pets on this world," Nero explains. "And since the domovoi take the guise of pets, they end up looking like cats, dogs, and sometimes like chinchillas."

"Wait, hold up," I say, examining him for any sign of mirth. "Are you saying dragons keep *humans* as pets on your world?"

In my head, I also wonder—what about vampires? And seers?

Put another way, am I Nero's *pet?*

"The word 'pet' is loaded with too many negative connotations." Nero smirks as if he read my earlier thought. "How about interspecies companions? Familiars?"

I put Fluffster on the ground and grimace.

"Humans consider it a big honor to live within a dragon's household," Claudia chimes in. "The right to do so passes from family to family."

"Many of the soldiers who helped in our campaign asked for such companionship to be their reward," Nero adds. "You have to remember, they revere dragons and—"

The doorbell rings.

Nero looks through the peephole, grunts approvingly, and opens the door.

A beautiful, slender young woman is standing there. She's dressed in tall leather boots and a leather jacket, and her frizzy curls are gathered into a big poof of a ponytail.

Since I can't see Cognizant auras at the moment, I can't tell if she's one of us—but if she's human, her ethnicity would be extremely hard to pinpoint. She looks as if some mad scientist took Zoe Saldana and spliced her with Emma Watson's genes, then sprinkled in a touch of Halle Berry.

"Bailey." Nero gestures for her to come in. "You're late."

So this is Bailey Spade, also known as Freda Krueger—the dream walker who works for Nero from time to time.

"Bowser," Bailey says with mockery in her voice. She looks at me with a good-natured smirk. "You're his Princess Peach, right?"

Bowser? She called Nero that before—referencing a video game character who happens to be the archenemy of Mario. When I first heard it, I thought she used the nickname because of Nero's deep voice, but now I realize that it might be the fact that the character in question is a very similar creature to a dragon: he can breathe fire and is scaly. That means Bailey knows about Nero's nature.

Processing all the information in a flash, I chuckle at my own Princess Peach nickname. In the Mario games, the princess is who Bowser always tries to kidnap and bring to his castle in order to marry her.

"Hi, Bailey," I say. "I'm Sasha. If you're here to help me, I'm sorry. I have no time to take a nap today. We'll have to do this some other time."

Out of the corner of my eye, I spot Claudia snatching Lucifur off the ground and scratching the evil one under the chin.

Instead of disemboweling the dragoness, the cat purrs contentedly and closes her eyes.

"Actually," Nero growls at me. "It will happen today. Now, to be precise. Vlad and the others aren't back anyway. There's time."

"There's bossy, and there's this." Bailey shakes her head and looks at me apologetically. "If he weren't my best-paying customer, I'd leave out of principle."

"It's fine," I say with a sigh. "I guess if we have the time, I'll do it—if just to shut him up. Besides"—I smile at her—"I wouldn't want you to miss out on your fee because of me."

"Thanks." Bailey examines me with unabashed curiosity. "You know, you're just as pretty in person as in his dreams. That's rare."

"Let's take this to the couch," Nero snarls before I can ask whose dreams Bailey is talking about—even though it's obvious they're Nero's.

"I'll meet you all there," I say and sprint for my room.

Once there, I fill my pockets with my favorite magic paraphernalia.

If there's any downtime between now and the end of the world, I hope I'll get to see how my vampire reflexes affected my repertoire. Also, if I get another chance to show off my skills to Claudia, I want to make sure I get her to pee her pants.

Do dragons need to urinate, by the way? *Do I?* Because I've been drinking my liquids, and I haven't felt the slightest urge… And what about poop?

"Just to clarify," Bailey says when I return to the living room, still puzzling over this. "We're not going to sleep together."

"That's good to know," I say, matching her snarky tone. "So how *will* this work?"

"Simple." She plays with a piece of strange furry jewelry on her wrist—a colorful thing that looks familiar for some reason. "You're going to sleep, and

I'm going to touch you. But not in a dirty way. Especially not in front of your jealous boyfriend."

Boyfriend?

I suppose that's better than princess-napper.

Or husband.

Or pet owner.

Nero grunts something unintelligible as Bailey, Fluffster, and Claudia chuckle at his—and maybe my—expense.

"Okay." I lie down, and Fluffster runs over and jumps into my arms.

"You're the domovoi, right?" Bailey asks Fluffster. "Felix mentioned you. It's great to meet you in person."

Oh, right.

She knows Felix.

I wonder if he'll be sad to have missed her.

"Is that your domovoi's girlfriend?" Bailey nods at the cat in Claudia's arms.

"No," I say. "It's his mistress."

"Hardy-har-har," Fluffster says mentally. Turning to Bailey, he asks, "What was that part about the fee? How much are your services?"

"Nero is taking care of it," I say quickly. The last thing I want is for Fluffster to rip anyone into bits over budget concerns. "Now, how about we start?"

"One second." Fluffster looks at the furry wrist-thing on Bailey's arm. "What is that?"

"It's Pom," Bailey says proudly. "He's a looft who is my friend and companion."

The bracelet-like thing changes color but doesn't respond in any other way.

Is it, per chance, an imaginary friend?

Then the term "looft" triggers a memory. We learned about them at Orientation. They live on cow-like creatures called moofts—which I saw on the cannibal gnomes' world.

I'm tempted to ask a bunch of questions, but I don't want Bailey to think I'm calling her a cow, so I close my eyes and even out my breathing.

I don't know if it's the presence of a dream walker or the relaxation from snuggling Fluffster, but I fall into sleep faster than I ever have.

CHAPTER TWELVE

I'M STANDING in front of five hundred spectators and my glossophobia/stage fright is speeding up my heart rate to supersonic levels.

Yet I don't faint.

I'm elated instead.

Performing magic is what I was born to do—and the adrenaline from my phobia is just a free stimulant my body produces to keep me sharp and alert.

"I need a volunteer from the crowd," I say into the microphone, my voice unshaken. "Someone who's good with firearms, like a police officer."

As the chosen lady cop walks to the stage, my already-prodigious stress response turns sharp and primal.

This is it.

I'm about to do the most dangerous of all illusions in magic—and I'm only allowing myself to do this because, as a vampire, I have a good chance of surviving a mistake.

I think.

"Please examine this gun," I say, handing the revolver to the cop.

She takes the weapon and finds nothing untoward.

"Now also check this bullet," I tell her, and she does.

"Initial the bullet, please." I hand her a permanent marker.

She does as I ask.

I then tell her to load the bullet into the gun as Nero—my scantily clad assistant—walks onto the stage.

Usually, revealing outfits are the way assistants draw attention from the illusionist, but today, I had Nero dress this way so the people can see he's not wearing some special gear underneath to explain away the effect.

Or at least that's what I told him. In reality, the outfit is there because I enjoy ogling his hard-muscled body.

"Please give the gun to my assistant and then stand behind him," I tell the cop as Nero and I take our places on the opposite sides of the stage.

She eyes him with obvious interest, then nervously walks over to give him the gun before taking her place behind his back.

Nero raises the gun.

I do my best not to think of a factoid I never told Nero—that twelve magicians I know of have died performing this very illusion.

Then again, unlike me, they weren't vampires.

As far as I know anyway.

Now that I'm not staring at a large audience, I feel calmer—even with the gun pointed at me.

Nero aims.

People in the audience inhale loudly.

Nero pulls the trigger.

The loud bang nearly deafens me, but everything goes as planned.

I'm not dead.

The only harm is to the enamel on my teeth—and that recovers vampire quick.

Everyone in the theater is dead silent.

The light guy moves a spotlight to me so everyone can see the metal gleaming in my mouth.

It's the bullet.

I "caught" it between my teeth.

Nero hands the cop rubber gloves and asks her to check the bullet.

She stumbles over and takes the bullet from my mouth.

"Are those your initials on that bullet?" I ask her.

"Yes," she says in wonderment. "This is the same bullet that was in the gun."

"Thank you," I say. "Everyone, let's have a round of applause for New York's finest!"

The cop leaves the stage as the audience members launch to their feet and start clapping like their palms are on fire.

As I bow, I grin like a lunatic.

This—the sound of ovations—is what gives my life purpose. It's a rush that's better than anything, barring sex with Nero.

And it gets better.

When I look at the adoring crowd, I spot Mom, who rarely comes to my performances, and Dad, who always does. Next to them in the front row are Felix, Ariel, Rasputin, Lucretia, Kit, and Vlad. All are cheering and looking at me with various levels of pride.

Except something isn't right.

There are people behind them that shouldn't be there.

Before I can say or do anything, an arc of black energy hits me in the head, completely paralyzing me.

The energy came from one of the people in the second row—the ones behind my friends and family.

I gape in horror.

Behind Mom is Beatrice, the necromancer, and behind Dad is Harper, Beatrice's succubus girlfriend.

And that's not all.

Behind Vlad is Baba Yaga, and she is where the paralyzing energy came from.

Behind Rasputin is Darian, and behind Ariel is Gaius.

Why can't I shake the feeling they can't be here?

Am I in denial?

Behind Felix is Koschei, and behind Lucretia is Woland—the chort who can stop hearts. Finally, behind Kit is the giant orc chieftain whose son Nero killed.

I strain to move, but I can't so much as twitch a muscle.

With evil grins, Beatrice, Baba Yaga, and the rest of my enemies take out identical, ceremonial-looking daggers and stab the person in front of them.

Mom, Dad, and everyone else I care about die in a horrible instant.

I strain to free myself from the paralysis so hard that a blood vessel bursts in my eye—to no avail.

I can't move.

All I can do is watch.

The audience starts screaming and running away.

Nero finally notices what happened.

Moving with supernatural speed, he reloads the gun, takes aim, and shoots.

Baba Yaga's head explodes.

My paralysis goes away just as a new person blurs onto the stage.

It's Yudo, a.k.a. the usurper—the dragon who killed Nero's parents.

Clutching a giant sword, the usurper blurs toward Nero.

"Behind you!" I yell as I leap across the stage, but Nero keeps aiming at the bad guys in the second row.

The theater audience stampedes for the emergency exits, and their panicked shrieks must be why Nero doesn't hear my warnings, or Yudo's approach.

Nero shoots again.

Woland's head explodes this time.

I'm halfway across the stage, but I might as well be on the other side of the world.

Yudo slices with his sword, and Nero's head separates from his body.

Something inside me snaps.

I close the distance between us, grab Nero's gun, and unload it into Yudo's head.

The dragon collapses, dead as a doornail.

I grab his sword just as Harper, Beatrice, Darian, Gaius, and Koschei get onto the stage.

"You'll all pay for what you did," I hiss at them, and to highlight my words, I disembowel Darian with the sword.

The rest of them step back, so I stalk toward them.

With fear in her eyes, Beatrice shoots multi-colored energy at all the dead, and they begin to reanimate as zombies.

Her moment of distraction gives me a window of opportunity to literally chop her in half.

As she dies, the zombies still.

"You bitch!" Harper screams. "You will—"

I'll never know what the succubus was going to say because my fist enters her chest and pulls out her still-beating heart—at the same exact time as I behead Gaius with the sword.

As Gaius's head rolls to the side, I toss Harper's heart at it with a curse.

Koschei—the only one left alive—grins at me. "You

know I'm not so easy to kill. They call me the Immortal for a reason."

"Good," I growl and chop off his right leg. "That means I get to enjoy this for as long as I want."

Koschei screams in pain.

Encouraged, I chop off his other leg.

He screams even louder and tries to crawl away from me.

As I stalk after him, a plan crystalizes in my head. I'm going to torture-kill him over and over, until the pain of losing my family and friends goes away.

Which it never will.

Just like my grief over losing Rose, his earlier victim.

Viciously, I carve him up with the sword until my arms go numb—and that's a long time when one is a vampire.

I don't know how many times Koschei dies and comes back before someone new walks out onto the stage.

The newcomer is slow-clapping and grinning like a maniac.

Wiping Koschei's blood from my eyes, I look at her.

Of course.

It's Lilith.

She's beaming at me with maternal pride.

"You." I clutch my bloody sword tighter. "If *you* set this up, I'll kill you slower than him."

I take a menacing step toward Lilith.

Which is when a figure appears between us—a

person it takes me a moment to recognize because we've just met.

It's Bailey Spade.

The dream walker.

Which means—

"That's right," Bailey says soothingly. "This is a nightmare."

"Oh." Intense relief replaces all the angst. "Of course, this is a dream."

How could I not see it sooner? Nero would never let me do a bullet catch, let alone "shoot" at me personally.

And Mom and Dad wouldn't watch a bullet catch so calmly either. Neither would my friends.

More importantly, Baba Yaga and the rest of the baddies are long dead—something I could've only forgotten in the dream world.

"I hope you don't mind that I cut into this dream before you got to matricide," Bailey says. "If you think that would be therapeutic, I could—"

"A dream," I mutter. "Just a stupid dream."

"Yep," Bailey says. "Now if you don't mind, I'd like to change the scene." She looks around at the blood and gore around us, and as soon as I nod, it all disappears.

We're on a cloud now—but unlike normal clouds that are just water vapor and thus would let us fall through, this cloud feels like a comfy down pillow under my feet.

Below the cloud is a soothing view of a never-ending ocean.

"Please get on the proverbial couch," Bailey says, and as she does, a couch appears on the surface of the cloud.

I take a seat and notice I'm no longer soaked in the blood of my enemies. Even my clothes are different now. Bailey clearly has control over every detail of what happens in this part of the dream.

"How do you feel?" she asks, perching on a cushy-looking chair that appears under her butt.

"I can't believe I didn't realize I was dreaming," I say. "It now seems so obvious."

"That's normal." Bailey crosses her legs. "Dreamworld is rarely logical. It takes a lot of training to notice the inconsistencies and realize you're in a dream. But if you learned to do that, you'd be able to do some of the things I can. The technique is called lucid dreaming, and I can teach it to you as part of our sessions."

She says more, but I get distracted when a fluffy creature appears to the side of Bailey's chair.

I stare at it.

It's an animal I've never seen before. An animal that seems to be a figment of someone's imagination.

"Hi," the creature says to me in a voice as cute as the rest of it, before it turns as white as the cloud below it. "I'm Pom."

"Pom, I'm working," Bailey says sternly to the creature. "We talked about this."

Pom's color darkens.

Bailey ignores the being and looks at me

apologetically. "This is what he looks like in the dreamworld." She waves her now-naked wrist in the air. "I guess he figured since you have a talking fluffy pet yourself, you wouldn't mind seeing *him*."

"A pet?" Pom asks indignantly, his color growing even darker. "I think you mean a symbiont."

"Sure," Bailey says sarcastically. "A symbiont. Not a pet, and especially not a parasite. Can you let me work now?"

"Wait, you mean this is the looft you had on your wrist?" I look at Pom. "The furry wristband?"

"I know." She grins. "In the dreamworld, he's pure, weaponized cuteness."

Pom puffs up, and his color goes back to a lighter hue.

"Don't you think your cat and even the chinchilla are ugly in comparison?" Bailey says to me with a wink.

"Yeah," I say, playing along. "Hideous."

"I like to say that Pom is cuter than your Earth's koala and panda bears," Bailey says. "Cuter even than the otters."

I chuckle. "He reminds me of a Pokémon," I say, getting into the spirit of this.

"Yeah." Bailey scratches Pom's fluffy ear. "It's like if Jigglypuff and Pikachu had a bastard child."

I laugh. Now that she said it, I can totally see the resemblance.

"Do I *have* to leave?" Pom asks petulantly. "I like Sasha. She reminds me of you."

"Thanks," I say. "I think."

"Oh, it's a compliment," Bailey says. "Pomsie thinks the world of me."

"Flatter yourself much?" the creature mutters.

"So, you want him to go?" Bailey looks at me. "For what it's worth, even if you don't see him, he hears and sees everything that happens in the dreamworld."

"I don't mind," I say. "Especially since I don't even know what's going to happen."

"Right." She steeples her fingers. "Actually, I didn't plan much for today outside of setting up our connection. That you're still asleep is rare but gives us a chance to do a little post-nightmare therapy, if you'd like."

"I guess," I say. "What does that entail?"

"Well, we can start by you telling me what you think that whole bloody business was about."

"I don't know." I shift my weight on the suddenly uncomfortable couch. "It started with a magic performance, and I can never do those again—so the nightmare could be my subconscious telling me how upset I am about that." I look at her expectantly, but she takes on an unreadable expression she must've stolen from Lucretia. "Or this dream could be more literal," I continue. "Maybe I'm afraid of losing Nero. Or my parents and my friends."

Realizing I'm sweating bullets, I stop and take a breath. Somehow—probably due to Bailey—a glass of water shows up floating in the air in front of me. I grab it and gulp down the water greedily.

"Any other theories?" Bailey asks soothingly when the empty cup evaporates from my hands.

"I could just be afraid of becoming a monster, like Lilith." I glance at Pom. "Or it can all just be random firings of my neurons and mean nothing. You're the expert, so you tell *me*."

Bailey clears her throat. "I like to compare dreams to virtual reality, only instead of it being the work of a team of designers and engineers, it's your own brain that's responsible for the experiences."

"That doesn't explain much," I say. "What do you think it all meant?"

"Me?" Bailey absentmindedly pets Pom on his head. "This isn't about me. It's your dreams, so you have to make sense of them. Your guesses are pretty insightful —especially for your first time."

"They are?" I lean back on the couch. "It might be because I do regular therapy with a shrink."

"Ah." She pulls her hand away from Pom. "That shows. You should keep doing that in parallel to our sessions."

"Sessions, as in plural? You mean I'll have to dream like this again?"

"Only if you want," she says. "Being a vampire, you don't need to sleep, and therefore, you're an unusual client as far as nightmares go. You will not suffer from sleep deprivation on a physical level. Still, dream therapy can help you work on every one of the fears you just mentioned—and your fear of public speaking as well. Assuming that's what you want."

I consider it.

Now that she's mentioned it, it would be great to not get so nervous when I have to speak in public—especially if that means I'd enjoy performing magic on a stage in my dreams.

Not sure I'd like to see people I care about die again, though, even in a nightmare.

"I think I might want some help from you," I say hesitantly. "But I don't want to delve into every one of my fears—at least not until after I save the world."

As soon as I say the words, I want to smack myself for forgetting about Tartarus so completely.

I don't have time for this.

I never had time for this.

Nero bullied me into this dream therapy, and I shouldn't have let him.

"Save the world?" Bailey raises an eyebrow.

"It's a long story," I mutter. "So what do you say? Can we continue this another time?"

"It's your boyfriend's money," Bailey says. "Besides, you did really well for your first session."

"Cool. So what now?"

"You wake up."

"Just like that?"

"Yeah," she says. "Will it, and it should happen. When you're ready for another session, just fall asleep again, and I'll do my best to visit you—though no promises. I have a ton of clients fighting for my attention."

"And you won't need to touch me again?" I ask, remembering what Nero said.

"No," she says. "And since you're a vampire, this should be easy. If I see you sleeping, I'll know you're doing it for therapy. That isn't the case with all my clients; they sleep because they need to do so."

"Great," I say. "How do I will myself to wake up?"

"Like Nike," Bailey says. "Just do it."

I stand up from the couch and will myself to wake up.

With a start, I open my eyes in my living room.

CHAPTER THIRTEEN

"YOU OKAY?" Fluffster asks in my head. "You squeezed me pretty hard in your sleep."

"I'm fine." I loosen my grip on my poor domovoi and sit up.

Just like the last time I woke up, I feel zero grogginess.

Must indeed be a vampire thing.

"How was the therapy?" Nero asks, entering the living room with Claudia, who's still holding Lucifur—and somehow still has all her limbs intact.

"Trippy." I put Fluffster on the floor and look at Bailey's furry wristband.

It must be the same Pom as in the dream, but it looks very different here. I wonder if its appearance in the dreamworld is a figment of Bailey's imagination, like the clouds and all that.

"It was a great start," Bailey says with an unreadable expression.

"Good." Nero glances down at his phone. Without looking up, he says, "Set up more sessions and put the bill on my tab in Gomorrah."

"Deal." Bailey touches her pet wristband.

"Are Vlad and the others back on Earth?" I ask, tearing my gaze away from the looft.

"Stepped through the gate a few minutes ago," Nero says. "Eric is going to come get us in a moment."

"Finally." I stand up. "Let's go."

Claudia puts down the cat, and we all walk Bailey out. When her elevator arrives, I tell her that it was nice to meet her.

"The pleasure was all mine," she says, then looks at Nero. "Not that there was any pleasure during our session. Everything was strictly platonic."

The elevator doors close in front of her, and Nero's phone dings.

He looks at a text, and I realize I haven't checked my own phone since we got back from the Otherlands —so I do so now.

I have numerous texts from Lucretia for some reason.

As an echo of my nightmare where I lost my newfound half-sister, my heart rate speeds up.

Then I see what the messages say and exhale in relief. Lucretia invited me to her new Mandate Rite. As a vampire, she has to go through that unpleasantness again, and it's scheduled for today.

A half hour ago, to be precise.

I scroll through all the messages she sent. After the

original invitation, her texts got more and more worried about my lack of reply. She even called me a few times.

I call her back, but it goes to voicemail.

I'm fine, sis, I text, grinning at the last part. *Sorry I missed your Rite, but maybe I'll catch you in the castle? I'll be heading there for a Council meeting in a second. Again, sorry about the delay in reply. I have a good excuse, I promise.*

As I look up from my screen, Eric appears in the corridor.

"Ladies first." Nero nods at his sister and me.

Eric walks up to Claudia and touches her shoulder. They poof out.

Then Eric reappears and grabs me.

I doubt I'll ever get tired of being teleported. One second, we're in my building; the next, I find myself on a familiar circular platform with the scent of sage incense tickling my nose.

Kit, Vlad, and the others are already here, standing next to me, dressed in those ceremonial robes with hoods on their heads.

As is customary, candles are lit up all around us— each of them seemingly floating, giving the place a Hogwarts Great Hall kind of vibe.

The rest of the Council is in their seats, also robed, their faces barely discernible in the gloomy light.

I look around for familiar faces but find none. I wonder if Chester—the probability manipulator who hired Beatrice to kill me, but later helped me and Nero defeat Darian—is back on the Council, as Nero promised.

I don't see him here, so probably not yet. Which makes sense, as Nero has been busy with his recent conquest.

"Kind of creepy to see them from down here," Kit whispers to me. "I feel like we're about to be judged."

Claudia studies the Council with amusement. She's clearly never seen *Eyes Wide Shut* and thus doesn't find this orgy vibe even slightly unsettling. Her lack of fear makes sense, though. As a dragon, she can probably decimate each and every one of these beings with a single breath.

Eric turns up again, bringing Nero, then disappears just as quickly. I guess he isn't on the Council.

Next to us, Vlad pulls down his hood, revealing his broody face. "I already gave the Council a brief overview of the threat," he says. "But we waited for you before discussing the plan of action."

A person gets up. Even with the hood of his robe, I can see that he's an elderly man who's gone bald on top but retained wispy long hair on the sides. Above his thin lips is a huge gray mustache. He reminds me of a mad scientist determined to take over the world—an honor for which he'll have to fight Tartarus now.

"How do we even know the seer is telling the truth?" He looks down at me with his slightly cross-eyed gaze. "The last time she was here, it was to discuss her TV performance."

"That's Easton," Kit whispers into my ear. "As a

dream walker, he's got something on everyone in the Council, which is why his annoying attitude is tolerated."

"I say we get proof," the dream walker says. "I can personally examine her dreams to—"

"Over your cold, dead body," Nero growls, his limbal rings turning dragony. "The same goes for anyone else who even thinks about touching her."

He sweeps his gaze across the room, and surprise surprise, no one wants to touch me all of a sudden.

"As everyone here knows, I can tell truth from lies," Nero says in a low, hard voice. "And Sasha is telling the truth. Unless"—he glares at the already-cowed dream walker—"you're doubting *my* word?"

Easton drops into his seat without a peep.

I guess he doesn't have something compromising on *everyone* in the Council.

A new person stands up. Under the hood, she's a gorgeous woman who—for lack of a better word—smells delicious.

Familiarly delicious.

"That's Tatum," Kit whispers huskily. "She's the most powerful succubus in the world and has had affairs with half the Council." Spotting my eyes narrowing on Nero, she adds hastily, "Not him, don't worry. He's never been with anyone on the Council."

Good. I don't want to have to kill yet another succubus—or anyone else on the Council.

I have a feeling they'd frown on such behavior.

"I think it's obvious what our next step should be,"

Tatum says in a sing-song voice. "Something of this magnitude can't be handled by our Council alone. We need to call a meeting of all the Councils."

"She's right," says a woman standing next to us—the one who helped Nero in his battles by summoning animals to do her bidding. "The Paris Council has their own powerful seer, and while no one here is doubting Sasha's vision"—she gives Nero a cautious look—"it would be prudent to hear what he has foreseen as well, and what he thinks can be done about the situation."

A seer on the Paris Council.

Why do I have a bad feeling about this?

"I agree," Nero says ceremoniously. "Does anyone disagree?"

Again, no one so much as makes a peep.

"Then we reconvene when the arrangements are concluded," Nero says with finality. Stepping aside, he approaches the guy who turned into a giant werewolf during the dragon world battles and says in a low voice, "We need to talk."

"Of course," the werewolf replies. "I'll meet you in the hallway."

Nero nods, then grabs my hand and drags me out of the room, with Claudia on our tails.

"Sasha, this is Eduardo," Nero says when we're out of the Council's earshot. "He's the alpha of the New York City pack."

"Nice to meet you." I extend my hand and shake Eduardo's giant one. "I saw you fight in a vision. It was an impressive sight."

"Thank you," Eduardo says, then looks expectantly at Nero.

"Tell him," Nero says to me.

"I saw a vision where I was attacked by a werewolf," I say to Eduardo. "A giant one. Bigger than you."

"Impossible," Eduardo says. "Are you sure fear didn't just mess with your mind? My kind can be rather intimidating up close."

I suppress an eyeroll. "No, I don't think so."

"Then describe him," Eduardo says with a frown.

As I do, the werewolf looks more and more confused.

"There is no such wolf in these parts," he says when I finish. "Are you sure it wasn't just Kit or one of her kind with their tricks?"

"No clue," I say. "How would I tell the difference?"

"You probably can't," Eduardo says. "Very few of us could—which doesn't help matters."

"Can you ask around?" Nero suggests. "Maybe he's a youngster who's not on your radar? Or a visitor from somewhere?"

"I'll do that," Eduardo says. "But don't get your hopes up."

And without so much as a goodbye, he stalks off.

Alrighty then.

Maybe werewolves are only good at socializing with other werewolves?

Shrugging, Nero starts walking down the catacomb-like path through the castle.

When I'm sure we're outside even super-hearing, I say, "The Paris seer is Nostradamus, isn't it?"

"That's right." Nero's face is dark. "But, despite what he did to you and your father, he *should* be our ally in this."

"I know," I say. "He wants Tartarus dead more than anyone. The question is, at what cost?"

"Right," Nero says grimly. "He's no doubt playing his own game."

My phone dings, attracting Claudia's curious gaze.

I check the device. It's a text from Lucretia.

I just came back to my senses and saw your replies. Are you anywhere near the recovery room?

"Where are we in the castle?" I ask Nero. "Lucretia is done with her Mandate Rite and wants to meet up."

"Tell her we're headed to the southwest tower," Nero says, then grabs Claudia's elbow and pulls her into a left turn. "She'll know where that is."

Following them, I text Lucretia back, and she tells me she'll see us there.

"She used the words 'came to,'" I say to Nero. "Does that mean the Rite is as unpleasant for a vampire as it was for me as a pre-vamp?"

Nero grimaces. "Almost everyone passes out from the Rite. And the stronger you are, the more painful the experience."

"Interesting," I say and notice Claudia listening with interest. "I guess I won't rush to get my second Rite any time soon."

"You'll need it ASAP, actually," Nero says. "Without

the Mandate aura, you're not recognized in the Cognizant society and therefore considered outside the law."

"Right. I guess it's like ripping off a Band-Aid—best to get it over with." Then something clicks, and I say, "The werewolf in my vision. I didn't see his aura."

"You didn't?" Nero raises an eyebrow.

"No," I say. "But I don't see anyone's aura right now —so I wonder if I'd nudge that future off kilter by going through the Rite before that attack."

"It's possible you didn't see the guy's aura because he was from another world," Nero says. "Then again, since you need to go through the Rite soon anyway, why not do it today?"

To highlight his words, he grabs one of the monks passing by and whispers something into the man's ear.

Nodding solemnly, the monk rushes off, presumably to make the arrangements.

"Would I see an aura of someone from another world?" I follow Nero and Claudia up a narrow staircase. "Assuming that someone is also from a world that uses the Mandate stuff."

"No," Nero says. "The Mandate is specific to each world—which is actually another reason for you to go through the Rite today, along with any other Cognizant on Earth who hasn't done so already."

"Oh?" I look at Claudia to see if she's following her brother's logic, but she just shrugs.

"When Tartarus and his children arrive, we'll be able to tell them apart from Earth Cognizant by their lack of aura," Nero says. "In fact, the Councils will probably issue an order to kill anyone without an aura on sight."

"In that case, I will go through this Rite as well," Claudia states. "We don't want the collateral damage of someone trying to 'kill me on sight.'"

Nero stops, frowning at her. "Are you sure? You're more powerful than most, and it'll be very painful for you."

Claudia shrugs carelessly.

"I don't know if it can even be arranged," he continues. "The Mandate is a privilege of the Cognizant who are born on this world. The Councils do make exceptions for some from other worlds, like me, but—"

"I'm confident they'll make the exception for me as well when I tell them it's the price for my help." Claudia winks at him, then looks at me. "I'd help regardless, of course, but they don't need to know that."

"We'll talk more about this later," Nero says and stops at the end of the staircase in front of a large door. "The southwest tower is through there."

With a screech of rusty hinges, he pushes open the door.

"There you are," Lucretia says, grinning, as we step into a room with circular stone walls—the kind where an evil dragon might keep his damsel in distress.

I better not piss off Nero. This place might give him ideas.

"Lucretia, this is Claudia," Nero says. "Claudia, this

is Lucretia—Sasha's half-sister. Like us, they just reunited as siblings."

"Nice to meet you, Sasha's sister," Claudia says to Lucretia with a mischievous smile. "Since I'm Nero's sister, we're practically family."

That not-so-subtle hint again. Claudia doesn't give up easily, does she?

I was hoping Lucretia didn't understand the variant of Russian that is the dragon tongue, but judging by the evil, Lilith-like grin on her face, my half-sister totally got it.

"How are you feeling?" I ask her, remembering she's just gone through the Rite.

"Yes, how are you doing?" Nero eyes her with concern. He's either a more caring boss than I'd realized, or more likely, he's thinking about what it's going to be like for me and his sister.

"I was surprisingly well as soon as I got my senses back," Lucretia says. "It seems like it's easier to handle the Rite the second time around."

"Oh, good," I say with relief.

I'm about to explain that I will be undergoing this myself shortly, but Lucretia grins and says, "I have a huge surprise for you."

My heart speeds up. I think I know where this is headed, but I don't want to get my hopes up.

"It's sibling related," she confirms, her grin widening.

Of course. When one goes through a Rite, their

family joins the ceremony—which means our mystery sibling was there for hers.

As if in reply to my thoughts, the door opens—and I can't believe my eyes.

This is my sibling?

You've got to be kidding me.

CHAPTER FOURTEEN

"I HOPE you can see why I needed to clear it with him first," Lucretia says.

"Yeah," I say as my brother walks in—followed by yet another surprise relative straight out of a *Jerry Springer* episode.

It's Chester and his daughter Roxy, a teen werewolf who, with her *Mean Girls* wolfpack, had attacked me, and more than once.

And now, it turns out, she's my niece.

In their defense, both father and daughter look chastened—and so do I, I'm sure. I already felt bad about what I did to Roxy, and that was before I knew we were related.

Hopefully, now all this will just be a story to laugh about at the Thanksgiving table—right after Lilith gets the Nobel Peace Prize.

Speaking of Lilith, now that I know what to look for, Chester does resemble her a little—especially that trickster smile of his. The same can't be said about Roxy. She takes after her mom—Chester's wife who was also Darian's lover.

Yep, definitely *Jerry Springer*. Cognizant style.

"I want to start by saying I'm very sorry I pointed a gun at you," I tell Roxy and extend a hand to her.

She stares at it intently, then shakes it with real enthusiasm.

With her usual queen bee demeanor toned down and her face relatively makeup-free, my niece finally looks her age—making me feel like a monster despite her acceptance of my apology.

Chester elbows his daughter.

"Right." She examines her Louboutin boots. "I'm sorry as well. I should've sensed that you were family. You look a lot like Aunt Lucretia." Meeting my gaze, she earnestly adds, "Nothing is more important to me than family. I hope you can believe that."

Poor girl. Losing her mom—and having Chester for a father—must've made her yearn for strong familial ties.

"Sasha has so many relatives," Claudia whispers to Nero, but loudly enough for everyone to overhear. "If you marry her, they'll be *our* family."

Great. Nero's sister must be in the same boat as my niece, having lost *both* of her parents at a young age.

I sneak a glance at Nero.

His face is unreadable. If he likes this preposterous idea, he shows no sign of it. Lucretia, however, grins widely, while Chester and Roxy's faces are unchanged.

Maybe they don't understand the Russian variant that is the dragon tongue?

Pushing all thoughts of Nero's reaction aside, I smile at Roxy. "Of course. Let's not ever mention our rocky start again."

"I, too, wish we'd started off on a better footing," Chester says, his satyr-like face unusually serious.

"You mean you wish you hadn't tried to kill her using Beatrice?" Nero growls.

Roxy looks at her father with wide eyes. I guess she didn't know the full extent of our history.

"I only knew Sasha was someone Darian was interested in," Chester says. More bitterly, he adds, "I had no idea our loving mother popped out yet another kid she could ignore."

"I don't think Lilith meant to ignore *me*," I say with a grimace. "And trust me, the absentee parenting you and Lucretia experienced was for the best."

"Right." Chester examines me as if he's seeing me for the first time. "Lucretia mentioned you've been spending time with Lilith."

"She—"

"Hold on," Roxy says to me, sniffing the air. "Something is different about you today. You don't just look like Aunt Lucretia; you smell like she does, too. At least how she started to smell recently. After she turned."

Great. Now I've failed my niece's sniff test.

"You're right," Nero says to her. "Sasha is now a

vampire. Lilith manipulated her into drinking her blood and then made sure she died."

My three relatives gasp as one, and Lucretia exclaims, "How could I have missed it? You don't have an aura. I can even sense—"

"Hold on," Chester says. "This is too much to process. Can someone start at the beginning?"

"Sure," I say. "It all started when I discovered a map to my father." I look to see if Nero reacts, since the map in question was in his safe, but his face is still closed-off. "I then organized an expedition to rescue him," I continue, "and ended up on a world that Lilith made her own. A world where people worship her as a goddess. That's where she'd been spending most of the time that she was, as you say, ignoring you."

"A goddess," Chester mumbles, and it's unclear if he's impressed or outraged.

Who am I kidding?

He's impressed. And I might've just given him an idea to take over some poor world and be their god of mischief.

Oops.

"Anyway," I say, "that's what we were up to when you helped us with your lion at the airport. After that, Nero locked me up, I escaped, and then Lilith, Nostradamus, and these chorts showed up." I proceed to tell them about the events that followed—ending with how Woland killed me.

I then describe my apocalyptic vision. Since they're

my family, I want them to evacuate if I fail to stop Tartarus.

Chester's face tightens as I speak, and Roxy's eyes grow wider with every word. "Earth is going to be destroyed?" she exclaims when I'm done. "Why didn't you start with that?"

"I hope to stop it," I say defensively. "That's what we're here for, by the way—to talk to the Council of Councils in a few minutes."

"Of course," Chester says. "I heard a meeting had been called, and I wondered what it was about." He cocks his head, studying me. "No offense, *sis*, but I wonder what it is about you that made Nostradamus think you can defeat Tartarus. I mean, our family is pretty impressive, don't get me wrong, but that guy is a legend of a different caliber."

"To start, she inherited two powers," Lucretia says. "Vampirism from Lilith, and seer abilities from Rasputin. Have you ever heard of a seer vampire before?"

"No," Chester says. "Double powers are pretty rare."

"Speaking of that," I say. "Could it be that I actually inherited *three* powers? Is it possible that because Lilith wanted a superpowered kid to save her, her prodigious probability manipulation made it happen for her?"

Chester scratches his chin. "You did manage not to die when I tried to make it happen. That's very difficult for someone without trickster powers. I thought it was your seer ability, but maybe—"

"She won against me as well," Roxy says, her cheeks

reddening. "And I'm under the protection of your luck, so the same logic applies."

Nero looks at me thoughtfully. "You know, now that you bring it up, this *could* explain your abilities with the stock market." He turns to the others. "I've been pushing Sasha to grow her seer powers by asking for stock recommendations, and she has obliged wonderfully. But, if looked at from the right perspective, her performance might've been due to probability powers instead of her seer ability. She was just too good—even for a seer of her power level." He looks at me admiringly. "Sometimes, I had a feeling that the mere fact that she gave me a stock *caused* the market to shift in that stock's favor."

He's right.

Without bothering to get visions of the stock market, I gave Nero stocks with tickers like EAT, CAKE, BEAT, HOG, LUV, FIZZ, YUM, NUT, COOL, WOOF, and even sillier ones without doing any research. I just pulled them out of my behind because they sounded humorous—yet they all made him money.

"To move the stock market like that would require a lot of raw probability manipulation power," Chester muses. "Did you encounter any other abnormalities like that?"

"I haven't exactly been lucky lately, if that's what you mean," I say.

Not lucky.

Right.

That's an understatement of the century.

"Bad things can still happen to probability manipulators." There's pain in Chester's eyes as he says this. "I've lost my wife, and more recently, my seat on the Council. Temporarily." He looks at Nero meaningfully, then sighs. "The universe is too complex to manipulate every aspect."

"Right," I say, trying to think of more examples that might fit with the probability manipulation theory. "When I need a vision, I often get just the right one. When I join minds with other seers, I get glimpses of very pertinent memories of theirs. I always thought it was my subconscious mind helping me out, somehow, but it could've been this instead."

"That's a good point," Nero says. "When she was but a novice seer, she managed to dream the exact visions she needed to thwart you and Beatrice, and also the Council."

He's right.

I haven't thought about those dream visions in a while, but they were laser-target accurate—and arrived just in time to save me.

"You know," I say. "According to many YouTube comments, my TV performance made a lot of people believe that my 'prediction' about that earthquake in Mexico was due to luck."

"I didn't even think of that." Chester grins, looking eerily like an evil villain. "That means you needed just the barest potential for probability manipulation as a basis, and then the TV performance would've boosted it."

"Wow." Roxy looks me over admiringly. "If this is true, no one will ever mess with our family. Assuming we survive Tartarus, that is."

"Right." I smile at her. "Now, if I were lucky enough to figure out how to check if I have these powers, I might start to believe in them."

Roxy looks at her father. "Can't she do the stupid test you made me do all my life?"

Chester pats his pockets and pouts. "I don't have a deck of cards with me today, but I guess I can devise another test that—"

"Wait." I put both of my hands into my pockets. In the right one, I wrap my trusty deck of cards in the flash paper I grabbed earlier, and in the left pocket, I grab a lighter. "What did you just say you need?"

"I said I don't have a deck of playing cards," Chester says, enunciating every word as if I suddenly lost forty IQ points.

"Well, I have this ball of paper," I say and pull out the wrapped deck. "Could that help?"

Before he can give a snarky answer, I ignite the paper with the lighter.

In a big flash of fire, I'm left holding a deck of cards.

Moving as fast as my vampire powers allow, I unbox the cards and spring them a few times from hand to hand, in part to show off, in part to prove this is a real deck that I made appear like that.

"That's neat," Lucretia says approvingly.

Neat? I prefer mind-blowing.

"She can do so much more," Claudia says proudly. "Show her the one where the cards turn over, or where—"

"Please don't ever do something like that at Orientation." Roxy gives me a pleading look. "At least if we're telling everyone we're related."

Wow. Is card magic *that* uncool with the youth of the Cognizant community?

"The test," Nero gruffly reminds everyone. "Now that a deck of cards 'materialized,' let's get to business."

"Right," Chester says and snatches the cards from me. "Sasha, I showed you this once before." He shuffles and spreads the deck—and it's in perfect new deck order.

"Yeah," I say, not even bothering to suppress my jealousy. "You showed me this. So what?"

"This is the test. As in, I want you to do the same thing," he says and shuffles the cards again. "Here." He hands them to me. "Try it."

I shuffle the cards and wish for them to end up in new deck order. I want it as much as I want to smack that smirk off Chester's face.

When I spread the cards, they're in a random order.

"Do you know how many arrangements of cards there are in a shuffled deck?" I ask Chester in frustration. "More than there are atoms on Earth."

"True," Chester says. "That just means you need to wish it—or will it—very hard."

"How about you give her some useful instructions," Nero growls. "There's got to be a technique to it."

"Fine." Chester blows out a breath. "How about you start by willing what you want so hard that you picture it manifesting into reality? When it works, you will see strands of possibilities available to you. The strands will have a hint of the outcome and power expenditure associated with them—but it takes skill and practice until you can use them properly, so don't fret."

"Wait," I say. "What do you mean 'strands?'"

"Some call them the threads of fate. When you see them, you'll know what they are," he says. "Try closing your eyes. It helps some novices focus."

I close my eyes as he says. Then, for good measure, I take in a few meditative breaths as if I'm planning to go into Headspace.

Shuffling the cards in my hands in a soothingly rhythmic pace, I try to will them to go into a new deck order.

No sign of any strands.

As I once had to do for my seer powers, I do my best to truly believe I have this new ability. With everything I have, I convince myself—and the universe at large—that I *am* a probability manipulator.

I am because I want it.

I am because my mother is one.

I am because it might be my only chance to defeat Tartarus.

Repeating "I am" over and over like a mantra, I

picture the deck separating, first into colors, then into suits, then sorted by values.

I dwell on how cool it would be to get the deck in order after this much shuffling.

Then an inspiration strikes me, and I start picturing myself performing this "shuffle into new deck order" as a magic effect.

It would make an awesome ending to a long card magic performance.

Another inspiration strikes. If I get the cards into new order secretly, many nifty effects become possible. For example, if someone takes a card out of the deck, it would be supremely easy for me to know which one it was if I glance at the cards in order.

This last possibility must be what does it.

Suddenly, I see faint colorful lines in front of me—even though my eyes are still closed.

I'm glad I was ready for something like this; else I'd think I'm losing my remaining marbles.

When I adjust to the whole business of strands, I notice they have different "colors"—for lack of a better word—and are of different "thickness." I do my best to "feel" the colors, and as I do, a bunch of them seem to "feel right."

I stand there, shuffling and introspecting, and it doesn't take me long to realize that the thickness of the strands matches the power expenditure Chester mentioned—the thinnest of the strands seem more bendy. More amenable to control.

Some of the thicker strands happen to be of the

colors that seem the most promising. When I attempt to mentally grab one, though, it feels unreachable.

Ignoring the unyielding strand for the moment, I try one of the thinner ones—ones with a color that doesn't feel as right.

Something seems to happen.

The strand "snaps"—again, for lack of a better word.

Opening my eyes, I spread the cards in my hands.

Wow.

They're not in new deck order, but they did end up separated into red in one half and black in the other half.

This is actually a secret starting point for a bunch of effects, so if I can repeat this in the future, I just greatly expanded my repertoire.

"I can't believe this," Chester says, staring at the ordered cards. "You did inherit the power."

"Are you sure?" Roxy looks at the deck. "I'm not a math whiz, but even I can tell there are more ways a deck can end up sorted into colors like that versus a single order."

"So you do remember what I taught you," Chester says proudly. "And you're right. The odds of this happening during a shuffle are much, much higher than the chance of the deck ending up in new order. Assuming she's powerful enough to pull it off, Sasha will need a lot more training to do anything practical with her power. But this separation proves the principle of the thing. There's no doubt in my mind. Sasha is a probability manipulator, like I am."

"That *would* explain her trickster personality," Roxy mutters.

Something is wrong with *my* personality? Talk about a niece pot calling its auntie kettle black.

"There will be none of that, young lady," Chester says sternly. He looks at me. "Try again."

Before I get a chance to close my eyes, Nero's phone dings.

"The lesson will have to be postponed," he states after glancing at the screen. "The Council of Councils is waiting for us."

EVERYONE WALKS DOWN WITH US, then we separate. Nero, Claudia, and I head to the Council meeting, while the others go to wait in the room where the Rite is usually performed.

"Did you know Chester was my brother?" I ask Nero as we turn the last corner on the way to the Council's meeting room. "Or Lucretia my sister, for that matter?"

"Not exactly," he says. "I only knew Chester was Lucretia's brother. That was the main reason I didn't kill him after I learned he was trying to kill you."

"I'm glad you didn't." I stop next to the door that's our destination.

"Lucky how that turned out." Claudia looks meaningfully at her brother.

Nero nods at her, then looks at me. "As far as Lucretia being your half-sister, I only learned that when you told me. And since you also mentioned

Lucretia didn't want you to know about your other sibling yet, I honored her wishes."

"Gee, thanks," I say, not hiding my disappointment. "If our roles were reversed, I would've told you something as big as that."

He leans in, his eyes gleaming. "You're right. Next time this type of situation arises, I'll prioritize your needs."

With that, he opens the doors and steps in.

Wow.

Was that an actual apology from Nero?

My luck powers must be fully active right now.

I let Claudia in, then follow her.

Once inside, I stop and look around.

That's odd.

I expected a lot more people here for the Council of Councils.

All I see is the same group from before.

The only thing that differs is that Dr. Hekima is sitting on the podium behind a wall of large computer monitors. We walk over to check out that setup, and find that each one is running a fancy video conference app—with multiple windows that show groups of people in hooded robes. In the background, some software seems to be translating their speech in real time—that, or some behind-the-scenes people are.

Aha. So we're not meeting the other Councils in person. Each Council is assembled in their own castle, and the technology is bringing us together.

I guess that makes sense. I just didn't expect the

"Council of Councils" to resemble a corporate meeting so much.

"It's all ready," Hekima says to us, then faces the rest of the room. "Please speak up if you don't want the illusion of immersion."

"He's an illusionist," Nero whispers to Claudia. "He can make the meeting feel real, but only if you want him to."

"Of course I do," Claudia says excitedly.

"Good," Nero whispers back.

No one rejects Hekima's offer, so I don't either.

"So be it," Hekima says and raises his arms with all the drama of a symphony conductor. Pulsing red energy streams from his fingers into everyone's heads, and in the next moment, we find ourselves in a room four thousand times bigger than the one we're actually occupying.

The place now reminds me of the Colosseum in its heyday.

Very cool. Looks like Hekima is creating the illusion of a giant in-person Council of Councils meeting for us. I bet someone with his power is doing the same for the other Councils.

"I will be representing New York today," Nero booms loudly enough that the New Jersey Council—assuming there is such a thing—might hear him in person, not just on video.

"And I will be representing Paris," says a tall man in a purple robe, speaking in a French-accented English.

"And I will be representing St. Petersburg," says a

stocky woman in a crimson robe in English that has no hint of a Russian accent.

For the next few minutes, more and more people introduce themselves, and when they're not speaking English, Hekima's illusion translates it for us, likely utilizing the software we saw on his screens. It's a bit like a foreign movie that's been dubbed—and it must be personalized for each listener, because Claudia looks as if she's following what's going on.

With the intros out of the way, the St. Petersburg lady says, "Before we start, I kindly ask that Sasha—the seer who foresaw the upcoming calamity—describe her vision to us all."

I recall Nostradamus saying that Baba Yaga was one of the nicer members of the St. Petersburg Council, and now I see it was true. What kind of monster would ask me to speak in front of so many of the most powerful Cognizant in the world?

Then again, they're not really here.

It's all an illusion.

I take in a few deep breaths as Lucretia had taught me, and ignoring the cold sweat pouring down my back, I tell them what I foresaw.

"Thank you," the crimson-robed lady says when I finish. "Now I'd like to ask Nostradamus—of the Paris Council—to weigh in on this prophecy."

She's good. She didn't exactly call me an unreliable liar, but the subtext is there.

Nostradamus stands up, and I feel a strong urge to punch him in the face for his attack in Headspace. But I resist because a) he isn't even here, b) even if he was, he'd probably see the punch coming and dodge, and c) even if I landed a hit, it would've been on a blind guy, which is a dick move.

"What Sasha foresaw is indeed one of the possible futures," Nostradamus says ceremonially. "I saw it in detail—including how every single person in this room who didn't evacuate died." The hooded figures around us shift uncomfortably in their seats. "Such a dire outcome need not come to pass, though," Nostradamus continues. "There is another way. One that involves Sasha—the first Cognizant I've heard of who has the combined powers of a seer, a vampire, and a probability manipulator."

He knows I'm a probability manipulator? Oh, what am I saying? Of course, he does. He's probably known it since before I was born.

Impressed hushed whispers accompany the revelation, followed by cold, calculating eyes examining me like a virus under an electron microscope.

Nostradamus waits for them to calm down, then continues. "Before arriving here on Earth, Tartarus is going to take over some other worlds, including a medieval backwater place ruled by Lilith."

A number of Councilors look unhappy at the mention of her name. Leave it to mommy dearest to make enemies everywhere.

"If we unite, with Sasha at the helm, we can face Tartarus and his children on that primitive world,"

Nostradamus says. "As there are no Cognizant besides Lilith there, we can reveal our natures indiscriminately. Winning there has many benefits—the key one being that humans on Earth will remain unaware of our existence."

There's a murmur of approval all around. These power maniacs like the idea of retaining the status quo here on Earth. They like it very much.

"Why did you steal Sasha's seer allotment for today?" Nero growls—and I can tell he's also reminding himself that attacking Nostradamus physically would be futile right now.

"I have a specific path for the future in mind," Nostradamus says, sounding contrite. "If another seer knew of this path, they could change it—by accident or out of misguidedness."

"Meaning you want to be calling all the shots, but Sasha is supposed to take on all the risk?" Nero's expression is thunderous.

"I foresaw that this august group will reward Sasha handsomely for the risk she's about to undertake," Nostradamus says. "And I also foresaw that if Tartarus gets to Earth, she will die futilely trying to protect her adoptive parents."

That does sound likely.

And, sadly, I notice Nero isn't calling out Nostradamus on any lies—which means he must be telling the truth.

"I understand you don't want to risk the life of the one you love," Nostradamus says to Nero. "But as far as

I know, there's no other choice."

The one he loves? Wait, what?

"That was a lie." Nero's eyes narrow into a death stare. "Lie to me again, and you die."

"I apologize," Nostradamus says, and I push aside his unsettling statement about Nero to focus on the matter at hand. "Obviously, there are other options. We could face him someplace other than Lilith's world, for instance. I'm just offering the best solution as I see it."

Nero's jaw tightens. Nostradamus must not be lying this time.

"Do we actually win on Lilith's world?" Nero demands. "Does Sasha survive?"

"Because of all the probability manipulators involved—Tartarus's child called Lug, Lilith, and Sasha herself—I can't guarantee any outcome with certainty," Nostradamus says carefully. "What we get is a chance."

"If you can't guarantee Sasha's safety, you will need to come up with another plan." Nero's voice is as close to a dragon's roar as I've ever heard it. "Earth and all of you"—he sweeps his gaze over all the Councilors—"can burn for all I care." And with that, he steps protectively in front of me.

"You don't really have a choice," says the St. Petersburg woman.

"Oh?" Nero's hands turn into claws. "You think anyone can force me to do something?"

"Not force," she says bravely. "You still owe me a favor from 1897. Or did you forget?"

I can't help but glance at Vlad, Eduardo, Colton,

and the rest of the people who helped Nero defeat the usurper in exchange for a favor.

He really did give out a lot of IOUs.

"Fuck that," Nero snarls. "Favors are implied to be reasonable."

"No one is asking you to kill your girlfriend," the woman says. "If she doesn't do what Nostradamus suggests, she dies here on Earth. Sounds to me like we all want the same thing—her alive and well, and Tartarus dead."

"That's enough." Nero grabs my shoulder. "We're leaving."

"Some of the contracts are written," the woman says. "If you break them, you'll die."

"He won't," Nostradamus says, unleashing another round of hushed whispers. "He's too powerful for that. But he will be gravely weakened—which wouldn't serve anyone."

"If he's weak, he can't oppose us," the woman says.

"Puny creature!" Claudia roars, her voice so dragony it sends a primal chill down my spine—and I'm not the one her ire is directed at. "Did you just threaten my brother?"

I glance at her.

Nero's sister looks on the verge of turning full-on scaly.

Did she forget that this giant Colosseum is an illusion? I doubt her dragon form would fit into the room we're actually in—not to mention, the person she wants to rip apart is safely sitting in Russia.

"We can't defeat Tartarus without Nero and his kin," Nostradamus says, perhaps seeing the same danger I do. "We must come to an amicable arrangement."

"Nero, Claudia," I whisper under my breath, knowing they can hear me with their dragon senses. "Please play along with what I'm about to say. No reason to start a war."

I can't tell if they heard or are likely to listen, but I prepare to speak up anyway—which is not easy, as I'm still shaking from my last bout of public speaking.

With a confidence I don't feel, I loudly clear my throat and wait for everyone's attention. "I'm tired of being spoken about as if I'm not here," I announce when all eyes turn to me. "I, not Nero, nor any of you, decide what I do and whom I fight."

I look at the woman in the crimson robe challengingly.

Nero takes out his phone, tilts it so that only I can see the screen and types in:

You better have a good plan.

"My parents' lives are on the line," I whisper back in a voice so low only he and Claudia should be able to hear.

Hopefully, that non-explanation sufficiently deflects him, as I don't really have a plan. For now, I'm thinking of going along with Nostradamus's, until/unless something better comes up.

Nero shakes his head, pulls up the text window

where he was ordering Eric around, and types in: *Get back here. Now.*

Eric doesn't show up.

I wonder what that's about?

To the Council peeps, I say, "Since *I* don't owe anyone any favors, I get whatever I want for *my* help—and my price will be steep."

I can see Nostradamus sigh in relief. We must be entering some favorable-from-his-perspective future.

Nero glares at his phone. I get the feeling Eric is in trouble.

"What do you want?" says the tall man representing the Paris Council.

I grin, channeling Lilith. "I want all of the favors Nero owes you to be mine."

"What?" the St. Petersburg representative exclaims. "Those are worth—"

"Exactly," I say. "Please don't interrupt me again."

Everyone gives the woman an angry stare, and she sits back down. My next demand might make her stand up again.

"I want complete amnesty for my father, Grigori Rasputin," I say. "Whatever he did to piss off the St. Petersburg Council is to be forgiven and forgotten. I want him to be able to come back to Earth and never have to look over his shoulder."

Sure enough, the lady leaps to her feet, but before she says anything, a couple of her colleagues whose faces I can't see walk over and whisper something to her.

"Agreed," she says grudgingly. "Anything else?"

"I want every Council on Earth to decree that my adoptive parents are never to be harmed or used as leverage against me—on penalty of death."

"I'm sure I speak for everyone when I say that won't be an issue," the Paris representative says, and the other Cognizant mutter their agreement.

"I want full citizenship privileges for Claudia." I nod at Nero's sister. "Her Mandate ceremony should be right after mine."

"I think that can be arranged," the Paris guy says. "But we may need to vote on it."

"And I want to be able to do magic again," I say on a whim. This isn't something I'm going to insist on, but since I have them all by their shorthairs anyway, why not throw it in?

"What do you mean?" the Russian Council lady asks, her frown deepening.

"Stage conjuring," I explain. "The New York Council forbade me from doing it, fearing it would expose the Cognizant to the world or gain me unfair powers. What I ask is to be able to do illusions that would be perceived by humans as merely that." I take out my deck and spring the cards from hand to hand a few times. "Things like this."

She looks around. Clearly, this request is trickier.

"The Mandate might prevent you from doing such illusions," Vlad says. "When the New York Council forbade you, it was in part for your own protection."

"I have an idea for that," I tell him. "When my

Mandate is reapplied, I want to be a Herald, like the late Gaius was. Isn't that kind of Mandate less restrictive?"

"It is," Vlad mutters. "That might work."

"Lastly, I want to be owed a favor from each and every Council member in the world," I say, deciding to really push my luck. "A written, binding contract that outlines how big a favor it shall be."

"You drive a hard bargain," the Russian Council lady says and looks at me with admiration. "This will require a vote. I assume that if the vote goes your way, you'll be willing to put all this in a binding contract on your end as well?"

"Right after I undergo my Rite," I say. "I believe the Mandate is a prerequisite when it comes to making such contracts?"

"It is," she says. "Does anyone have a problem with this deal? Stand up if you oppose it."

Very few people stand up.

Great. I get my way—for all the good it will do me once Tartarus kills me dead.

"So, it is decided," Nostradamus says with relief in his voice. "Your Mandate Rite awaits."

Before either sibling can start a world war, I grab Claudia and Nero by their hands and drag them out of the room.

When we're outside anyone's earshot, Nero frees his hand and angrily dials Eric.

"Voicemail," he mutters and resumes walking. "We're going to have words, Eric and I."

"Maybe the Councils knew you might use him to get me away and did something about it?" I say, hurrying to keep up.

"Unlike the two of you who don't have your Mandates, Eric isn't outside the law," Nero says, but he doesn't sound certain. "In any case, good job de-escalating the hostilities in there." He darts a careful glance at his sister. "Few on Earth know just how truly dangerous Claudia and I are. If they attacked, you could've been hurt in the crossfire."

"Crossfire," I repeat, picturing him and Claudia turning, then breathing flames from their giant maws at the hapless Councilors. "Literally."

Claudia chuckles, and Nero's lips twitch, but then his expression darkens again. "What is the *real* plan?" he demands. "Don't tell me you want to dance to Nostradamus's tune."

"Honestly, I don't have one," I say. "But you and Claudia killing all the Councilors didn't seem like a good idea."

"Then I'll tell you what we're going to do." Nero's stride lengthens. "As soon as your and Claudia's Mandate Rites are finished, we will leave this world. Let them try and make demands once we're among my dragons. They wouldn't make it past the gate hub."

Claudia nods approvingly.

"We can't do that." I huff as I try to keep up. "What about my parents? What about everyone who works for your fund? Not to mention, the whole human population of Earth?" My hands ball into fists. "Do we need to rehash our earlier argument again?"

He stops, and so do I and Claudia. "How about another plan?" he says. "After the Rite, we join Rasputin on Atlantis."

I frown. "How is this different from the first plan?"

"It buys us time—in the most literal way possible." He resumes walking, and we follow. "Given how fast time flows on that world, you can practice your vampire and trickster powers for months before any time passes here on Earth. I can train you to fight— and, most importantly, you and your father will stockpile enough seer juice to make sure you can see for yourselves if Nostradamus's so-called plan is indeed the best and only way to defeat Tartarus."

Right. And you'd have plenty of time to talk me into staying on Atlantis or hiding out on dragon world, is what I don't say out loud.

If Nero thinks he can convince me to abandon my parents, he's going to be sorely disappointed.

"That's a decent plan," I say grudgingly. "But won't the Councils mind us leaving just like that? How do they know we plan to return?"

Nero looks at his phone again, then behind us, where the Councilors are.

"Since I can't reach Eric, I think it best if you both go through the Rite as if nothing has changed," he says. "You're also going to sign a contract with people on this Council. We'll just add clauses to it."

"Like a 'no suicide missions' clause?" I ask. "And

'unless another seer comes up with a plan that's better than Nostradamus's' clause?"

"Something like that," Nero says. "With the contract in place, everyone will relax, which is when you and Claudia will say you're not feeling well—something that's normal after the Rite. After that, we'll all go to 'meet up with a healer,' but instead, we'll surreptitiously meet up with Thalia and the limo—or Eric, if he replies to me by then. Then we head straight to the JFK hub and Atlantis from there."

"It could work," I say as we enter the familiar torture-chamber-like room with a sacrificial slab in the front—the very one where I suffered through the Rite the first time around.

"It *will* work," Nero says darkly. "I'll make sure it does."

When he notices the monk dudes fussing around the grim place, he falls silent.

Spotting us, the monks grab me and Claudia by the elbows and drag us into the alcove in the back.

A blood bag, two masks, and two uncomfortable robes hang on golden hooks, waiting for us.

I greedily consume the thoughtfully provided snack, then take my mask—the one with the serene feminine face made from marble. This is the exact one I used the first time. It's missing eyes and has an extra eyeball in the middle of the forehead. A mask that marks me as a seer.

Claudia's mask is blander. I guess they don't know what kind of Cognizant to designate her as.

I press the mask to my face, and like the last time, I can see through it thanks to the tiny holes someone drilled in the eye area.

"This will hurt," I tell Claudia as I begin to strip. "And it'll hurt *you* more than it will hurt me—the more power you have, the harder it is when the Mandate magic interweaves with yours."

"I'm not afraid," Claudia says and slips off her dress to reveal a body that human models would sell their souls for. "Sounds more like an adventure."

"They might offer you a Mentor," I say, throwing on the sandpaper-like robe. "Nero will probably take the job—just as he did for me."

"Like he can teach me anything I don't already know." She smirks. "What does it actually feel like to see the auras?"

I do my best to tell her what everyone with the Mandate aura looked like to me before I turned into a vampire, and then she asks what it would be like to break the Mandate.

I explain that I've never done it, but that I heard it's deadly. "My friend Ariel, whom you already met, once tried to say something the Mandate didn't like. She bled out of everywhere as a result," I say, shuddering at the memory. "My advice? Get your kicks some other way."

Claudia grins. "Gotcha. Well, you better go." She nods at the alcove entrance. "It sounds like everyone's already here for you."

"Thanks," I say. "Dragon ears strike again. Good luck with your Rite."

"Same to you," she says and puts on her mask.

I leave the alcove and find that she's right.

The candles in the torture chamber are festively lit, like the last time, and the New York Council members are sitting on the stone benches, with their creepy masks on. Lucretia, Chester, and Roxy lift their masks and wave at me.

How nice. It's not just the Council. This time around, I have family here, too.

Colton is performing the ceremony once again. He's probably the only one who can hold that giant staff for the Rite without looking silly.

"Get on," he booms. "Try to relax."

Yeah. Sure. That's what he said the last time—and then I was in hell.

With great reluctance, I lie down on the slab and open the robe.

Like before, Colton's staff glows with a circle of magical energy.

"Wait a sec—" I start to say, but he brands me with it before I can finish the sentence.

Until this moment, I think I was blocking the memory of how much this hurt before.

Now it's violently coming back to me.

My skin doesn't sizzle where the brand touches it. I almost wish it did. Instead, the agony is internal, and much worse than any burn could be.

It feels like my essence is on fire. Like I am getting

violently rearranged into hydrogen, oxygen, carbon, calcium, and phosphorus—and then those atoms are getting smashed back together again.

I convulse on the slab, an inhuman roar coming out of my throat.

My vocal cords rip apart, but my vampire powers repair them right away, allowing me to scream more, which I promptly do.

Blood—either mine or what I drank earlier—spews out of my mouth.

Why haven't I passed out yet?

The worst of it comes before long—the part where the magical energy overstimulates my nerve endings. It's the worst agony imaginable, and when the pain reaches a particularly unbearable height, something inside me breaks and I feel like I'm falling.

Yes.

Finally.

With one last vocal-cord-tearing scream, I black out.

CHAPTER SIXTEEN

I WAKE UP TO SILENCE.

Sitting up, I rub my eyes.

Something about this silence is reassuring, but I don't know what.

Then I look around.

The bland room doesn't have any furniture besides my bed, and there are no windows.

Wait a second. The room also smells vaguely of medicine—reminiscent of a nurse's office or a hospital room.

Oh, crap.

Memories rush back to me—both of the Rite I've just undergone, and my vision where Lilith used her sire bond over me to force me to kill Ariel and Felix.

The events in that vision took place *here*, in this very room.

Thank goodness I made my friends stay on

Gomorrah. Avoiding medical establishments was clearly not enough to overcome this future.

This must be the room where they take you to recover after the Rite. In fact, Lucretia even mentioned some recovery room in her texts to me, but it didn't click that I'd end up there too, or that it might be the room from my vision.

My heart rate skyrockets.

If I'm right about this, I have seconds before Lilith arrives.

Where is Nero?

Come to think of it, where was he in my vision?

Ah, right. Claudia was going to have her Rite after mine. He must be there, watching it or participating in the Mentor selection.

Unless it's over and he's on his way here?

Either way, I'm not waiting for him to save me.

I will save myself.

Leaping to my feet, I rush for the gray door with all the speed of a vampire.

Before I reach it, the door breaks into shards.

Hovering a few inches from the ground is Lilith—just as I foresaw.

"Sasha, dear, how are you feeling?" she croons, looking me up and down.

"What are you doing here?" I blurt out—but then instantly realize I said the exact same thing in my vision, so I know what she'll reply with.

"I'm here to check on you." Her beatific smile shows

off her fangs. "Your well-being is very important to me."

Yep.

Just what she said in my vision.

If I were to follow the script, I would next accuse her of being behind the chorts' attack, which would lead her to—and I quote— "stop playing nice mommy."

By which she means using the sire bond to make me kill Ariel and Felix.

Nope.

I don't like that script at all.

Even without my friends here, I don't think I want her to stop being 'a nice mommy.' Not if that means she'll invoke the sire bond and force me to do her bidding.

Much better to play nice and stall until I get an opportunity to escape—or until Nero gets here.

"I got the Council to make me a Herald," I tell her with exaggerated enthusiasm. "Also, each and every one of them will owe me a favor."

"That's great." Lilith looks around furtively. "Do you mind telling me all about it on the way?"

"On the way?" I look at her as guilelessly as I can. "Where are we going?"

"Long story," she says. "I'm not exactly welcome in these parts. Are you ready?"

I know that if I say no, she'll *make* me go.

Then again, if I seem overeager, she might catch on to my strategy—which also might lead her to use the sire bond.

"You have the gate sword." She extends her hand. "Please give it back to me."

Oh, right. The sword I've thought of as mine all this time was originally hers.

This is when I also realize that someone dressed me in my own clothes when I was unconscious. Hopefully, that someone was Nero, though I strongly suspect it was actually the monks. The return of my clothing means that the sword is indeed on me—but I *really* don't want to part with it, especially if that means it will be in Lilith's hands once again.

"I'll let you play with it some more later," she says reassuringly. "Now give it to me."

If I don't, she can make me anyway, is what I tell myself as I hand her the sword.

With an evil grin, she activates it.

Remembering what she did to Nero with that thing, I decide I *don't* want him to come here to try and save me, after all.

"Make haste," she says and grabs my hand.

With a jerk, she gets me out of the room—and I nearly trip on the dead bodies of the Enforcers and the monks who must've been guarding the recovery room.

Would it help if I screamed?

Probably not.

When we get to the end of the corridor, I spot Eric —Nero's teleporter ally.

Yes!

If anyone can get me out of this mess alive, it's him.

The best part is that I don't need to break the "good daughter" act. He'll know to save me on his own.

"Ready?" Lilith says to Eric.

"At your command," he answers in that robotic speech pattern everyone under glamour exhibits.

Oh no. Is this why Nero couldn't reach the guy? Because he fell into Lilith's clutches?

"Not fair," I say to Lilith, continuing my act. "When I tried to glamour this guy the other day, he said, 'Your vampire mind tricks won't work on me.'"

"A shame," Lilith says as Eric places a hand on each of our shoulders. "Just goes to show how urgently we need to grow your powers."

Before I can ask for a clarification, Eric poofs us away.

When we reappear, I recognize the entrance to the JFK gate hub.

The nearest gate is a leap away, but I know Lilith can catch me without breaking a sweat, so I don't bother with the futile gesture.

"Thank you," Lilith says to Eric. "Now you will teleport back to your little apartment and forget this ever happened."

"I will forget," Eric says, then poofs away.

Except I doubt Nero will *let* him forget.

They will figure out Eric is missing time—and hopefully why.

Of course, by the time they do, it might be too late for me.

"Through there, dear," Lilith says, pointing at an unfamiliar gate. "We have a trek ahead of us."

I walk to the gate and gesture for her to enter first—figuring once she does, I can dive for the nearest gate and hope it doesn't lead to a nuclear wasteland.

"You first," Lilith says, crushing my hopes.

"No, after you," I say, doing my best not to sound pushy.

What I almost said was, "Age before beauty"—but I'm glad I didn't. I have seen her rip people apart with her bare hands before, and don't want to be on the receiving end of something like that.

Besides, she doesn't look a day over twenty-five.

Lilith's lips tighten anyway. "I insist."

Crap. Better walk in on my own than get sire-bonded into it.

"Thanks," I say lightly and leap into the gate.

Lilith stays on my heels, and the world we end up in is a barren wasteland that doesn't present any opportunity for escape.

In my head, I repeat the color and location of the gate we just entered. When I escape, I'll need to know the way back.

"Can you tell me where we're going?" I ask Lilith politely. "As fun as it is to just hang out with you, I was in the middle of something super-important when you showed up."

She pouts, then heads for a green gate. "What could be more important than spending quality time with your mommy?"

"Saving the world," I say, mentally updating the route I'm trying to memorize. "Nostradamus told me how to defeat Tartarus, and I was about to train for it with Nero."

"What a coincidence." Lilith gestures for me to enter the gate. "Training you and then killing Tartarus is exactly what this little trip is all about—only we'll do all that without meddlesome Michel cramping our style."

Oh yeah. She calls Nostradamus "Michel." Maybe I should also be on a first-name basis with the guy. After all, he's the source of a lot of my headaches.

The world on the other side of the green gate has a veritable rainbow of colorful moons in the evening sky, and in a far distance, I see some sort of giant creatures walking about. All this, I file away for the return trip.

"So we're going to your world?" I say with fake excitement. "That's where Tartarus will attack, according to Nostradamus."

"Yes and no." Lilith walks toward a purple gate at our two o'clock. "We're going to a place Tartarus will attack, but not my world. According to Michel, the attack you speak of is slightly further in the future. Before attacking my world, Tartarus is going to destroy another—one more like Earth. *That* is where we're headed."

"But why?" I ask. "Why don't you want to follow Nostradamus's plan to face Tartarus on your home turf?"

"You mean besides the billions of people we'll save

on the world we're heading to?" She lifts an eyebrow. "They'll all die if we don't show up, you know."

"Right." I suppress the urge to say that she didn't strike me as someone who gave two craps about some distant world being sucked dry.

"Besides, if we follow Michel's stupid plan, all the years of hard work I've put into my world will be ruined," she says, gesturing for me to enter the purple gate. "Worlds with humans but without Cognizant are pretty rare."

We step out of the gate into a snowy cave and get blasted with a freezing cold.

Lilith points at a yellow gate nearby and continues. "Also, being a goddess comes with certain responsibilities to my worshippers. I doubt Michel mentioned how many of them will survive his plan, but that number is pretty close to zero."

"He didn't go into that much detail," I say, memorizing the next step of our path. "Don't take it the wrong way, but I didn't think you cared about your people this much."

That's putting it mildly. She's enslaved them, and has drunk their blood and fed them lies for generations.

She shrugs. "Well, it's like having a pet—or cattle. I don't want someone to just come and harm them."

Can that be true? Does she have *something* resembling a conscience? If she cares about her people at least a little bit, there may be more to her than just the thirst for power.

Then again, she did just compare them to cattle.

We walk through a red gate onto a watery-looking world with a pink sky, and she adds, "Also, Michel's original plan would've brought Earth's Cognizant to my world—and even if we'd defeated Tartarus, I might not have been able to get all of them to leave."

Now the truth comes out.

Her world is an all-you-can-eat blood-and-power buffet that she doesn't want to share.

I make a mental note of the next gate she walks toward and say, "Are you sure Tartarus can be defeated on this alternate world you're taking me to? Nostradamus said—"

"That the chances of killing Tartarus are better on my world," she says. "I couldn't help but notice how he never said *my* chance of survival was greater in that circumstance."

"So you think Nostradamus wants to get rid of you *and* Tartarus at the same time? Why would he do that? I thought you two were pals."

We step through another set of gates. "He and I are allies in that he really, *really* hates the guy who is prophesied to kill me," she says. "I long suspected Michel would double-cross me in a heartbeat if that meant Tartarus would die—and my intuition recently told me I was on my way to a sacrificial slab." We walk up to a lavender-colored gate. "No thanks." She gestures for me to walk in. On the other side, she continues. "As you have no doubt learned by now, you can never trust a seer. Present company included." She winks at me. "I've made use of Michel for as long as I could, but now I have to make my own plans."

Real lesson: you can trust Lilith even less than a seer.

"Why steal me then?" I ask. "Why not come to the Councils and convince them to help on the world we're going to?"

"They'd sooner kill me than listen," she says. "But also, if we do defeat Tartarus and play our cards right afterward, this juicy world full of humans will be ripe for a takeover."

"As in, you again don't want to share," I blurt out, forgetting the good daughter act.

"You got it," Lilith says after we pass through another hub and enter the next gate. "Something else too: thanks to their level of technology, the world in question provides more opportunities for a fast power-up."

Oh? I resist the temptation to clarify or ask any more questions in general. It's getting hard to keep the route in my short-term memory as is.

In fact, if we go through a few more gates, I'll start losing track of our path—if I haven't done so already.

Maybe I could risk Lilith's ire by taking out my phone and making notes?

I could palm it and—

"We're here," Lilith says as we enter a hub that looks a lot like the one at JFK.

"We are?" I sigh in relief and rerun the route we just took in my mind.

"Yep." She looks at an old-fashioned wristwatch. "We better hurry. Your big TV appearance is in an hour."

CHAPTER SEVENTEEN

"MY BIG WHAT?" I shout, walking fast because she's herding me like a pig to slaughter.

"Didn't I mention it? You're going to be famous on this world." She grins. "Isn't that what you've always wanted? To be a TV phenomenon?"

"Err," is all I can say. Taking a breath, I try again. "I wanted to be a famous TV magician. *On Earth*. And that was before I knew Tartarus was coming to kill everyone."

"Well, this will be pretty much what you've wanted, and this is the best way to get you ready for Tartarus." Lilith leads us into a corridor. "Now focus on thinking up tricks that will convince people you're a vampire, a seer, and a probability manipulator."

"Wait, you knew I was a trickster? Am I the last to know these things?"

"Michel told me," she says. "He saw a vision of you and dear Chester speaking about it. How is he, by the way? I hear I now have a granddaughter. Foxy, was it?"

"It's Roxy, and she's in her teens now," I snap, then take another breath. "Wait. Don't change the subject. Why am I going on TV?"

"Remember how you boosted your seer powers? That earthquake prediction?"

"Yes."

"Well, this is the same thing," she says. "The more humans believe in your powers, the bigger the boost you'll get."

My head spins.

In one way, this is a dream come true.

In another, this is my worst nightmare—to have to perform in front of a large audience unprepared.

Maybe I should run?

No. Bad idea. I've gone this far without getting sire-bonded, so I might as well keep up the pretense.

If this works and I do become more powerful, it should make it easier for me to escape—and deal with Tartarus as well, on whichever world.

A part of me isn't even sure Lilith is wrong.

Maybe this world *is* a better place to fight Tartarus.

Regardless, what I need is to notify Nero and the others of my whereabouts. Lilith didn't include them in her plans out of greed for the spoils of this world, but I don't have her ambitions and I think more people mean a better chance at winning.

Except I don't know how to reach anyone.

If I could go into Headspace, I'd ping Rasputin, or

the bannik, or even Nostradamus, but I'm all out of juice.

Or am I?

I check for the umpteenth time and verify that Headspace isn't reachable.

Maybe Rasputin will see a vision of this? He *is* on a faster world now, so his powers might've recovered.

Then again, as a probability manipulator, Lilith can shield us from seer eyes, and she's probably doing that.

We get to a door that leads out of the secret hub corridors, then follow a path until we reach the main lobby of the airport.

Except I realize this isn't an airport.

It's a giant train station, like New York's Grand Central Terminal, only a hundred times bigger.

The place is teeming with strangely dressed people with haircuts heavily inspired by the eighties.

To continue the eighties theme, most teens are walking about with gizmos that look eerily like Sony's Walkman cassette players. In their ears are little orange headphones attached with wires—no Bluetooth in sight.

"Do they have internet on this world?" I ask Lilith in mock horror.

"No," she replies. "But thanks to that, more people than ever will be tuned in to see you on TV."

Oh, right. I almost forgot I'm about to perform.

Now that I recall that, monster stage-fright jitters settle in my stomach.

"When is this show?" I ask, dodging a lady with a mullet who's wearing a jacket with giant shoulder pads.

"In an hour," Lilith says.

"And how far is the studio?" I ask as we exit onto the street, and I see cars that look like they came out of the 1985 portion of *Back to the Future.*

"Ten minutes walking distance," Lilith says and starts jaywalking in the middle of heavy traffic. "We're in the center of New Langdon."

Not a single car hits us as we cross, which gives me an idea for how to pull off some of the effects.

"I need a convenience store and a hardware store," I say, thinking fast. "And your help with the show."

"Of course," she says. "Whatever you need."

We walk to a grocery store on the corner, and I ask the young clerk if they sell lottery tickets.

"We do, miss," he says with a strange accent that reminds me of a mix between British and Australian. "They will announce the numbers in fifty-five minutes or so."

I'm not surprised things are falling into place so well. Lilith is helping me already.

"Can you use your powers to choose the winning numbers?" I whisper to her.

"Does a drekavac make you shit in the woods?" Lilith whispers back, then starts to confidently name numbers at the clerk.

"What is it for?" she asks when we exit the store, with me clutching the hopefully winning ticket.

"Unless we stop Tartarus, this world won't last long enough for you to collect the winnings."

"You'll see," I say. "Now we need a hardware store."

We walk by antiquated stores that include a VHS tape rental place that's clearly the local version of Blockbuster, then another store that sells music on cassette tapes, and yet another that looks like Radioshack's evil twin.

The hardware store is normal enough, though, and it doesn't take me long to locate what I need—the scariest-looking nail gun they sell.

"What's this for?" Lilith asks, looking over the device while I grab a box of nails. "I know plenty of creative torture methods that don't require props."

"I'll have someone shoot me with this to prove how lucky I am," I explain as I walk to another shelf and pick up a welder's mask. "I assume you can use your powers to make sure every nail will miss my body?"

"Of course." She grins. "You won't need that mask."

"The mask is to make that part of the performance more dramatic," I say. "It will heighten the sense of danger."

The mask is also there because I don't trust Lilith not to let a nail hit me in the eye for laughs, but this I keep to myself.

"You have a great instinct for drama," she says, eyeing the mask approvingly. "I have a feeling you're going to make me proud today."

"I hope so. Now, next stop should be an office supply store. I know some mentalism routines that—"

"No time," Lilith says, looking at her watch. "We're late as is."

She proceeds to drag me through this town's equivalent of Times Square and into a skyscraper with the fanciest lobby I've ever seen.

"We're here for the Pacifica's Got Talent," Lilith says to a burly security guard.

"You're too late," the guy says. "Contestants were supposed to be here an hour ago."

Lilith's eyes turn into mirrors. "You will take us there. Now."

Glamoured, the guy leads us to the elevator. When we reach the studio floor, Lilith has to repeat the glamour trick a few more times until I'm rushed into makeup.

"Make her look even paler," Lilith says, looking me over disapprovingly. "More regal, if possible. More like a vampire should look."

"She's already sickly looking," the makeup lady says with the accent everyone here seems to have. "I think she—"

Lilith uses glamour yet again, and I'm made to look so pale some folks might think I'm wearing a porcelain mask. Afterward, the hair girl does her own thing, ending the treatment by emptying a bottle of hair spray onto my head.

"Let's go. You're on soon," Lilith says, dragging me out of the makeup room.

In front of us stands a line of other contestants: one

looks like a singer, one like a juggler, and the last one has creepy clown makeup on.

This is when it hits me again.

I'm not just going on TV.

I'm going to participate in a competition.

If this show's format is similar to the talent shows on Earth, I have to worry about getting scored by judges on top of being stared at by hundreds of spectators.

I didn't think my heartbeat could speed up further, but it manages somehow.

"I'm famished," Lilith says, and before I can make a snide comment, she glamours the clown in front of us and tells him not to scream.

The other contestants are so preoccupied with their own stage fright, they don't notice when Lilith bends over the clown's neck and sinks her fangs into it.

They also don't pay attention as she gulps down copious amounts of the poor guy's blood.

Her luck at work, maybe?

Done with her grisly task, she detaches the clown's red sponge of a nose and wipes her mouth with it. "You should feed," she says to me. "You'll be stronger if you do."

"I think I'm okay," I say.

"Don't be overconfident," Lilith says. "Drink him."

Before she uses the sire bond to insist, I bite into the clown voluntarily. At least this way, I can be sure he'll be alive after my meal.

A few sips later, I let him go.

"So." Lilith looks at me with a deadpan expression. "Did that taste funny to you?"

I resist a groan. She no doubt chose the clown just to make that corny joke.

"You will forget this ever happened," Lilith commands the clown. "Oh, and you're now going after us."

The poor guy gives up his place in line and stands behind me.

Crap.

He might've been an easier act to follow.

Oh, well. The juggler doesn't look too impressive either.

"I do feel better," I say to Lilith, and it's true. "I hadn't noticed blood doing this before."

"Oh, it can make you feel amazing things," she says. "You don't just feel good, you're more powerful for a while after a feeding. Sometimes you can be a *lot* more powerful. All depends on the source of the meal."

"Powerful?" I can't help but be intrigued.

"Indeed," she says. "You won't feel it as much when you drink from a human like that, but with a Cognizant, you will. The more powerful they are, the more powerful you get after drinking from them."

That's cool, in a disturbing way.

I wonder if this is why Gaius got Ariel hooked on his blood. Or why—

Wait. I *did* experience what Lilith is talking about.

Maybe even more than once.

When I drank from Nero the first time we had sex,

I felt incredible. More to the point, whatever we did afterward caused a crater in the ground and felled trees.

More powerful indeed.

Oh, and does this explain my nonstop run to save Nero? It happened when I drank all of Woland's blood.

I ask Lilith if the amount matters.

"Definitely," she says. "The more you drink, the more power you gain. My rule is: when I get a chance to drink from a powerful Cognizant, I always drain them to the last drop to maximize the benefits."

Great.

Kill them is what she means.

Kill them over a temporary burst of superpower.

Boy, do I hope I got more of my DNA from my father.

"You're up next," Lilith says as the juggler stumbles onto the stage.

I start breathing deeply in an effort to calm my escalating panic. When the light above the stage entrance turns green, I shuffle onto the stage, mask under my armpit and the nail gun dragging behind me.

Someone wires me with a microphone, and I walk on, feeling like a zombie.

At first, the stage lights are too blinding to see anything. Then my eyes adjust, and I realize the situation is *much* worse than I thought.

It's not a TV studio, like during my performance on Earth.

This is a full-on theater, with thousands of

spectators in hundreds of rows. At the front are seven judges, and all of them are staring at me with homicidal hunger in their eyes.

But that's still not the worst discovery.

According to all the signs and warnings, this show is being broadcast *live*.

It's every glossophobic's nightmare come to life—and there's no Bailey to save me.

CHAPTER EIGHTEEN

"HI THERE. What are you supposed to be?" says the leftmost judge haughtily. "A goth or a geisha?"

I nearly choke on my tongue.

It's bad enough I'm freaking out as is. Now this guy wants to add extra stress with his stupid commentary?

Sucking in a breath, I remind myself that he must be the obligatory rude "Simon Cowell" type, and it's just show business.

It's not that he doesn't like *me*, specifically.

"I'm supernatural," I say, my voice a little shaky. "I understand how difficult that is to believe, which is why I'm going to demonstrate the things I can do."

He—a grown man—rolls his eyes at me, and murmurs, "That patter needs work."

Deciding that my best bet is to ignore him as if he were a regular heckler, I say, "To start, I will demo my ability to predict the future." I put down the nail gun and the mask, and fish out the lottery ticket. "Here." I walk over to a gorgeous lady judge farthest from the prickly one and hand her the ticket. "I came up with this because everyone always says, 'If you can see the future, why don't you win the lottery?'"

Speaking to the nearest camera man, I say, "Can you show that to the viewers at home? I want everyone to know there's no fishy business with the ticket."

The guy is good. The camera instantly zooms in on the numbers, and someone even puts the whole thing up on a bulky CRT TV screen above the stage.

"Remember those," I say, pointing to the screen. "Now, would it be possible to tune that TV to the lottery drawing?"

The camera man gives me a thumbs up, so I step away from the judge to make sure no one can suspect me of switching anything, or secretly erasing numbers and printing new ones somehow.

My chances of looking like a fool are astronomical because Lilith's luck needs to work on multiple levels here. Firstly, the ticket needs to really be the winning one, and secondly, the lottery result needs to be announced right now.

As someone puts the right channel on the screen, one part of the plan falls into place—the broadcast shows a large wheel with white balls covered by numbers.

As the thing spins and spins, it builds the suspense for everyone—especially me.

The first ball falls into place, and the number on it matches my ticket.

The second one matches as well.

The lady judge murmurs my favorite phrase for a spectator to say: "No way."

When the third number matches, I relax.

Even if the rest of them are wrong, I still have a strong effect on my hands.

My favorite thing about this demonstration is that I really am fooling everyone. I'm not using my seer powers like I claimed. They're on hiatus for now. Like in every magic effect, there's an underlying method behind what I'm doing that has nothing to do with my pseudo-explanation.

It just so happens that the method I'm using is supernatural in nature and impressive in and of itself.

The next number comes up matching, and the next.

When the last number is exactly the same, the audience breaks into mad clapping.

My pulse skyrockets, and I become aware of an odd sensation—like I'm filling up with wonderfully warm energy.

Oh, yeah. I remember this feeling. I had it when I was on TV on Earth. It must be what it feels like to get a faith-based power boost.

That's good. It means some people out there believe I really did predict the lottery. They're convinced that what just happened isn't an illusion.

Phew.

It used to annoy me when people thought my mentalist powers were real. Now, though, I'm super grateful for human gullibility.

"You're amazing," says the judge I gave the lottery ticket to. "Why are you even here? You just made yourself a millionaire with your gift."

"Well, I enjoy performing," I say honestly. "I'd do it even if I had all the money in the world."

"It *was* a nice trick," the prickly judge says with a modicum more respect than earlier—but not much. "Especially good for a girl magician. And you *do* look like you're enjoying yourself." He looks me up and down and crinkles his nose. "You just need to work on your showmanship and your stage presence. Also, it's obvious you somehow—"

"I'm not actually done yet," I say through gritted teeth. "Save your criticism for the end and your theories about my methodology for the tabloid magazines."

He raises an eyebrow, and I can tell he's about to say something else snide.

A burst of anger overrides my stage fright.

His behavior, especially that "girl magician" bit, needs to be addressed.

Wait a minute. I can get revenge and do an impromptu demonstration that's worthy of Lilith herself.

If this works well, it should boost one of my core vampire abilities.

"I have a few more impossibilities planned," I say, speaking over whatever the judge just said. "I want the viewers at home to have no doubt that what I do is real. It's not—as you put it—tricks."

"Now that's a tall order," the annoying judge says. "Lots of idiots come here and think they can sing, but they screech like broken records. Like you, they believe their own—"

"If you're such a skeptic, how about you volunteer for the next demonstration?" I say sweetly. "It's going to involve mind control, but since you're convinced all I do is tricks, it should not work on you, should it?"

Usually, I'd never choose a heckler as a helper—that's audience management 101—but this isn't a usual situation.

Here, the more skeptical he is, the stronger the effect.

"If you mind-control me, you'll get my full support." He raises a little paddle with a 10 written on it. "Now, do you need me to come join you on the stage?"

"No." I turn my eyes into mirrors—and the audience gasps. With honey-laced voice, I say, "I want you to crawl to the stage on all fours."

The room goes dead silent.

They think this must be a bad joke.

Then the judge robotically gets up from his seat, gets on the ground, and starts crawling onto the stage like a good puppet.

The silence grows heavy.

I can almost hear everyone's incredulity.

The other judges and camera people look even more astonished than the audience behind them. As I surmised, my victim is a real primadonna, and no one can imagine that a performer like me could've bribed him to humiliate himself like this—which is the best non-supernatural explanation.

"Good job," I say when he crosses the stage like a dog. "Now you will kiss my shoes and stand up."

Am I getting too BDSM-y for family television?

Oh, well.

He gives my shoes a smooch as I commanded, then slowly rises, his expression still blank.

"Please give my brave volunteer a round of applause," I say, and that finally breaks the tension. Everyone claps with insane enthusiasm.

Just like before, I feel a warm sensation of power—and it's getting stronger.

Uh-oh.

I hope it doesn't get as bad as the last time. I don't want to faint again.

I take a deep breath.

I can't think about fainting—or other potential pitfalls—as that way lies a freak-out on national TV. In a world that's not my own, but still.

"Thank you," I say when the ovations subside. "The other power I wanted to demonstrate is my ability to control luck itself."

I pick up the welding helmet and put it on in such a way that I can still use my microphone.

"Is there anyone in the audience who owns one of these?" I wave the nail gun in the air.

A large man rises, and I ask him to join us on the stage.

"Take this." I hand the man my nail gun. "Please

check to make sure this is a regular nail gun, but be careful. I don't want you to shoot your foot off, in case this show isn't insured."

Everyone chuckles, and the man verifies the gun is indeed a regular one.

"Please hand it to him"—I nod at the judge—"and return to your seat to a round of applause."

As the hardware expert leaves, with the audience cautiously clapping, I walk over to the end of the stage, where I press my back against a wooden wall.

"You ready?" I ask the judge.

He nods robotically, clearly still under glamour.

"Good." I take in another calming breath. "I want you to shoot me with one of those nails. Do your best to aim and don't worry. My power over luck is going to make it so not a single one will hit."

This is as close to the truth as a magician's ever gotten.

The method will indeed be power over luck—only Lilith's power, not mine.

The prickly judge points the nail gun at me.

I theatrically spread my arms.

Everyone in the audience moves to the edge of their seat, dead silent.

I've always wondered what's going on in an average person's head when they're witnessing a dangerous stunt like this. Does anyone want to shout, "Stop!" as would probably be the moral thing to do? Or do they secretly hope the performer gets hurt?

Humans do have a morbid curiosity—that's why they always stop to stare at an accident on a highway.

Bang!

The first nail hits the wall an inch away from my shoulder.

The audience collectively gasps.

The next nail hits in the space between my legs.

Wow.

If that was just half an inch higher, I would've gotten nailed in a very literal way.

The next nail is so close to the top of my head that it scrapes a little paint from the welding mask.

The next one hits between my outstretched fingers.

Lilith must have great control over the trajectories of these nails—and she's doing her best to make this look good.

What seems like a week later, the gun finally runs out of nails.

I step aside and look back.

There's a silhouette of me made out of nails.

"And there you have it," I say. "I'm very lucky indeed."

The applause is rapturous now. It goes on and on—and I notice everyone, even the judges, are on their feet to show their appreciation.

My knees feel weak, and the warm energy sensation is back, but much stronger this time.

A veritable flood of it.

Crap.

I need to get off the stage before the orgasmic part

arrives and makes me fall on my face—possibly undoing some of the effect.

"Thank you so much," I gasp. "Vote for me!"

With that, I run off the stage.

The ovations don't stop.

The lady judge I left the lottery ticket with shouts that I should perform something else as an encore.

Lilith meets me with a proud grin, and even hugs me.

I take off my welding helmet so I can breathe, and then an idea hits me.

They can have their encore, and I could impress them even more without breaking a sweat.

Muting my microphone, I urgently tell Lilith, "Switch clothes with me."

Ignoring the stunned stares of the other contestants, I begin to strip.

Being at least as devious as I am, Lilith catches on quickly and undresses without question.

When our clothes are swapped, I give her the mask, and she puts it on.

Yep.

No one will be able to detect the switch.

"Go out and prove that you can fly," I tell her.

I can't see her face through the mask, but I'm sure she's grinning in anticipation.

Gracefully, she walks onto the stage.

I go into glamour mode and make the other contestants forget what they just saw.

As I do this, it occurs to me that I can use this as a chance to escape.

First, though, I have to make the most of this effect. I locate a CRT TV that's showing what happens on the stage and turn my mic back on.

Lilith gets to the middle of the stage and bows.

The insane ovations subside.

"Before I perform the next demonstration, please check me for any hidden wires or magnets," I say into my mic, and Lilith walks up to the still-on-stage-and-probably-glamoured prickly judge.

Without getting too handsy, he checks her for wires and finds none.

Lilith slowly floats up.

This time, the impressed gasp is so audible I can hear it from here.

Someone gets the brilliant idea to put on New Age-sounding music in the background as Lilith soars higher and higher.

I'm extremely pleased with her performance.

If this effect had been done on its own, I doubt anyone would've believed I can really fly. David Copperfield performed a levitation illusion that looked just like this back in the early nineties without being a goddess-vampire—as far as we all know, anyway. But combined with my other demonstrations, people should believe this is real.

At least, I hope they do.

"I'll now fly to the members of the audience so you can check for wires too," I say, and Lilith does as I said

—landing next to random people who obviously can't find any secret wires.

As the viewers at home form their beliefs, the warm feelings intensify further.

My extremities start to tingle and I sit down, worried I'll fall.

There goes my chance to escape. I got carried away with the performance.

My toes curl and I feel a faith-related orgasm crashing over me, akin to the one I had during my first TV appearance.

The power-gasm—or whatever you'd call it—is followed closely by another, and another.

Just like that first time, the pleasure morphs into pain as I feel like my whole body turns into a raw nerve ending that someone zapped with a taser.

The room spins around me, and I get lightheaded.

Then a new wave of the warmth hits me, causing my brain to short-circuit.

I collapse on the floor, and my consciousness goes bye-bye.

CHAPTER NINETEEN

I COME to my senses and sit up.

My head was on Lilith's lap, and we're inside a moving car, with no sign of the TV studio in sight.

"How did we get here?" I ask, looking out the window at the countless people milling about the busy streets of the city around us.

"When I finished our performance, I came out to find you passed out on the floor," Lilith says. "Before the adoring fans could gang up on you, I carried you out and we took this cab."

Wow.

Before, I only passed out for a short time. Maybe I gained even more power today?

"How can I tell if it worked?" I ask Lilith in a hushed whisper. "Am I a more powerful seer and probability manipulator now? And, more importantly, can I fly?"

"Your guess is as good as mine," she says. "I imagine that as a seer, you won't feel the difference that much—

apart from the fact that your daily seer power supply should be much greater."

To check this theory, I attempt to go into Headspace but fail again.

Maybe the boost will kick in only after I recover from Nostradamus's attack?

"Now, as a probability manipulator, with greater power, you should have access to lower frequency events—those that look like thicker strands," she continues.

I take out my deck of cards, shuffle it, then close my eyes and try Chester's test again.

I picture the deck separating, first into colors, then into suits, then sorted by values. I remind myself how cool it would be to get the deck in order and, like before, picture myself performing this test as card magic—or using it as a secret methodology.

It's easier this time.

The colorful lines—the strands of fate—appear in front of me faster than before.

Examining them carefully, I focus on their thickness.

As before, the thicker strands feel more "right"— and I now have an idea why. It's as Chester mentioned: the thicker strands require more power expenditure. And Lilith just said thicker strands are of lower-frequency events.

Combine that information together, and it makes sense that a less likely event—like a one out of fifty-two factorial chance—will use up more probability manipulation power and be represented by a thicker strand.

Like the last time, the thinner strands seem easier to control, more elastic, while the thicker ones are unreachable and unyielding.

I mentally grab the thickest strand I can see.

It's as though I tried to grab a sea eel with oily hands.

Fine. I ignore the unyielding strand for the moment, and try one that's a little thinner—one that doesn't feel as "right."

This one escapes my clutches as well—as does the next thinnest one and the next.

Eventually, though, I find a strand that's about medium thickness in reference to the others—and when I metaphysically put pressure on it, it snaps.

Opening my eyes, I eagerly spread the cards in my hands.

Yes!

I made progress.

Instead of just separating by color, like before, the cards also separated into suits. The values in each suit are still in a random order, but I'm closer to my goal.

The TV appearance is already paying dividends.

I do the test again.

Getting the same result feels easier this time.

Another try, and I manage to bend a thicker strand to my will—and half the spades are sorted as a result.

"That's excellent," Lilith says, looking at my handiwork. "Just be careful overextending yourself so much in the beginning. There are limits on how much you can manipulate in a day." She takes the deck from me, gives it a shuffle, then spreads the completely ordered deck with a wink. "Those limits expand as you get more experience—like a muscle growing—but right now, you might not have a lot left to play with."

Crap.

That would've been useful information before I wasted my trickster mojo on playing with a deck of cards.

Then again, I need the practice. I'm nowhere near being able to do something useful with my newfound power.

Deciding to ignore Lilith's warning, I shuffle the cards and try to repeat the test—but no strands show up, no matter how hard I focus.

I guess I reached the limit she was talking about.

Oh, well. There's something much cooler I need to figure out how to do.

"How about flying?" I ask Lilith eagerly. "How do I do *that*?"

"I honestly don't know," she says. "When I need it, it just happens." She floats slightly off her seat, but not so high that the cabby would notice. "I never had to practice flying like I did probability manipulation. All vampire gifts are effortless like that. You just do it, and that's that."

Okey-doke.

I will myself to fly.

Nothing happens.

Maybe I don't want it badly enough—especially sitting in a moving car as I am?

I will myself to fly again.

Still nada.

Fine. I'll experiment with it later.

Since Lilith is staring out the window and not paying attention to me, I use the moment to ponder what my plan should be.

Do I escape her and rejoin Nero and the rest of the Cognizant on Earth so we can face Tartarus on Lilith's world, as Nostradamus suggested? Or do I face Tartarus here, on this world, as my mother wants?

The cab stops at a red light, and a large group of schoolchildren start crossing the road.

Their faces are cherubic and so innocent that it's like a bucket of cold water in my face.

Why is this even a dilemma?

This is a world with *countless* people—each someone's child, mother, father, brother, sister, husband, wife.

All of these people deserve to keep living as much as everyone on Earth.

If I can, I should protect them—especially since some of them now believe me to be a superhero of some sort. To paraphrase the famous quote from *Spider-Man*: when someone imbues you with a great power, you have a great responsibility to them.

There's really no other choice.

I have to try to help them. It's the only way I'll be able to live with myself.

If I survive, at least.

So that's that. I'm staying.

Now I need to figure out what this means when it comes to Lilith.

Do I still run from her? Or do I go along with her plans?

Yeah, a hard pass on that last one. There's a huge problem with what she wants—for Earth Cognizant to stay out of this conflict.

That's her greed and folly speaking. We stand a much better chance of defeating Tartarus if I can somehow get the word out to Nero, so he and the others can join and help.

But how?

Do I reason with Lilith?

No. That risks unleashing the sire bond and limiting my freedom significantly.

If I had Headspace access, I'd be able to reach Rasputin, but there's no time for me to recover my powers.

I need some other inter-Otherland form of communication—that or I have to run away and bring the news to Nero personally, a move that seems unlikely to succeed given Lilith's vigilance and the constant threat of the sire bond.

Then it hits me.

I *do* have an alternate way to communicate from anywhere in the Otherlands.

All I have to do is trick Lilith into allowing me to utilize it.

"No matter how much I try, I can't fly," I tell Lilith, not faking my frustration. "In general, I feel worn out." I massage my temples. "If I were still human, I'd say I need a good night's sleep. Or a vacation. And a spa treatment or two."

"You poor dear." Lilith strokes my back in a bizarrely caring gesture. "You *have* been through a lot. When I'd just turned, I slept for the first few nights, just to adjust. How about you take a nap when we get to the hotel?"

"Are you sure?" I yawn, inwardly hooting at my success.

"I'm positive," she says, just as the car pulls up to a hotel.

As we walk through the lobby, a few people look at me with curious expressions.

"I think they recognize you from your TV escapade," Lilith whispers. "Until Tartarus arrives, you're all they'll be talking about."

As if to confirm her theory, a teenage boy accosts us by the elevators, pleading for me to autograph his Rubik's-cube-looking toy.

I write "The Amazing Sasha" on the cube, then curse myself for not having thought of a cool superhero name and for having used up all of my probability power on shuffling cards.

If I still had it, I could've created a cool effect where I take the puzzle behind my back, turn it randomly, and sort out the colors thanks to my trickster powers.

Even if a few squares didn't align, it would've been an impressive feat.

Oh, well.

I pull out my deck of cards and perform regular slight-of-hand stuff where the card the boy names ends up in my pocket.

"How did you do that?" the kid asks, mouth agape.

"Can you keep a secret?" I whisper to him conspiratorially.

"Yeah." He leans in, his eyes widening.

"So can I," I say with a wink, then grab Lilith by the elbow and escape into the elevator.

Once inside, she presses the 25th floor and says, "You'll have to teach me some of your conjuring ways. It can help on my world."

"Sure." The elevator stops, and we get out. "But maybe when I'm not feeling so pooped."

"Fair enough." She opens a door, and we enter a bland, TV-less hotel room. "Why don't you rest now." She nods at the bed.

"Yeah." I take off my shoes. "As I sleep, why don't you practice this?" I give her one of my cards and show her how to keep it hidden in her hands. "This is called palming—and to master it, I urge you to walk around with this card in your hand until it feels like the most natural thing in the world. You might feel some guilt when palming at first, but—"

"Guilt isn't a problem of mine," Lilith says, awkwardly grabbing the card into her palm.

The urge to respond to that comment is strong, but

I resist it with every shred of self-preservation I possess.

I've come too far to get overtaken by the sire bond over such triviality.

Lying down on the bed, I close my eyes and say, "Nighty night."

"Rest, my dear," Lilith croons softly, almost maternally.

Nah. I imagined that last part.

Lilith is about as maternal as an AK-47.

Evening out my breathing, I set a new record for how fast I fall asleep.

CHAPTER TWENTY

I'M PERFORMING the bullet catch, with Nero as my sexy assistant.

The bullet is in my teeth—and the ovations begin when I notice my family and friends in trouble.

Before anyone is killed, a familiar figure appears in front of me and freezes time around us, so only she and I can move.

Yes.

My plan worked.

This is a dream, and she is its walker—Bailey.

"I hope you don't mind that I cut in before this pleasant dream turned into a nightmare," Bailey says. "For therapeutic purposes, we—"

"I'm not here for therapy," I say urgently. "I went to sleep in the hopes that I'd see you again. I need to send a message to Nero. It's very important."

Bailey blinks at me, and we again find ourselves on a cloud with the never-ending ocean below us.

"Tell me what the problem is," she says as the couch appears on the surface of the cloud.

Pom—her cute companion—materializes here as well, and watches me with his huge, pretty eyes.

Figuring I might as well get comfy, I take a seat and say, "It's Lilith. She stole me."

I proceed to tell Bailey everything, including the part about Tartarus—how the original plan was to face him on Lilith's world, and how I think that plan should change based on what I recently learned.

"How can you be found?" Bailey asks. "That's the first thing Nero will demand to know."

Grateful I memorized it earlier, I give her a step-by-step path from Earth's JFK hub to this world.

"Let's make sure I have it correctly," Bailey says. But instead of saying it back to me, she shows me a dream of herself walking the route I just described.

"You got it," I say and tell her about the hotel I'm currently in. When it's clear that Bailey has this down too, I ask, "Do you know where Nero actually is?"

"On Earth, I imagine," she says. "I myself am on Gomorrah but can be on Earth soon. From there, I'll just call him."

"Good," I say. "You do that, and I'll wake up and do my best to handle Lilith in the meanwhile."

"Be careful," Bailey says, stroking Pom. "I still hope to work on your nightmares one day. You've had an interesting life so far."

I smile at her. "It's a date. If I survive Tartarus, I'm

sure I'll have brand-new nightmares for your professional enjoyment."

With that, I stand up and will myself to wake up.

It works.

With a start, I open my eyes in the hotel room.

CHAPTER TWENTY-ONE

NOT GROGGY IN THE SLIGHTEST, I look around.

Lilith is nowhere to be seen.

I get up and spot a handwritten note on the bed next to me.

Went out to get something to eat. Be back soon.

-Mommy

Something to eat? I hope it's not a small child, or a nun, or a kitten.

I mindlessly make my way into the bathroom.

Just my luck—as soon as I decide I don't need to escape Lilith, she gives me a chance to do so.

Unless I *should* run away?

I can always reconnect with her later, once Tartarus shows up.

On autopilot, I grab a disposable toothbrush the hotel has provided, squeeze some toothpaste onto it, and attack my teeth.

Then something clicks in my memory—and a wave of dread follows.

How could I not have realized this sooner? I had a vision about brushing my teeth in a hotel bathroom!

I was standing just like this right before—

My realization comes too late.

My vampire super-hearing picks up the same noise I heard in my vision—that of someone opening the door and creeping into the room.

Like in the vision, I don't even bother spitting as I toss the toothbrush aside, then zoom out of the bathroom with top speed.

At least I avoid smacking into the giant intruder this time.

But just barely.

As I look at him, whatever doubts I had disappear.

It's the same growth hormone turned into a man.

Except he isn't a man, as I learned. He's a werewolf.

I take a step back as some of the puzzle pieces fall into place—the weird circa-eighties hair on his head, the outfit, the polaroid photo.

It all fits.

It's normal on this world.

I also understand why he lacks the Mandate aura.

He's not from Earth.

This is why Eduardo, the alpha werewolf, was so sure he doesn't know a werewolf like this.

I back up some more, recalling what I tried in my vision so I don't do it again.

Not that I have many options: it's either glamour or fight.

Well, glamour didn't work—which is disappointing, given that it's now boosted by faith.

Unless my vision was of a future where I didn't go on TV?

No.

Can't risk it.

This guy might be the local alpha and thus too powerful for glamour—or, for all I know, werewolves just can't be glamoured.

Which leaves the option to fight—but that also didn't work.

Unless I can do it better this time? Or at least, differently?

It would be good to stall him and pray Lilith arrives in the nick of time.

Worth a shot.

One way to stall is to chat, so I say, "Hi. How can I help you?"

The guy cocks his head, then looks at the photo in his hand, then back at me. Grunting, he shines with energy.

Not a talker, this one.

Just like in my dream, his clothes rip into shreds as he turns into his giant wolf form.

I back away, my heart hammering more desperately than in my vision.

Damn the future and its predictable patterns.

Growling, the werewolf bares his massive teeth and advances on me.

My fangs extending, I dodge a swipe of his paw—and the corner of the bed gets ruined once more.

I push my hands into my pockets, pull out all of my remaining flash paper along with a lighter, and blind us both as I light it up.

He recovers first, and swipes at me with his other paw.

Knowing how stubborn the future can be, I expected this maneuver, so even though I'm blinded, I twist to the side with supernatural speed, and the dresser gets decimated instead of my face.

Last time, I kicked him in the ribcage—so I kick at his head now.

It doesn't work any better than in my vision.

The guy dodges the strike and clamps his teeth on my thigh, just like before.

Gritting my own teeth in frustration, I strain to keep my balance.

He tosses me back and forth, and I lose the fight, my head smacking on the corner of a nightstand as I fall. He then drags me through the room.

Again.

Flailing, I fight with all my might. If I don't change the future now, I'm going out the window, and that's that.

It doesn't work.

His teeth just clamp on me tighter, and he growls as he jerks his head and throws me into the air.

There's a familiar moment of weightlessness before my back hits the window.

Glass shatters around me, slashing my skin as I grapple for the window frame—only to get my palms sliced to shreds as the momentum carries me out.

This is it.

I drop like a stone.

CHAPTER TWENTY-TWO

THE ADRENALINE OVERDOSE makes the descent seem slow.

I marvel at how quickly my head wound and skin lacerations heal, but I also know no healing ability can save me from this fall—or the landing, to be more accurate.

Plummeting by the nineteenth floor or thereabouts, I recall something important.

The TV demonstration.

There should be people out there who believe I can fly.

I hope.

I certainly wouldn't have believed it, and Felix wouldn't have either. But Ariel might have.

So yeah. There's got to be believers out there.

That, plus the fact that vampires—or at least Lilith —can fly, adds up to potentially good news for me.

Except I'm *not* flying.

I'm falling.

Why isn't it working? Lilith said there wasn't a special technique to it, but when I tried flying in the car, I couldn't. At that point, I wondered if perhaps I didn't want it enough—but I do now. I want it more than anything.

Another floor goes by.

I will myself to fly with all the desperation born of my current situation.

Another floor.

I picture myself lighter than air. I even hum "I Believe I Can Fly"—at least until I recall who sings that song. I then hum "Learning to Fly" by Pink Floyd instead.

Two more floors pass by.

As wholeheartedly as I can, I try to believe that I can do this. I remind myself that flying is nothing compared to the ability to see into the future. After all, birds and planes can fly, but no creature or machine can do what a seer can.

Still nothing—and not many floors left to work it out.

Closing my eyes to help focus, I remind myself that I'm a vampire.

And not just *any* vampire.

I'm Lilith's daughter, so flying is mine by birthright.

Something happens near floor five, and I feel an amazing lightness spread through my whole body.

Air resistance ceases and my descent seems to stop —but I'm afraid to open my eyes.

What if this is how everyone feels after hitting the ground? What if this is the lightness of my soul leaving my body?

I hear some sort of excited cries in the distance.

My ears still seem to work. That's reassuring.

Here goes nothing.

I gulp in a breath and open my eyes.

I'm hovering in the air, fifty feet above the ground.

CHAPTER TWENTY-THREE

I LOOK DOWN.

There are people staring up and pointing at me.

So that's where the noise was coming from. Too bad they have no cellphones with cameras on this world. This feat could've gone viral.

All right. Time to figure out how this flying thing works.

I wish to float up.

To my amazement, I do.

Now that it's finally working, flying reminds me of the way I float during Headspace joining with other seers—only I feel even lighter.

Slowly, I float up to double-digit floors. Then, moving faster and faster, I reach the twenties and locate the broken window from which I came.

The giant wolf is staring out of the frame at me, ears pinned back and his teeth bared in a snarl.

"We have some unfinished business, you and I," I

hiss at him dramatically. "I have a lot of questions, and you'll answer them for me."

Clenching my hands into fists, I extend my arms Superman style and speed up.

As I close the distance, a part of me wonders why I'm returning to fight the guy instead of fleeing. I think it's because if I can't prove to myself that I can defeat a mere werewolf—no matter how big and strong—I'll never believe I can face someone like Tartarus.

Also, I'm sick and tired of random strangers trying to kill me. Enough is enough.

Maybe if I make a few bloody examples, my name will go on a list of people never to mess with.

The werewolf growls and lunges at me as I whoosh into the window just above him. His teeth clank together a hair below my shoulder.

I zoom up and kick him in the snout.

The werewolf flies through the room and crashes into the door with such force that it shatters.

He starts to get up, but slowly, as if stunned.

Hovering in the air, I grab his hind paw like a baseball bat and swing him up—which results in his head smacking into the ceiling.

Plaster rains down as he drops to the floor, his hind paw still in my grip and his head lolling to one side.

I either knocked him out or he's faking.

If it's the latter, it's a miscalculation.

Gripping his hind paw tighter, I fly toward the window.

He's still out—or faking—as his head rams into the window frame.

There's a sound of claws shredding the carpet behind us.

Damn.

He wasn't alone.

A group of smaller werewolves rushes into the room.

Was probability manipulation on my side again? If our fight had lasted just a few seconds longer, I'd be dealing with a whole pack.

"You're too late," I shout at the newcomers tauntingly as I float out of the window.

They watch me with so much anger in their canine eyes that I worry one or more might actually risk leaping at me. My catch in tow, I fly up to prevent that from happening and only relax when I leave the hotel roof far behind.

Now that I'm up, I keep going toward the clouds, until the people on the ground look like ants. That's when my captive starts to come to—and by now, I'm sure he wasn't faking.

His recovery is slow, so I give him a good shake.

His eyes finally open—and widen in an unnatural-for-a-wolf way. That is, if a supernatural creature can be said to do something unnatural.

His gaze drops to the people below us, and his whole body stiffens as blood starts to pour from his ears, maw, and nose.

Oh, crap.

He must be under this world's version of the Mandate, and it's punishing him for showing his furry form to the Muggles.

"Dude," I say. "I doubt anyone on the ground can really see you with much detail. Get your act together."

He doesn't say anything and keeps bleeding—and I can't resist the lure. Lifting him up higher, I bite into his furry paw.

How can something so gross be so good?

The guy must be very powerful indeed. His blood is like chocolate-covered heroin.

Snarling at my bite, the werewolf shines with that now-familiar energy, and the furry paw in my grip turns into a human leg.

A naked human leg—attached to a naked everything else that's dangling upside down.

Well, this is awkward.

Then again, it could be worse. I could be the naked one, and he could be the one enjoying my bodily fluids.

"Let me go," the werewolf snarls as the blood outpour from his orifices ceases.

I look down at the distant ground below us, then back at him, and channel Lilith with my smile. "Are you sure? I understand it sucks to be slapped around by someone a third of your weight, but that's no reason to give up on life just like that."

He pales, realizing his choice of words. "Please," he grits. "I don't like heights."

"You don't like heights?" I ask, feigning concern.

Then, as if I lost control over my flying, I jerkily dip down a foot.

The look of horror on his face is priceless.

"What do you want?" he growls.

Did my probability manipulation deliver me a werewolf with acrophobia, or is it merely a happy coincidence? Can there even *be* such thing as a coincidence for me anymore?

"Nothing," I say and repeat the drop-down tactic.

He pales another shade of white. "How do I make you stop?"

"By telling me why you tried to kill me," I say, and to highlight my opinion of his actions, I dip down another couple of feet.

"You're clearly Cognizant, yet you went on TV and displayed your powers by winning the lottery," he says shakily. "We checked—it was no illusion—so you must've used your trickster powers to do so. Now it turns out even your flying was real—which I still can't believe." He looks down. "What did you expect would happen?"

"I had extenuating circumstances," I say, and as I do, I realize how interesting it is that Lilith omitted any mention of the local Cognizant. In fact, she made it sound like they didn't exist when she was saying that she didn't want to share the spoils of this world with any Cognizant from Earth. Did she take it as a foregone conclusion that Tartarus would kill all local Cognizant?

"You can make all the excuses you want, but the

Councils will have your head," he says a bit too boldly for my taste, so I dip another three feet to calm him down.

He snarls in response and says sulkily, "I wasn't the only one sniffing you out. My Enforcers are out there—and you're as good as dead. Especially if you kill me."

"What's your name?" I readjust my grip to make sure he doesn't slip. Sweating bullets like he is, he's as slippery as an overused stripper pole.

"Obo," he growls.

"What, like the woodwind instrument?"

"No," he says. "That's an oboe—with an 'e' at the end. My name is short for Oboroten'."

I grin. "As in, werewolf in Russian?"

"My parents were not very subtle people," he says gruffly.

"And the apple didn't fall far from the tree," I say. "Fall, get it?"

"Yes, very clever," he says sarcastically.

"All right, Obo. Let's get back to the matter at hand." I regrip his leg to make sure he doesn't slip out and prematurely end our conversation. "I'm here from a different Otherland, and I plan to save your world from destruction. I don't expect much in the way of thanks, but assassinating me isn't going to help anyone."

"What are you talking about?" Obo crunches up, his abs flexing. "How can you, a single vampire, save a whole world? And from what? The biggest threat to our existence is you. By going on TV, you risk revealing our nature to the humans."

"I had to go on TV to boost my powers in order to help you all. As to what or whom I'm saving you from —how much do you know about Tartarus?"

He lets himself hang. "I've heard of Tartarus. Isn't he just a myth they tell you about at Orientation to scare you from running off into the Otherlands?"

"Sadly, no. Tartarus is a real entity, and he's coming to devour your world."

"Sure he is. And you came here to save us—out of the kindness of your vampire heart." His words are dripping with so much sarcasm, I strongly contemplate dropping him, but I just dip down to scare him instead.

It works. He starts breathing faster.

"If you're such a skeptic, why do *you* think I'm here?" I ask when he calms a bit. "Why would I put a target on my back like that?"

"Maybe you're dumb and power hungry," he says. "It's happened before."

"I think it's dumb to call me dumb," I say and loosen my grip slightly, causing his leg to nearly slip from my hold.

He starts sweating bullets again. "Fine, whatever. It doesn't matter why you did it. It's not my job to know. I leave such questions for the ones in charge."

"What *is* your job, then?" I ask as a possibly bad idea occurs to me.

"I'm an Enforcer," he says proudly. "I bring

Cognizant like you to face the wrath of the Council. Dead or alive."

I sadistically plummet a couple of feet to remind him who's in charge. "You're in luck," I say, deciding to implement my dubious idea. "I'm going to let you do your job."

He stares at me uncomprehendingly, audibly panting. The last plunge was clearly sobering.

"You're going to take me to speak with your Council," I say. "Hopefully, they're not as thickheaded as you."

He crunches up again, his eyes as wide as if I'd spouted tusks. "Is this a trick? You *want* to face them?"

"No trick," I say. "I'm here to save your world, as I've said—but I can't do it alone. You and your Council will need to help me save you, and the first step is for us to have a chat."

He blinks. "If you're sure about this, then take me down so I can put a blindfold on you and we—"

"Take you down?" I chuckle. "That's not happening. We're going to fly there together."

"But—"

"I'm going with my eyes wide open," I say firmly. "If anything unforeseen were to happen to me, I still have a chance to let you go."

"Fine." His jaw muscles tense. "Let's fly there. If you don't mind, I'll keep my eyes closed as we go."

"So long as you can give me directions without looking, I can blindfold *you*."

He shrugs—which is clearly hard to do upside-down. "Go north."

I do, and as I fly, I notice that the metropolis below us is built on an island shaped like a triangle that has two equal sides.

"If I have my terminology right, that landmass is an isosceles triangle," I tell my captive. "That's pretty neat."

"A golden triangle," he says without opening his eyes. "The west and east sides of the island are in a golden ratio to the south side."

"Impressive," I say sarcastically. "I didn't realize trigonometry was such a basic skill for a werewolf Enforcer."

"Every Cognizant child here knows this," Obo says, taking on a tour-guide tone. "You see, long ago, this landmass was a pentagram—a shape that has golden triangles at the tips. Then one of the descendants of Rūaumoko caused a major earthquake that left only this island above water. Soon after, we implemented the Mandate. I hope you can see why everyone on this world is sensitive when it comes to flashy displays of power." He opens his eyes and narrows them at me.

Great. It will be that much harder to justify my TV performance to these people. Assuming I can do it at all.

Biting my lip, I fly silently for the next few minutes and do my best to figure out what I'll say to the Council.

Obo corrects my course a few times until it

becomes clear that we're flying to where the narrowest part of the island points like an arrow.

"What's with the geometric shapes?" I ask when I see another island in the distance. "That looks like a pizza with a slice missing—though I'm sure there's a better mathematical term for it."

"That shape is called a sector and the reason there are so many patterns to the landmasses on this world is Rūaumoko—the most powerful earth mover Cognizant who's ever lived," Obo explains. "Believing himself a god, he ripped apart the original cohesive continent into shapes he thought pleasing. This world has many legends about those apocalyptic events—and even modern scientists explain it by using a dubious symmetrical tectonic plate theory." He stares at the fast-approaching shape. "Anyway, it's called Pac-Man Island and is where the local Council resides."

"Wait, what?" I nearly drop him. "Pac-Man? That's a game we have on my world. How do you know it?"

He wipes the sweat off his forehead and takes a calming breath. "Do they also have Orientation on your world?" he manages to say after a moment.

"They do," I say defensively. "Maybe I didn't exactly finish the whole thing, but that's not my fault."

"Well, if you did, you'd know that all good ideas for games, books, and movies get routinely 'borrowed' by the Cognizant from different worlds," he says. "That's why you'll often find similar languages, popular culture, technological advancements, and much more."

Of course. Why didn't I think of that? It sounds like

I could bring the abacus to the dragon world and be the next Bill Gates there as a result.

Wait a second.

Is Bill Gates a Cognizant? Did he get the idea for *Windows* from someplace like Gomorrah? If so, why didn't he jump right to AI or VR instead? Or hover—

"Some technologies are controlled by the Councils," Obo says, clearly reading my mind. "Books, comics, and music are where the world sharing is most rampant. Unless they're books about political ideologies ahead of their time."

I make a mental note to talk more about this with Dr. Hekima—assuming I survive.

Now that we're close enough to Pac-Man Island to examine it, I study it with all the intensity of my new and improved vampire vision.

Unlike the concrete jungle that was the city island we left behind, this one looks like a forest preserve—only on major steroids. Anywhere the eye falls are four-hundred-foot-tall sequoia-like trees that jointly blot out any visibility of what's happening on the ground.

As in, I could land in the middle of an ambush and not know it.

How lovely.

"Do the humans not come here?" I ask Obo as I reluctantly begin my descent.

"We made sure a lot of animals are protected on this island," he says proudly. "It's warded against random sailors getting an idea to dock here. If someone from the government ever comes to check on things, our illusionists make them see what we want them to see. And if any poacher-types manage to break through the wards somehow, they'll either be eaten by the very animals they came to kill, or glamoured to never come back."

Eaten? Talk about overkill.

I wonder what they'll do in a few decades when Google, or this world's equivalent, decides to create satellite images of everything and put them online. That, and small drones, might one day be a problem for this Council.

If they're around after Tartarus arrives, that is.

Which is why I'm here.

"Land there." Obo points to where the Pac-Man's eye would be.

As I clear the bushy tops of the enormous trees, I spot the place he meant.

It's a meadow, and on the grass are people who look like a cos-play convention—or extras in a movie about wood elves.

Many point their fingers at me, while some point actual guns—which clash with the medieval fantasy vibe they have going.

I carefully fly down and make sure Obo doesn't break anything critical as I drop him on the ground.

Then, ignoring the threatening displays all around, I land and wave at them. "Howdy. I'm here to have a very important conversation with y'all." For some reason, I say it with a Texas drawl. Must be all the guns.

"Looks like we're going to have a hearing," says a dude with a bushy beard that doesn't go with his elven outfit. Then again, for all I know, elves might have beards, especially if they're also hipsters.

"A hearing is what she wanted," Obo says.

The bearded guy nods, then takes out a walkie-talkie from under his tunic and fiddles with the controls. When the gizmo hisses, he says, "Lizzy, bring the TV here so we can review the evidence."

A young woman with a kind, round face poofs into existence.

This must be Lizzy, and she's a teleporter, like Eric.

With her is a black, multi-level stand with a big CRT TV and VCR. It reminds me of the setup our Sex Ed teacher used when he showed the horror-flick-like documentary from the eighties called *The Miracle of Life*. The graphically depicted live birth in it was, for me, the best motivation for abstinence for countless years after—not to mention, something that still gives me nightmares on occasion.

Maybe I should get Bailey's help with *that*.

The bearded guy walks to the contraption and grabs the electrical plugs that lead to the TV and VCR.

After a moment of concentration, sparks show up between his skin and the plugs. Then the TV comes to life.

Interesting.

Is he a technomancer like Felix?

But no. Lizzy is working the controls, so the bearded guy must just have electrical powers.

I'll call him Sparkles, I decide.

The VCR comes to life next, and a grainy video starts, showing me on stage, performing the lottery prediction and the rest.

It looks great and I don't look like I was freaking out, even though I totally was. As tempting as it is, I resist the urge to ask Sparkles for a copy of the tape.

I'm probably expected to act repentant at this juncture.

"Now tune it to live TV," Sparkles says, and Lizzy complies.

A TV news show is on, and they have a picture of yours truly.

"We checked on the lottery ticket," says the newscaster guy. "It's genuine, and was bought just before the performance. The folks at the lottery assure us there is no possible way the system could've been—"

Sparkles stops supplying the TV with electricity, and it cuts out. Seeing that she's no longer needed, Lizzy sets the remote down on the VCR and poofs away.

"Thank you for coming," Sparkles says to me nastily. "You will now pay for that heinous crime."

As if on cue, Obo turns into his wolf form, and the fingers and weapons of the others point at me again—more menacingly this time.

CHAPTER TWENTY-FOUR

I ASSESS my chances of flying away if they all shoot at me at once.

Very low.

Probably zero.

"I can explain," I say quickly. "I came to save all the humans on this world from a horrible fate. I didn't realize there were Cognizant here as well; else I'd have spoken to you first."

The Councilors look confused—and, as a result, slightly less ready to shred me into little pieces.

"I'm a seer," I continue, speaking at a rapid clip. "I foresaw Tartarus destroying the world I'm from, and then I learned that he's also coming to this world—and much sooner. So I came to stop him here."

As I pause for breath, I notice that not a single person has shot me with either a bullet or their magic mojo—and some have even lowered their arms.

Good.

I might survive yet.

"Did you say *Tartarus?*" an older woman with lapis-colored eyes asks and frowns. "Maybe we should get Jaylen to join? He survived—"

"Oh, please," Sparkles says, rolling his eyes. "We're not going to bother the poor illusionist with these lies."

"I'm not lying," I say. "Tartarus is coming and I was prophesied to be the one who kills him. And because I wasn't sure that I'm powerful enough, I did the TV performance to grow stronger. Again, I didn't realize I'd step on your collective toes—though it doesn't really matter anyway. The purpose of the Mandate is to prevent humans from learning about the Cognizant. But as soon as Tartarus arrives, there will be no humans left here—nor Cognizant."

I pointedly omit any mention of Lilith's involvement. They may have heard of her, and being the daughter of evil incarnate is not going to help my case.

Sparkles sighs theatrically and shakes his head. "Wow. She'll say anything to save her hide."

"My hide is only in danger because I chose that." I nod at Obo. "Why would I come here if not to warn you and get you ready? I could've easily flown to a hub and hightailed it home, leaving you to fend for yourselves in the apocalypse to come."

A lot more people look thoughtful, and some—like the older lady who spoke about some survivor—even look convinced.

"You knew we would hunt you down no matter

where you ran," Sparkles says, but he sounds less certain.

"Actually, I have powerful allies on the world where I'm from," I say. "You wouldn't be able to touch me there."

"This *could* explain where Criswell went," says a slender woman who was one of the first to lower her gun.

"Who is Criswell?" I ask Sparkles.

"A seer who disappeared a few months ago, along with his friends and family," he says gruffly, his expression more troubled.

"There you have it," I say. "He must've foreseen the end of the world but didn't like the rest of you enough to warn you about it."

Sparkles strokes his beard for a few long seconds. "I still don't trust you," he says, and the few people still aiming at me nod approvingly. "You broke the most sacred rule we have."

"Don't you have anyone with the power to tell if I'm being truthful?" I ask, looking around for limbal rings in people's eyes and finding none.

Where's a dragon when you need one?

Speaking of dragons, I really miss Nero—and not just because having him here could save my non-lying hide.

"We can use one of the stones," the older woman with the strange eyes says.

"And waste an invaluable artifact?" Sparkles grunts.

"The stakes couldn't be higher," she says. "We have ten stones left. We can spare one for this."

Frowning, Sparkles pulls out his walkie-talkie again and fiddles with the controls.

"Yes?" a feminine voice says.

"Bring the stones," Sparkles orders and puts the walkie-talkie away.

Lizzy poofs into existence once more. This time, she's holding a beautiful bejeweled box in her hands.

When she opens it, I see a bunch of large stones that shine with magical, ocean-blue light.

Ah.

This rings a bell.

There's a necklace in the box as well—one where a stone would fit into.

That confirms it.

When I faced the New York Council for the first time, they used the same thing on me. That time, it was Nero who shot a blue stone to make it shine like that— and after he did it, it took on his truth-telling abilities. Here, though, some dragon already pre-loaded the stones with that power.

Maybe Nero himself?

Since now isn't the time to ask if the hot guy I'm sleeping with gave this to them, I wait quietly for Lizzy to put the stone into the necklace and then drape it over my neck.

Sparkles puffs up. "With that, you will speak only—"

"The truth," I say. "Yes, I'm familiar with this magic

and want to start by saying that if you need more stones, I know someone very intimately who can recharge them for you."

My necklace shines green—which proves beyond a shadow of doubt that I am telling the truth.

As I intended, everyone's eyes bulge out of their sockets.

They must know about dragons—which I guess makes some sense, given the *Lord of the Rings* vibe of this group.

In case the implied threat wasn't clear, I add, "And before you make your decision about my fate, you should know the person in question would be extremely upset with you if I were harmed."

My necklace shines green once again.

"In fact," I say, feeling bolder at the horrified and impressed impressions all around, "I suspect that if you kill me, Tartarus's arrival will be the least of your worries."

The stone confirms my words again.

"Are you done with your threats and boasts?" Sparkles asks.

"I was just stating facts," I say, and the stone glows green. "How about you ask me what you need to know, so we can focus on what's important—saving everyone from Tartarus?"

"Are you really a seer?" he asks.

"Yes," I say to a green confirmation.

"Did you really see a vision of this world perishing?"

"No," I say. "I ran out of seer power before I could do so. I foresaw my own world ending, then someone else told me the same is going to happen here."

"Who is this someone?" he asks. "Is it another seer?"

Crap.

I really would rather keep Lilith out of this.

"It wasn't a seer, but she said a seer gave her the information," I say, choosing words carefully to make sure the stone doesn't call me a liar. "I believed her because she has no reason to lie—which should be the reason you believe *me*."

"Let's say we believe you," the slender woman from earlier says. "The fact remains that Tartarus is a destroyer of worlds. What can we do, besides run?"

"As I said earlier, I was prophesied to be the one who kills Tartarus. The prophecy was made by a seer who is more powerful than I am. Oh, and besides being a seer, I'm a vampire—as you can tell. And a probability manipulator."

The stone confirms my words, and everyone, even Sparkles, looks impressed with my rare trifecta of powers.

"I also studied deceit and illusions—the conjuring kind," I say. "Which might help in this situation."

"How?" the older woman from earlier asks with a frown.

Maybe deceit and illusions weren't the best thing to bring up when trying to sound like the paragon of honesty.

"Do you have many Heralds on this world?" I ask as an idea that was jelling in my mind starts to crystalize.

She nods as Sparkles frowns.

"And can you, the Councilors, speak of things usually forbidden by the Mandate?" I ask.

She nods again, but more warily. She must be anticipating where I'm going with this.

"Okay. Then I think you should all go on TV and gain more power, the way I did," I say before they can start booing my idea. "And I can help design illusions to make your abilities seem even greater."

"She's insane," Sparkles says. "She may believe her delusions, but that makes her no less crazy."

"I'm perfectly sane," I say, and the stone confirms my words—though I guess it would do the same in any case, as long as I believed the truth of my words.

"The scope of this conversation is growing far beyond what this Council can handle," says the older woman from before. "We need to bring representatives from other Councils here—and Jaylen as well. He knows the most about Tartarus, having survived him."

A survivor besides Nostradamus? That's interesting indeed.

"Doing that is as good as admitting we believe her," Sparkles says, looking unhappy.

"I believe in the power of those stones," the woman retorts. "I also don't see any reason for her to make this up."

Grudgingly, Sparkles fiddles with his walkie-talkie.

Before the device can come to life, Lizzy shows up, an expectant expression on her round face.

"We need to gather as many representatives of the other Councils as we can," he says to her imperiously. "Also, we need to speak with Jaylen—if he's available, that is."

"Got it," Lizzy says and teleports away.

Nothing happens for about a minute, so I check if I've regained my seer powers.

Sadly, no.

After a couple more minutes, Lizzy comes back and brings another person with her, this one dressed in a toga—perhaps from a Council with a different aesthetic, more reminiscent of ancient Greece?

The next person Lizzy brings is dressed in regular clothes, and the one after that is in a cocktail dress.

Unlike on Earth, where all Councils like their robes and masks, it appears this world has a theme free-for-all.

As more and more Councilors gather, I mentally outline the details of my idea on how to improve our chances in this fight.

My musings are interrupted when I notice that besides Lizzy, there are now a dozen more teleporters bringing people in—at a faster and faster rate.

The newcomers are exchanging heated whispers with the local Councilors, and my face burns under the weight of all the curious stares.

A few more minutes pass, and Lizzy shows up holding the shoulder of an ancient-looking man.

"Hello, Jaylen," says the older woman who insisted he be brought here. "Sorry to disturb you, but this visitor has something that you, of all people, might want to hear."

Curious, I study the new arrival.

When Samuel L. Jackson is a hundred-and-ten years old, he might be able to play this guy in a movie—assuming any actor would be able to project the bottomless sadness in Jaylen's eyes.

"I'm always glad to see your face, Roslin," he says to the woman in a raspy voice.

Flirting? Good for him.

Blushing slightly, Roslin looks around at the noisy people, then points her hand at the ground.

The meadow vibrates with a mini-earthquake—which gets everyone's attention immediately.

"Please tell everyone what you just told us," Roslin says to me.

I do as she says—only pausing midway, when the stone around my neck stops shining, likely having run out of dragon truth-telling mojo.

Being able to lie is nice, so I embellish parts of the story a bit, claiming I came here of my own free will instead of admitting that my psycho mother kidnapped me.

As soon as the name Tartarus is mentioned, Jaylen's expression turns as dark as the one I've seen on Nostradamus's face.

He hates Tartarus, that much is clear.

"Am I to understand that everyone believes the

nonsense that just came out of her mouth?" Sparkles asks loudly, staring at his colleagues.

The majority of the Councilors nod with varying degrees of enthusiasm.

"How about we vote on it?" Roslin says. "Those who think we should treat Tartarus's arrival as a credible threat, please raise your hand."

Almost all hands go up—even those of people who didn't nod when Sparkles asked if they believed me.

Shrugging, Sparkles lifts his own hand. "Fine. I guess there's no harm in being prepared," he grumbles. "But if Tartarus doesn't come, this one will have a lot to answer for."

"I wish I were making all of this up," I say. "For everyone's sake."

"Right," Roslin says. "With that settled, I want Jaylen to take over. He's the only person I know who survived Tartarus's arrival on a world. And, as an illusionist, he can show us what to expect."

Right. She said that earlier, but it only now clicks. No wonder Jaylen had that expression on his face when I mentioned the upcoming invasion.

Tartarus must have hurt him deeply.

"Anyone who minds seeing my illusion, please speak up," Jaylen says, looking around.

No one has any objections, so he raises his thin arms and shoots red energy at us.

The forest around us is replaced with the hub Lilith and I came from.

"Let's start on my home world," Jaylen's disembodied voice says. "I'll take you there now."

Our viewpoint flies into the gate Lilith and I stepped into this world from, then quickly travels the path to Earth that I memorized—only we don't exit on Earth but follow another set of gates, which are also familiar.

When we exit at our destination, I see that my suspicion was right.

Jaylen took us to a world I've been to. The one with all the mummified bodies I kept seeing on the way to and from Lilith's and Nero's worlds.

Only here, Jaylen's world is very much alive—the airport bustling with frantic activity reminiscent of New York's JFK.

Like a movie on fast-forward, the viewpoint rushes out of the airport and travels over the highway, then through a city block, up the staircase of a building, and into an apartment where a much younger Jaylen is sitting in front of a TV.

On the screen is a man who vaguely resembles Jaylen, especially the older one of today.

"When you look at Tartarus, you see someone you look up to or worship," Jaylen's disembodied voice says. "That's why I see my long-dead grandfather."

Right. Nostradamus saw *his* mentor in his memories.

Tartarus has a green screen in the background—as if the studio execs wanted to CGI something behind him, but then forgot to do so.

"Behold," Tartarus says sonorously. "I have finally come, and your worries and tragedies are over."

As he speaks, I get an odd sensation. It's like he means every word of that cryptic message. Like I should believe him. Like his word is the truth, maybe with an upper-case T.

When I mention this, Jaylen explains, "Tartarus has the power to make you want to believe his words. Fortunately, it doesn't work on those of us who know better."

Interesting. So Tartarus can look like something sacred and make you want to believe him—no wonder whole worlds lose to him.

"I am known by many names," Tartarus says with the same trust-invoking manner. "Know that those who had faith in me will now be rewarded." He smiles beatifically, and I wonder how many billions of people see him as their deity. "But worry not, those who did not have faith in me," he says with an even brighter smile. "Now that I am revealed, you can believe. It's never too late."

The gall of this guy. He's doing the same thing Lilith did on her world, but on a grander scale. And, unlike Lilith who left her subjects more or less alive, Tartarus plans to have them sucked dry right after he makes himself their god.

"Soon, I shall bring your essences—your very souls —to join with me," Tartarus says, his eyes radiating celestial warmth. "We will become as one."

What a clever charade. If people believe this last bit

—and many will—their belief will enhance his core power, that of consuming life energy. What's most diabolical is that nothing he said in that last statement is a lie. When he drains someone—or gobbles their essence—they do become "as one," in a very strict sense of the word.

"Now my children will arrive," Tartarus continues. "Treat them with the respect you would treat me, as they are an extension of me. We serve the same purpose."

Again true. They're all here for an all-you-can-eat buffet.

Finally, Tartarus disappears from the screen, and the programming cuts to a newscaster, who right away starts to speculate on what the viewers just heard, dropping phrases like Judgment Day and Second Coming.

Young Jaylen isn't interested in this part. He overhears something happening outside, so he stands up and walks to his third-floor window to look out.

A shining plasma gate opens in the middle of the street.

It looks like the gates at the hubs, only smaller and fainter.

"Some of Tartarus's children are teleporters powerful enough to open temporary gates," Jaylen's disembodied voice explains when someone gasps. "These gates will only exist for an hour and a half—but that is more than enough time for these villains to suck the world dry."

As he speaks, a stream of people rushes out of the gate, all looking like someone Jaylen reveres and loves, to varying degrees.

The humans on the street stare at them in awe. Some fall down on their knees, while others just stand there, as if frozen. They must be seeing angels or their own long-dead relatives.

Tartarus's children slowly spread out from the gate, then extend their hands as if in prayer.

Arcs of energy jump into their hands from the humans nearest to them.

Before anyone can so much as blink, the humans turn into the mummified husks that now cover this world.

Despite being far away, Jaylen starts to feel his life force being drained as well—but not as quickly.

"I apologize, but I don't want to relive the next part in detail," his voice says as the world around us momentarily goes black. "Let me just say that those monsters will methodically seek out every living being. The humans they will suck dry right away, but the Cognizant they will separate into food and breeding stock. The latter will be used to make children with useful powers for their father. Out of my whole family, I was the only survivor."

Though I can't see Jaylen, the darkness around us grows heavy with his pain.

"The next parts are my extrapolation, rather than a factual account of events," he says in an unsteady voice as he shows us a room covered with TV monitors.

It's like a surveillance room in a bank, only big enough to cover dozens of locations all over the globe.

On each screen plays out a similar scene.

Somewhere in the world, a gate opens, Tartarus's children run out of it, and destruction ensues.

On one screen, this is happening in the desert. On another, on an island in the ocean. Most, however, show cities.

On one larger screen, Tartarus walks through what looks like a TV studio and is soon joined by a dozen or so of his children. He and his posse suck dry every person who crosses their path, leaving husks in their wake.

A teleporter woman appears, blocking Tartarus's path—and she brought a regal-looking man with her.

"That's two of the most powerful Councilors we had," Jaylen explains. "I later shared a cell with them in the breeding pits. If anyone had a chance to defeat Tartarus, it would've been them."

Tartarus looks the newcomers over and focuses on the woman, pointing his arms at her just as his children attack the noble-looking dude.

A purplish energy flows from the woman into Tartarus. She screams in pain and starts to visibly shrivel, as if aging at a rapid pace. Draining her of energy seems to be a slower process than with humans, but that just extends her agony.

In the meanwhile, the regal-looking guy turns into a werewolf even bigger than Obo, and starts ripping

Tartarus's children into pieces as they attempt to drain him of energy.

They're clearly not as skilled at sucking as their daddy.

As the werewolf finishes with his last victim, the teleporter woman lets out a tormented shriek and poofs away.

Wow. She just left her comrade to fend for himself. That's not cool—and totally futile, since judging by what Jaylen said about the breeding pits, she gets caught later anyway.

With the teleporter gone, Tartarus points both hands at the werewolf and orange energy starts to flow to him.

The werewolf's ears drop, his tail slinking between his legs as he starts to howl, his furry body turning increasingly raisin-like.

Without letting up on the energy-sucking, Tartarus approaches him and knocks him out with a single punch to the snout.

On that optimistic note, Jaylen's illusion is over.

I'm back in the meadow, surrounded by greenery and all the Councilors—who now look quite grim.

Like me, they're not looking forward to the upcoming fight.

Unlike them, I know Tartarus is someone I'll *have* to face.

It's apparently my destiny.

If I wasn't sure about my prospects before, I'm even less confident now. For starters, I didn't think Tartarus would have so much backup. "Defeating him" always meant killing just one very powerful guy, not a whole army of his grown children. But now it looks like he's just a piece of the puzzle. He will arrive, go on TV, and unleash his spawn on everyone—a chain of events much harder to deal with.

I guess we need a bigger plan. A plan that will include killing all of his hellish spawn.

As I'm pondering this, Lizzy, the local teleporter, shows up next to the TV setup.

Her eyes are wide and she's paler than some of the vampires present.

"Turn on the TV," she says to Sparkles hollowly. "You have to see this."

Sparkles grabs the cables, bringing the TV to life.

Her hands trembling, Lizzy tunes in to a channel.

My heartbeat skyrockets as I wait for the image to appear.

If this is what I think this is, all my efforts have been for nothing.

If Tartarus is already here, making his speech on TV, this world—and I along with it—is doomed.

CHAPTER TWENTY-FIVE

THE IMAGE SHOWS UP, and I realize the world isn't doomed.

I am, though.

The screen is showing Lilith. She's floating a few feet above the ground, the way I've learned to do.

"My name is Lilith. The one who revealed herself to you earlier is my daughter, Sasha," my mother says into the camera, and the Cognizant around me turn from the screen to stare at me, their expressions darkening.

"I am a goddess of blood and luck," Lilith goes on. "And I will prove this for your viewing pleasure."

Her eyes turn mirror-like, and she casts her gaze onto the people in the first row of the studio audience.

Having gotten their attention, she says, "Come. I will drink your blood."

The spectators begin to get up, one by one, and walk onto the stage.

When the first man gets there, Lilith makes him kneel and pray to her. Then she drinks him for the longest ten seconds in TV history.

The rest of the audience screams and attempts to flee.

Undaunted by the humans' reactions, Lilith drinks from the rest of the glamoured people before she does that remote feeding trick she performed on the chorts, where a small stream of blood goes from every single member of the audience into Lilith's greedy mouth.

Everyone around me—even the vampires—gape at the TV with horrified expressions.

I guess they didn't realize this last trick was even possible.

On my end, I can't help but wonder if *this* was what Lilith meant in her handwritten note when she said she'd "get something to eat."

Talk about major understatements.

Of course, what Lilith is actually doing is growing her power in the exact same way I did. She must've gotten jealous of my TV coverage and decided to get some of her own.

Before I can process this any further, Sparkles drops the TV cable and turns to me with lightning dancing on his palms. "You were stalling us with your tales of Tartarus so she could be free to do *that*," he grits out. "Now you're dead."

Guns and weaponized fingers fly up to point at me again.

Damn.

I knew Lilith could be the end of me, but I didn't think it would happen in such a roundabout way.

CHAPTER TWENTY-SIX

A FAMILIAR ROAR rings out from above the treetops—
one that sounds like it has human words in it. In the
most blood-chilling way possible, it seems to say,
"Touch her and die!"

In case it wasn't obvious what kind of creature the
roaring belongs to, a big dragon swoops out of the sky
and knocks down five IKEA stores' worth of tree
branches on everyone's heads.

The Councilors freeze in their tracks.

The dragon lands, shines with magic, and turns into
a mouth-wateringly naked Nero with his hands still
claw-like and his limbal rings out of control.

My heart jumps, and I realize how overjoyed I am
to see him—and not just because he stopped me from
becoming mincemeat. It may have something to do
with that hard-yet-kissable mouth, perfect abs, chiseled
pecs, and don't even get me started on what's going on
below the waist.

Yeah, I've really missed my bossy Mentor—and I never thought I'd say that.

"Put down your weapons, now," Nero growls menacingly, bringing me out of my horny reverie. "Your real enemy is Tartarus—just as Sasha has already explained to you."

Shell-shocked, they do as he says.

"You're him," Roslin says, her lapis eyes roaming over Nero's body with such avid interest that I get the urge to smack her. I resist, though, because she's been pretty nice to me so far. "You gave your power to the stones in exchange for an earthquake from me," she continues. "Do you remember?"

Nero looks at her, his limbal rings shrinking.

"Yes." He walks up to me, takes off the used-up jewelry from my neck, and strikes it with an arc of light that recharges it instantly. Handing the necklace to Roslin, he says, "We're wasting valuable time. Just vote on whether to trust us so we can either help you or leave."

He says it in such a way that it sounds like he strongly prefers the latter.

Sparkles pushes out his chest. "You don't tell us what to do. And who says she'd be able to leave?"

Nero shakes his head in annoyance, then blurs into motion and strikes with his claws before anyone can let out a peep.

I half-expect Sparkles to rain on us in pieces, but Nero is clearly in a merciful mood today.

His claws just severed Sparkles's beard at around the chin level, giving the atrocious growth a trim.

In the time it takes the pube-like remnants of the beard to hit the grass, Nero blurs back to my side.

"Anyone else want to threaten Sasha?" he asks harshly.

"No, no. We're ready to vote." Roslin gives the still-recovering Sparkles a narrowed-eyed stare.

Not surprisingly, they vote to trust us.

"Your audience," Nero says to me, a slight smile touching his eyes.

"How did you even get here?" I whisper. "How did you know where I'd be?"

"Bailey told me about your conversation, so that's how I knew the path to this world, and Rasputin foresaw you dragging an Enforcer werewolf to this very distinct-looking island," he explains quietly. "We can talk about this later, though. You have a family matter to resolve first."

"Right." I face the crowd. "That woman on TV is indeed my mother. She is insane, maybe criminally so, but I think she can be of help. She's very powerful, and she hates Tartarus." I take a breath and look around. "I have an idea of what we should do next, but I need you all to keep an open mind. As I started to tell you earlier, it has to do with your Heralds and Councilors going on TV and revealing your powers."

I stop to let that sink in.

Sparkles glares at me. "That's a terrible idea. Say this Tartarus of yours comes, and we defeat him. If we reveal our existence to the humans, they will get rid of us—or make us get rid of them."

"Not necessarily," I say. "Not if this is handled in the way I have in mind. If implemented carefully, my idea should allow the Cognizant to coexist with humans after Tartarus is gone."

Everyone except Nero looks curious.

Did Rasputin already tell him how this will go? If he did, it's not fair. I wanted Nero to bow and say how clever he thinks I am.

"Sounds too good to be true," Sparkles says.

"Maybe," I say. "But I think this would undo some of the damage Lilith and I have caused—and hinder Tartarus's power grab if he manages to get on TV as per Jaylen's memory."

"She's right," Roslin says. "Humans are already wondering things we don't want them to wonder. If we battle Tartarus's spawn on the streets, they will know even more."

"Exactly," I say. "But we're going to give humans a framework that will make sense to them. It will be a deception of unparalleled scope—but luckily for you, I happen to be a master magician."

"Stop building it up and tell them already," Nero says impatiently. "Lilith needs to be stopped."

"It's simple," I say triumphantly. "We will pretend to be superheroes."

CHAPTER TWENTY-SEVEN

"WHAT?" Sparkles attempts to tug on his beard, but finds most of it gone.

"Super. Heroes," I enunciate. "Like Superman. Do you have that comic book or movie here?" I look at Obo, who vigorously nods.

Sparkles frowns. "I don't understand."

"We'll say we're superheroes, and then prove it on TV," I say. "We'll also paint Tartarus as a supervillain. This way, we can fight him in the open, and the humans will even help."

Most Councilors still look dubious.

They might be thinking back to their comic book lore and remembering stories like *X-Men*, where the specials and the humans aren't exactly getting along as peacefully as they should.

Note to self: make sure not to call us "mutants" or "more evolved," as that's bad PR.

"It's pure hubris," Sparkles says.

"Oh, really? Then what do you suggest?" I ask him.

"We can glamour the humans," Sparkles says uncertainly.

"Using glamour on billions will be pretty much impossible," a vampire Councilor says. "There's not enough of my kind to make that happen in a dozen lifetimes."

Jaylen clears his throat. "Our ancestors called themselves gods. That's what Tartarus and that TV woman do. Maybe we do the same?"

"I considered that," I say. "But your world seems too modern for that, and at the end of the day, there isn't a huge difference between something like pagan gods and the superheroes in comic books. On Earth, there's a superhero named Thor, who was a god of thunder in mythology." I look at Sparkles meaningfully, as his kind might've been the inspiration for that specific myth. "The key difference is that people think of superheroes as good guys who are looking after their interests. Gods, on the other hand, can be seen as selfish and self-serving—not the best PR."

Sparkles—and many others—still look uncertain.

"Time is of the essence," Nero reminds everyone. "If this is too high of a price to pay for preserving your lives, Sasha and I will be happy to leave. Keep in mind, though, once she's gone, you won't find anyone to sell this lie to humans as well as she can."

Is Nero bluffing about leaving?

If so, he's good.

I totally buy it—and I'm very good at reading those

sorts of cues.

"I say we vote again," Roslin says.

"I agree, but just remember that this will change our society forever," Sparkles says pompously.

"And that there will actually be a society to experience the changes," I retort.

"Those for Sasha's plan, raise your hands," Roslin says, her arm shooting into the air.

Almost all the hands in the meadow go up, though some, like Sparkles, raise them reluctantly.

"That settles it," Roslin says. "Looks like we're going to have to trust Sasha to make us into superheroes."

I suppress a satisfied grin.

This will be my best deception ever. An illusion so amazing that no magician, even one as great as Houdini, would ever dream of performing it.

I look at Lizzy and say, "Can you take me and Nero to that studio?" Glancing at some of the teleporters, I add, "Can you also bring along the most powerful Councilors and Heralds, especially the ones with the showiest powers?"

Lizzy walks over to me and Nero, and grabs our shoulders. As we're about to poof away, I belatedly hope she isn't against my superhero idea to a treacherous and self-sacrificing degree. After all, she *could* teleport with us into the middle of a volcano. Or the bottom of the ocean.

Before that thought can bloom into full-fledged anxiety, we teleport—and as we appear in the new place, I look around in horror.

CHAPTER TWENTY-EIGHT

WE'RE in the TV studio. However, since we took our sweet time on the Council's island, Lilith fed on most of the remaining audience—some in very creative and disturbing ways.

Oh, and the cameras are still rolling.

She must've used glamour on the camera dudes because any regular semi-sane person would've escaped long ago.

"Mother, hear me!" I scream as pompously as I can, and float up, getting into the range of the camera.

Lilith looks at me first, then spots Nero and the other Councilors who are popping in. Angrily baring her fangs, she clutches the hilt of the gate sword at her hip.

"We come in peace," I say quickly. "I represent the heroes of *The Defenders' League*. A great threat is coming to this world, and we decided it's time for us to team up."

Lilith cocks her head as I float closer to her.

Making sure the camera is at my back, I lower my voice so only someone with vampire hearing would hear my next words. "I learned more about Tartarus—and the only way we can win is if the Cognizant of this world, as well as the ones from Earth, help us with the task. I have a plan, but I need you to play along. We're going to villainize Tartarus and tell the humans we're superheroes whose goal is to stop him. Say something grand, along the lines of wanting to put aside our differences, then turn off the cameras so we can talk."

I've got to hand it to Lilith's decisiveness and quick thinking. Almost instantly, she looks at me with kindness and love on her face—something I didn't think her facial muscles were capable of. Spreading her arms as if to embrace me, she says, "My daughter. Tartarus—that villain—put me under a spell that caused me to hurt all these poor innocent people." She gestures at her recent snacks. "As soon as I heard you speak, the mother's love conquered the foul magic. I'm back!"

A little inconsistent with what I said, and too melodramatic, but she did improvise on the spot.

"Let's turn off those cameras so we can have a private moment," she says to the camera guys.

They do as she commands, and as soon as the spotlight is over, all semblance of maternal care disappears from her face.

"What's this plan of yours?" she asks, her eyes narrowing as she takes in more and more of the arriving Cognizant. "I told you I wanted this world for myself after Tartarus is defeated."

"And I'm telling you that he can't be defeated by just the two of us," I retort. "Do you realize that when he comes, he brings along a whole freaking army?"

"He does?" Lilith frowns. "Michel never mentioned his children were *that* numerous."

I clench my jaw. "Don't get me started on that bastard Nostradamus. And let's join the others, so I don't have to repeat myself."

She nods, and we fly toward overwhelmed-looking Councilors from this world.

I open my mouth to speak, but at that moment, Eric teleports in, holding Vlad and Kit by their shoulders.

"Just in time," Nero says as I gape at them. "Bring the rest of them."

"What are you guys doing here?" I exclaim.

Before either Vlad or Kit can reply, Eric comes back with Ariel—as well as a robot that looks a lot like the one Felix used in the fight with Baba Yaga.

"Hello," the robot says. Then its face plate opens, and I see Felix's grinning face inside.

Wow.

This must be Golem version two, the power suit edition. Felix said he'd work on it with Itzel, so this must be the result.

"I can't believe you're here as well," I say, rushing forward to hug them both. Only Felix is all metal, and Ariel is so stiff she might as well be a robot, too.

My vampire state of being must still be freaking her out.

Carefully, I retreat and give them a big smile. "Not that I'm not happy to see you, but why did you come?"

"They need a boost," Nero says. "Everyone critical to the defense effort does."

Okay, then. Sounds like Rasputin did foresee my superhero plan; otherwise, Nero wouldn't be so prepared.

"I don't know if I want my friends to be part of the defense effort," I hiss at him.

"We insisted," Ariel says.

"Strongly," Felix adds.

"And you don't tell me what to do," Kit says.

"What she said," Vlad says.

"Fine." I sigh. "I'd like to go on record as saying that this is a bad—"

Eric comes back, this time with Lucretia and Chester.

"If this isn't a family reunion," Chester says sarcastically when he spots Lilith. "Mother, you look lovely, as always."

Lilith replies with something snide, but I don't hear it because I'm busy hugging Lucretia. Like with Felix and Ariel, I'm glad to see her, but I don't like the idea of her being put in harm's way.

"Time still isn't on our side," Nero cuts in. "How about we let Sasha explain what's about to happen?"

I look everyone over. "Here is my plan. We get someone to make superhero costumes for everyone present. We also create backstories and, most importantly, plan demonstrations of powers for you all —which I can help make as spectacular as possible. Once you're better at whatever your power is, use it to defeat Tartarus and his henchmen."

"And this needs to happen quickly," Nero adds. "Tartarus shows up at 6:45 p.m."

Everyone looks at the clock behind him. It's already 2:15 in the afternoon.

"Why didn't you lead with that?" I ask Nero.

"I didn't get the chance," he says. "Anyway, we're still on schedule to make it."

"And how do you know *that*?" Sparkles asks.

On cue, Eric teleports in, holding Rasputin by the shoulder.

"This is my seer father," I explain when I recover from my surprise. "I bet he's the reason Nero knows what the future holds."

"Indeed," Rasputin says, and I can't help noticing the longing look he darts at Lilith—which makes it official. He's a masochist. "I stockpiled some power and used it to learn every place where Tartarus's forces will gate into this world, and when. I also know where his base world is, and—"

"What do you mean 'base world?'" Sparkles asks.

"Tartarus repopulated a whole world with countless descendants who share his energy-draining power," Rasputin says patiently. "They call the world Tartarus, and to really win, we need to make sure that world becomes isolated from the rest of the Otherlands."

Wow.

How are we supposed to do that?

"If you've seen the future, did you foresee us winning?" Sparkles asks.

That's a great question.

I wish I'd asked it first.

"I don't know," Rasputin says, looking at his shoes. "I was about to see visions in that regard when Nostradamus attacked me in Headspace again and stripped me of the remainder of my power."

"Nostradamus is another seer," I explain for the locals. "He's the reason why I'm powerless right now as well."

To make sure I'm actually still out of juice, I try to go into Headspace.

Nope. Still need to recharge.

"Stupid Michel," Lilith mutters under her breath. "For someone who claims to want Tartarus dead, he sure likes to mess with everyone's ability to actually kill the bastard."

"At least we know where all those gates will open," Vlad says, his face broody, as usual. "This gives us a fighting chance."

"And I'll share those locations with you as soon as we're done here," Rasputin says and looks at Nero. "Do you want to fill them in on the rest of it?"

"Right," Nero says, looking at the locals. "The Cognizant from Earth and a few allies from elsewhere are already taking their battle positions here on this world."

"What?" Sparkles's face tightens, his fingers sparking with hints of lightning. "You just marched in without consulting us?"

"Yes, we did." Nero doesn't look the least bit intimidated. "There was no time to wait for your approvals. We did more than just waltz in. Our Enforcers glamoured key leaders in your human governments and military organizations to make them help us—whether Sasha's plan works or not. But we still need everyone present to boost their power."

"To that end," I chime in. "Why don't we focus on the superhero plan?"

No one objects, so I quickly tell them my ideas so far: that Roslin can be a hero named Earth Shaker, Sparkles can be Sir Lightning, and Lizzy will be the Ether Runner.

They like it, so I name a bunch of others before I'm interrupted by Ariel, who says, "I want to be Batwoman."

"And I'll be her Joker," Chester says and winks at Ariel.

"Hey." Felix makes his robot strike a heroic pose. "In that case, I call dibs on Ironman."

"All those characters already exist in the comics," Obo says.

Felix frowns. "Stupid cross-Otherland plagiarism. How about Steel?"

"How about we keep the names as original as we can?" I say.

"Fine," Felix says. "In that case, I want to be Neo

Golem. Not because of Neo from *The Matrix*, mind you, but because this Golem is the new one and neo means new."

"Whatever," I say. "Before you ask, we aren't going to invite an orc to the team and call him Hulk."

"Or Horc," Felix says.

"Is Batman seriously out of the question?" Ariel looks like a kid given a scratchy sweater on Christmas. "How about Sugar Glider? They're the closest thing I can think of to bats, and it sounds kind of cool."

"It sounds like a good porn star name," Felix mutters and slides back his mask just in time to avoid getting slapped.

"I'll be Jester," Chester says and grins like one. "Instead of a purple suit like that of the Joker, I can wear one of those pointy hats."

"And look like Harley Quinn from the cartoons," Felix mutters under his breath.

I sigh.

When I pictured the end of the world, I never thought there would be this much joviality.

"I'll be Ninja Fox," Kit says and turns herself into an actual fox wearing a black ninja outfit. The result is more adorable than a meme of a cat in a bunny onesie.

"Kit is going to be the easiest superhero to sell to people," Felix says. "She's basically Mystique who can also turn into animals and monsters."

"I think Mystique *could* do that too," Ariel says. "Though I think it was when she was boosted by A—"

"Focus," I say with an eyeroll. "Does anyone *else* want to choose their own name?"

A bunch of them do, and I let them. Then we hash out the elements of their outfits and backstories. Apparently, Sugar Glider was originally an Amazon—something Felix and I reluctantly allow. We do make it clear, though, that Ariel's outfit will look nothing like that of Wonder Woman and that she can't have a lasso prop.

"Every teleporter should go and get the top movie prop designers of this world to quickly make the prerequisite outfits," I say. "Take a vampire with you in case you need anyone glamoured."

They follow my suggestion, and I have Eric take me to a local magic shop to get a long list of supplies to complement those I was already carrying in my pockets.

By the time we get back, some of the "heroes" are already wearing their outfits, making the place look like a cross between Comic-Con and a Halloween party.

"Now let's talk about the power demonstrations," I say and take out the props from the magic store.

For every hero, I make up a suitable performance and add showiness by using every magic methodology I can think of. Some of the illusions I invent are so good, I almost wish another magician was here, just to appreciate the level of my deviousness.

"What about me?" Lilith asks midway through my spiel. "What is my superhero name and backstory?"

Oh, right.

I have such a hard time thinking of her as a hero, I forgot to do this for her.

"How about Lady Night?" I say, looking her over.

"Maybe Lady of the Night?" She floats up and takes a strange pose.

"No, that makes you sound like a courtesan," I say. "How about Night Lady?"

"Fine." She lifts her chin. "What's my story?"

"You already kind of boxed us in," I say. "How about: you were cursed to drink human blood by Tartarus himself, and you're an anti-villain driven mostly by your love of your lovely daughter—and hatred for the one who turned you into this monstrosity."

"What's an anti-villain?" she asks.

"Kind of like an anti-hero, but the opposite," Felix chimes in with the robotic voice that comes out of his suit when the faceplate is down. "It's someone who has good goals but goes about achieving them through immoral means. Oh, and probably refuses to do typical villainous things like eating babies."

"So *not* Lilith," Rasputin says under his breath. "She eats babies without any compulsion."

"I heard that," she says. "It's not my fault baby blood is so delicious."

Everyone—especially the local Cognizant—exchange uncomfortable glances that seem to wonder if she's kidding.

I strongly suspect she isn't kidding, but I don't tell

them that because I want my superhero team to have good morale.

Lizzy and a bunch of other teleporters come back with more outfits, and people start putting them on. In the meanwhile, I send teleporters to local hospitals to locate people with horrible injuries. This will allow the vampires and the healers among us to demonstrate *that* ability for real.

I resume naming people and the rest of it until Nero grabs my shoulder and whispers, "We should talk."

He says it in a such a way that I know resistance would be futile—not that I even want to resist.

"Felix, Ariel, can you take over for a minute?" I say. "Name and dress whoever hasn't gotten a name yet, and decide in what order everyone should go on TV."

Before they can reply, Nero drags me behind the stage.

Crap.

He's another person I almost forgot about—which is why he doesn't have his superhero outfit on, or anything else for that matter.

That or my subconscious did it on purpose because I like seeing Nero naked.

"I think you should get a boost with everyone else," I say to him huskily, hyperaware of all that maleness so close to me.

"Oh?" Nero frames my face with his big hands, his expression growing strangely tender. "And what should my superhero name be?"

"Big Snake?" I say, glancing down at the thing between us that's making it hard to concentrate. "Or Mighty Dragon—"

Nero silences me with a hungry kiss, and for the next few moments, I'm reminded why I have to win.

I have a lot to live for.

All sorts of wonderful things.

Big, hard things.

"We shouldn't," Nero murmurs eventually, pulling away from me.

"We totally should." I pull him back. "This is very motivational."

He groans. "We can't. We'll destroy this whole place and all your heroes."

Right. Sex outside his warded dragon castle leads to me drinking his blood, and then to inconveniences such as craters in the ground and felled trees.

I lick my lips. "There's got to be things we still *can* do. Maybe you—"

"Not safe," he growls. "And this is not why I brought you here."

"It's not?"

He blows out a frustrated breath. "I wanted to try to talk to you about something for the last time. Rasputin told me it will be futile, but I still owe it to myself to try."

"Let me guess. It's about bailing on the battle with my tail tucked between my legs?"

"I'd call it 'retreating and letting someone else fight the fight,'" he says.

I grit my teeth. "I don't care what you'd call it. How many times do we need to rehash the same argument?"

"It's different now," Nero says. "Even if Tartarus survives today, the plan we put into place will set him back centuries. He needs his army to invade Earth—so if they take great losses today, there will be no invasion."

"Rasputin didn't see any of that. That's just optimistic conjecture." I shake my head. "We've been through this. Tartarus needs to be stopped."

Nero's eyebrows snap together. "You're not actually a superhero. You're pretending to be one. Or did you forget?"

"I know what I am—which is why there's nothing you can say to change my mind."

"Are you sure?" His eyes glitter with a strange light, the limbal rings expanding. "Not even 'I love you?'"

CHAPTER TWENTY-NINE

I BLINK AT HIM.

He leans in, his gaze drilling into me. "If you die, I will not be able to stand it."

I just keep blinking.

And blinking.

And blinking—as if my brain crashed and now needs a reboot.

He *loves* me?

Of all the arguments I expected him to make, *that* wasn't on the list—which is maybe why he said it.

But did he mean it?

I mean, I know he cares about me, in his growly, overprotective, often-overbearing way, but this—

"We're ready to start the TV demonstrations," someone's voice announces, interrupting my scrambled thoughts. "We took a vote and decided Sasha should go first and Nero second, so we need you guys."

"I'm coming," I say, purely on autopilot.

Giving me an unreadable look, Nero blurs away.

As I follow, I belatedly recall that when someone makes a statement of the kind Nero just dropped, you're expected to say something back—ideally, how *you* feel.

Except I didn't get a chance to do so, and I'm too overwhelmed to figure anything out.

What the hell was he thinking, starting this kind of conversation *now?* It would be too much even if there *wasn't* Armageddon around the corner.

When I come back out, I see Rasputin hand Nero two spandex monstrosities with scales and glitter glued to them. "These are two copies of your outfit. We realized you didn't have one and found something in one of the fitting rooms here. Also, since Sasha didn't name you, you'll be Drakon."

"How original," I manage to say. "You named him 'dragon' but in Russian."

Not caring what his name is, Nero dresses as I stand there, still processing his revelation. Then someone hands me something that's meant to be *my* superhero outfit.

"Wait a second," I say, getting some of my speech back thanks to outrage. "This will make me look like a stripper playing a dominatrix."

"You didn't specify what you wanted, so Lilith suggested a copy of her own getup—which was also something that was lying around here," Felix explains and nods at Lilith—who is indeed wearing an identical excuse for an outfit. "Just put it on and go do your demonstration."

Shaking my head, I go to the back of the stage and change into the getup.

"You're on," the camera guy says when I walk back out.

Crap. I didn't prepare any patter for myself. This is happening too fast; I need at least a month for this.

Oh, well.

Taking in a deep breath, I walk in front of the camera, doing my best not to give in to the stage fright nibbling at me.

"Dear citizens, it's me again—this time coming out of my superhero closet." I float off the ground to remind them of our last meeting. "I call myself *Vespa*, and I'm a superhero destined to defeat Tartarus—a villain who will try to take over the world today."

The Cognizant in the crowd clap, but I wish there were some uninjured humans around, so I could gauge normal people's reactions.

With my vampire-boosted hearing, I hear Ariel and Felix making fun of my superhero name in hushed whispers.

Really? It's not like I named myself in honor of my deceased vehicle. I came up with Vespa based on an acronym V.S.P.—as in, Vampire, Seer, and Probability Manipulator.

Sugar Gliders, Neo Golems, and others in glass houses shouldn't throw stones.

Anyway, I'm stuck with this hero name because of

selflessness. Being a nice person, I gave all the cool ones I could think of to others.

"You've met my mother, Lady Night." I gesture into the distance. "She got her powers when Tartarus cursed her with vampirism—and I got mine because she was pregnant with me at the time."

Did I just rip off the backstory from *Blade?* Nah. Not if I didn't become a vampire slayer.

In any case, the power demo is what's key—not what I actually say.

"Now, as the saying goes, 'Extraordinary claims require extraordinary evidence.'" I land gently on the stage. "I don't expect you to just believe that I'm a superhero. I will show you my powers, under test conditions. Then, and only then, you can decide for yourselves what you will or will not believe."

I proceed to demo the powers I didn't get a chance to show the last time I was on TV.

To start, I heal a badly injured woman that one of the teleporters brought from a local hospital. I do so by cutting my wrist with a knife and letting the woman drink my blood.

I sure hope Ariel isn't watching this part.

The woman's injuries heal without a trace—which impresses even me.

No illusions here.

The woman comes to her senses and looks around in confusion as a couple of Cognizant come to take her away.

The feeling of pleasure I experienced the last time I

was on the air hits me again—but not as intently as before. Whatever boost to my vampirism I just got, it must be a subtle one.

"Now I will prove my own super-healing abilities," I say, and instead of actually cutting myself for real, I perform the effect where I appear to cut off my hand, then "heal" the lost limb with my powers.

The pleasant feeling grows stronger, but I ignore it and keep going.

"I move faster than the fastest person alive," I say. To "prove" this, I perform my version of the classic stage illusion called "teleportation"—the one where the illusionist goes from one location to another using sneaky business instead of mystical superpowers.

The pleasant feelings grow stronger still.

People are clearly believing even the fake part of the demonstration—as I hoped they might.

Thanks to the stuff I did for real, stage illusions aren't perceived as such anymore.

This bodes well for what we have prepared for the rest of the Cognizant—and they need the boost more than I do.

"My senses are keener than anyone else I know," I continue, then take out a special blindfold and perform my favorite "seeing without sight" routine.

The pleasant feeling is borderline overwhelming.

I need to stop because if I keep pushing, I will pass out again.

"The next superhero you will meet is a close ally of mine," I say theatrically. "His name is Drakon."

I step off the stage, allowing Nero to take my place.

Perhaps it's my demonstration already boosting my vision, or just good lighting, but Nero looks spectacular standing there, looking into the camera with his strange eyes.

Without a single word, he turns into his dragon form, his outfit bursting into shreds.

Oh yeah.

On a world with eighties-level special effects, it doesn't get any better than this as far as demonstrations go. Nero as a dragon is so massive he takes up the entire stage, and even with the super-tall ceilings in the theater, the top of his scaly head brushes the ceiling. Slowly, he blinks into the camera, showing off the dragony limbal rings and, just for fun, exhales a small stream of fire.

The Cognizant who are sitting there in place of the audience let out startled screams, adding to the drama of it all.

With another flash, Nero turns back and gives the ladies at home something to drool over before he dons the intact version of his outfit and blurs off the stage.

Kit goes on after Nero. She tells everyone she is Fox Ninja, then turns into a whole zoo worth of creatures and people, including a white-haired man that she claims is this country's president.

Felix goes after Kit. For the most part, he lets his space-age suit speak for itself, but he also demonstrates his ability to control random electronics around the globe.

Then Ariel goes on, displaying feats of strength even greater than what she's capable of by using a neat little tidbit I learned from a magic book written by a guy who worked as a martial arts teacher for many years. Apparently, a lot of those very impressive "fist breaks concrete" videos on YouTube are done by cheating—the exact method of which the magician in me enjoyed learning and loves implementing today even more.

Next go some of the folks from the local Council, with Roslin as Earth Shaker and so on.

After about an hour of demonstrations, I get tired of watching it all and decide to locate Nero to continue our earlier chat.

Not that I know what I'll say when I find him. I just know something must be said.

I sprint down a corridor to see if my performance boosted my speed as I hoped.

Yep.

I'm not yet blurring like Nero, but this is as close as I've ever gotten.

Looping through the studio passageways at breakneck speed, I find Nero—except he's not alone.

On the floor next to him is an unconscious werewolf, while in his right hand is a neck.

A neck attached to a person whose feet are dangling ten inches off the floor.

An extremely familiar person.

"Nostradamus?" I say, stunned. "What are you doing here?"

The seer grunts something unintelligible. I guess having your throat crushed can do that.

"Nero, let him go, please," I say. "I want to know why he'd come here after everything he did."

With a growl, Nero drops his victim—who falls on the ground next to the werewolf that I now recognize as Marius.

"I guess from your point of view, I deserved that," Nostradamus rasps, rubbing his neck. "Sasha, I'm sorry I took your powers, and your father's. I had to. I swear."

"You did?" I cross my arms over my chest. "I'd love to hear why—especially in front of Nero, who can tell if you lie."

"I'm actually counting on his lie detection." Nostradamus takes out something from his pocket and puts it under Marius's nose.

The werewolf recovers instantly, and whines like a dog as he returns to his feet.

Was that bits of bacon or smelling salts?

"Speak," Nero growls at the seer. "Convince me not to kill you."

"Tartarus is arriving on this world in twenty minutes." Nostradamus pats the ground to locate his dark shades, then hides his ruined eyes behind them.

"No." I look at Nero. "Rasputin said the gates open at 6:45 p.m. We still have about an hour."

"That's when his army arrives." Nostradamus soothingly pets the whining Marius. "Tartarus and a select group of his offspring always arrive sooner, so he can make it to his TV appearance."

Crap. This jives with Jaylen's experience.

"You still haven't given us a reason for why you took Sasha's powers," Nero says harshly. "Or Rasputin's, for that matter."

"I did," Nostradamus says. "It's as I told you at the Council meeting on Earth. Everything needs to play out just right, and I can't have another seer meddling with the outcomes."

"But I'm destined to win, right?" I ask. "That's what you foresaw long ago, before I was even born?"

Nostradamus sighs. "Your father derailed that specific future when he stole you from your mother and let you be raised by humans. So we all have to readjust. I've seen over twenty million versions of what's about to come—and therefore know of countless ways to fail. In one future, though, there is a chance. The problem, as always, is that probability manipulation is at play, so I can't tell you for certain that we'll win."

"Not good enough," Nero hisses, reaching to choke him again.

Marius growls at Nero as Nostradamus rattles out, "I'm one of the people who needs to be there when you face him, Sasha. In every future without me, we fail."

I look at Nero, and he angrily nods. Nostradamus is telling the truth.

"Fine. You live," Nero says grimly. "But if you can't guarantee a victory, I'm not letting Sasha risk her life."

Before I can remind His Imperial Majesty that I

make choices for myself, Nostradamus says, "She has to face him today. Otherwise, she's as good as dead."

Nero's hands grow claw-like, and he slams a fist into a wall next to Marius, shattering it into pieces.

Undaunted by the destruction, Nostradamus continues. "Without Sasha, Tartarus won't be killed. That's for certain. And if he survives, he'll investigate why the people here were so well prepared for his arrival. He'll learn about Sasha, and he'll set his sights on her, not stopping until she's dead—no matter where you hide her."

The seer must not be lying, because Nero breaks another wall in a burst of fury.

"Not that I'm going to run, but how can that last part be true?" I ask as Marius whimpers. "How can Tartarus kill me on, say, the dragon world?"

"He can drain energy from dragons, same as from other Cognizant." Nostradamus soothes Marius with a scratch behind the ears. "It will take him decades to rebuild his forces and attack, but attack he will. Oh, and since he'll know he'll be facing a seer and a probability manipulator, he'll breed an army accordingly."

Before Nero can bring the whole place crashing down around us, I put a hand on his shoulder. "Stop, please. I have to do this. We don't have a choice."

Nostradamus nods. "This surprise attack is *the* best shot at Tartarus. It's a culmination of years of planning on my part and—"

"Wait," I say. "I thought you wanted us to face him on Lilith's world?"

"He lied when he said it was the only option," Nero growls. "Now I see why. He knew there would also be *this* opportunity."

"I did," Nostradamus says. "As always, I had a hard time anticipating what Lilith would do because she's a probability manipulator."

"Speaking of that," I say. "How did you even manage to foresee Tartarus's arrival this time? Doesn't he still have that Lug guy?"

"I'm a much, much better seer now," Nostradamus says darkly. "But you bring up a good point. Lug is yet another reason I can never be sure of an outcome. He will be there, at Tartarus's side."

"If we know where he'll be, why don't we put a bomb there with a timer?" Nero clenches and unclenches his fist. "Or send a squadron of humans to gun him down?"

"Because of Heph, Tartarus's son who can create something like forcefields around himself and his father." Nostradamus takes out some kind of beef jerky and hands it to Marius. "Bullets or fire from an explosion can't penetrate Heph's fields. Only the gate sword can."

"A force manipulator?" I say. "How come we don't have one?" I look at Nero accusingly.

"I looked for one for centuries, but they're exceedingly rare," he answers. "They also don't look traditionally human—so they can't live on modern worlds with a Mandate."

"And Tartarus destroyed the world where most of them lived," Nostradamus adds. "Their force fields couldn't stop his power."

"Great, so even if we had one, it wouldn't help," I grumble. "The news just gets better and better."

"We have to make haste," Nostradamus says.

"Hold on," Nero says. "What else can you tell us about this fight?"

"I can tell you who should go, and who shouldn't," Nostradamus says. "I can also tell you who can use their powers and how. And who shouldn't." He gives Nero a pointed look.

"If you say *I* can't go, I will call this whole thing off," Nero growls at him.

"No, you must go." Nostradamus pushes his glasses higher up his nose. "You just can't turn into your dragon form. In every future where you do, it all goes to hell."

"That's just great," I say. "Can we breathe when we get there? Can we use our arms?"

"I'm only trying to help," Nostradamus says defensively. "My life will be on the line as much as yours. I'm one of the people you have to bring."

"Fine," I say. "Tell us who else should go on this suicide mission."

"Besides me and the two of you, it should be Lilith," Nostradamus says. "And Vlad, because vampires are harder for Tartarus and his kind to drain. Also Roslin, because her earth-controlling ability will help us deal with the gate. Additionally, Chester would be helpful in dealing with Lug, but we have to convince him to join us. With his probability manipulation powers, I can't predict what he'll do." He takes a breath. "Any local vampires who are willing should join as well, for the same reason as Vlad—but not Lucretia, as worrying about her fate will make you lose. For that last reason, we also can't bring Ariel, Felix, or Rasputin."

I glare at the seer. "Are you trying to say I don't care what happens to Nero and Vlad? Not to mention, my half-brother Chester and my biological mother—"

"It's what you hedge fund types would call a cost-benefit analysis," Nostradamus says. "Lilith, Chester, and Nero are so critical to the mission, they must go despite your feelings on the matter. And Vlad needs to go because I saw him in the version of the future where there's a chance of winning."

"That's just peachy," I say. "Anything else?"

"The teleporters can only take us there, but they can't stay and fight," Nostradamus says, ignoring my sarcasm. "I saw a million futures where Tartarus manages to force a teleporter to take him to safety."

"What if we glamour them?" a familiar voice says from around the corner.

Is that—

Yep.

Lilith steps out from her hiding spot, where she likely eavesdropped on the whole conversation.

"If they're glamoured, they're as good as dead," Nostradamus answers, unfazed.

Lilith's smile is predatory. "That's a sacrifice I'm willing to make."

Nostradamus shakes his head. "Why have them die when they can greatly help in the fights with Tartarus's spawn? If they stay with us and die, they're of no use to anyone."

"Fine," Lilith says. "But I'm now in the mood to glamour *someone*."

"You'll get the chance," Nostradamus says. "Can we go?"

"Let's," Nero says, and strides down the corridor.

When we turn the corner opposite the one where Lilith hid, we bump into Chester—who also seems to have been eavesdropping.

How lucky that he was in the right place at the right time, just like his mother.

"I heard everything," he says, confirming my suspicion. A satyr-like grin appears on his face as he announces, "Mommy, sis, I'm coming with you. Of course, I have some ideas as to my compensation."

"Freaking probability manipulators," Nostradamus mumbles under his breath.

We resume walking, and Nero and Lilith work out what they'll do for Chester as a thank-you for his help. He lets himself get convinced rather quickly—which makes me think he would've helped regardless, but is milking the situation since he can.

Once we get to the stage area, we locate everyone else, except Vlad.

"What do you need Vlad for?" Kit says when I ask if she's seen him.

"He's going to help us in an epic fight." Chester pulls violently on the ear of his Jester hat.

"How fun. Can I also go?" Kit is all but jumping up and down with anticipation.

"You will help greatly in your currently assigned post," Nero says.

"Fine." Kit pouts. "I'll go get Vlad for you."

She goes away, and while we wait for Vlad, we tell Eric about the people Nostradamus insisted we bring, and that, unlike Vlad, he and the other teleporters can't be there during the fight. Afterward, we recruit Roslin —who then convinces a bunch of local vamps and teleporters to help us as well.

Vlad walks out from backstage. He's wearing all black and is holding one of the lances that were used to pierce dragon hide during Nero's campaign—the ones with the super-hard diamond-like tip. The weapon is part of his superhero getup. Perhaps not very creatively, we dubbed him *The Impaler* after a Vlad from Earth's history that the locals haven't heard of.

It's one of the many superhero names we've given people that could also work if they decide to pursue a career in the porn industry.

"Where are we going?" asks one of the local teleporters.

"It's called Fun Palace," Nostradamus says without a

hint of mirth in his voice. "It's on Avenue S and North 24th Street."

"I know it," the guy says.

"Can you show me?" Eric walks over to him.

The local teleporter nods and takes Eric by his shoulder. They poof away and come back almost right away.

Next, each teleporter grabs two local vampires by the shoulder and takes them to their destination before coming back to transport Vlad and the rest of the vamps.

"Your turn." Eric walks up to me, glances warily at Nero, and carefully lays a hand on my shoulder. He then touches Nero, and we poof once more.

We arrive in a giant open space lit by blacklights and filled to the brim with ancient-looking arcade machines that beep and ding all around us.

I recognize *Galaga, Donkey Kong, Pac-Man, Space Invaders, Dig Dug, Defender,* and *Frogger* because these are all games Felix made me try at some point. That they exist here is further proof that the Otherworld game rip-off business is a real thing.

The place is almost empty. The few people that are here are clustered around a wall of TVs in the back rather than playing games.

They're watching the very show we just left behind, and no wonder.

When was the last time they showed genuine miracles on TV?

"I can't believe this is happening," one lanky teen

says to another. "Real superheroes. How can this not be a hoax?"

"You saw that hot chick fly," his friend says. "There were no wires or anything. This shit is real, I'm telling you."

Am I the hot chick in this conversation, or is it my mother?

"You wanted to glamour someone?" Nostradamus says to Lilith as soon as he turns up. "Why don't you go and glamour those humans to leave?"

She saunters over to the TVs, and the people gasp. They recognize her as one of the superheroes they just saw on the screens.

I half-expect Lilith to drink their blood, but she must be too full from earlier because she merely glamours them to leave, as Nostradamus suggested.

"Did you leave your pet werewolf behind?" I ask Nostradamus, looking around for Marius.

The seer nods somberly. "If I didn't, he would've died in vain."

He puts such emphasis on the "in vain" part of that answer that I get a hollow feeling in the pit of my stomach.

I'm almost sure Nostradamus has foreseen people in our party dying "not in vain."

"Leave and don't come back," Nostradamus says to Eric and the rest of the teleporters when they bring Roslin and the last of the crew. "It's very important."

When they poof away, Nostradamus says,

"Everyone, hide behind the arcade machines so when they arrive, they don't see us until it's too late."

"Where will they be?" I ask. "We need to know their viewing angle."

Nostradamus points at the very center of the room. "The gate will open there."

We all spread out and duck behind the arcade games.

"Here is the plan of action," Nostradamus says from behind the *Galaga* machine. "Dirk is Tartarus's grandchild, the one responsible for the stable gate that's about to open. He'll arrive first. He must be eliminated quickly, or Tartarus will be able to escape."

"Leave him to me," Vlad says from behind the *Multipede.*

"Great," Nostradamus says. "The other two critical targets, besides Tartarus himself, are Lug, the probability manipulator, and Heph, the force field master."

"I can deal with the trickster," Chester says from behind the *Missile Command.* "Should be a no-brainer."

"He's more powerful than you," Nostradamus says. "But don't worry. I will help you."

"How will we know who's who?" Lilith says from behind the *Space Invaders,* and I hear the whoosh of the gate sword activating.

"Heph and Lug will stand out as the two spawn who look like what they are. The rest of them will have Tartarus's ability to appear as someone you revere," Nostradamus says. "Aside from that, Heph doesn't look traditionally human, and Lug is the one with the wild eyes."

"I wonder who I'll see the rest as?" Lilith mutters.

That's a great question. Who does the evil incarnate revere?

Lucifer, maybe?

As in, the devil, not my cat.

"There's no more time left," Nostradamus says urgently. "Roslin, your goal is to make the earth swallow the gate—and as many of Tartarus's allies as possible."

"I'll do it," Roslin says gravely from behind the *Defender*.

Suddenly, I feel an extremely strong rush of anxiety. It's as if someone not only walked over my grave but also nuked it for good measure.

Doing my best to stay calm, I peek from behind my hideout.

The air in the middle of the room shimmers, and a gate materializes there.

A gate that looks just like the ones in Jaylen's illusion. The orange plasma glow is fainter than that of the permanent gates, clearly weaker.

My heartbeat spiking, I watch as a man steps out— and I can't help but gape at who it is.

CHAPTER THIRTY

LOGICALLY, I know this is Dirk, the teleporter who created the gate. Nostradamus said he'd be the first to come out.

What I see, however, is Criss Angel—the TV magician who made such a strong impression on me when I was young and, well, impressionable.

Does that mean I revere him? I guess it's close enough. I mean, I do admire the hell out of the guy—but then again, I almost equally respect every famous magician, and countless underground ones as well.

The weird part is that, at one point, I had a crush on Criss Angel. Now, though, I feel nothing as I look at him—and not just because I know this is a villain's minion instead of my idol.

Apparently, now that I've had a taste of Nero, I'm ruined for all other men, no matter how good at stage magic they are.

Two more people step out of the gate.

One is Lug from Nostradamus's memories, and the other must be Heph.

Wow.

Saying Heph doesn't look "traditionally human" is like calling a drekavac unpleasant-looking. Heph is vaguely humanoid, but has more in common with a grizzly bear than a person. Given that Heph is the result of a breeding program, Tartarus probably forced someone to procreate with something that was even more bear-like than this—a frightening thought.

The next people to step out of the gate all look startlingly familiar. One guy is David Copperfield, another is David Blaine. The next pair look like Penn and Teller, while the following two are Siegfried and Roy. As I watch, open-mouthed, A-list magicians keep coming and coming, followed by some slightly less known ones. There are even some long-dead stars like Dunninger, and folks who left a mark as writers of magic books—like Tony Corinda, who wrote the classic *13 Steps to Mentalism.*

The next person to walk out of the gate can only be Tartarus. Who else would I perceive as the man I truly revere, to the point where I even have a poster of him hanging in my room?

With those signature triangular eyebrows and a mysterious gaze that seems to penetrate your very soul, Tartarus is Harry Houdini.

Grr. If I needed another crime to add to Tartarus's infinite list, I'd add "tarnishing the great man's image."

Tartarus/Houdini and the rest of them begin to spread out to make room for more arrivals.

Roslin must spot Tartarus as well, because the floor of the arcade begins to shake and rips apart in the middle of the room—swallowing the gate along with a bunch of Tartarus's spawn.

Yes!

Except Tartarus himself and a large number of his henchmen remain.

Too many, unfortunately.

Roslin isn't done, though. The asphalt outside the building begins to shake and rise. A moment later, the space around us gets darker because all the windows and doors get covered by the earth—blocking the way out.

"Get that earth mover," Tartarus shouts and points at the *Defender* machine, behind which Roslin is peeking from.

The henchmen point in the same direction as their progenitor.

Purplish arcs of energy flow from Roslin to each of them.

Screaming her lungs out, Roslin shrivels up and turns into a raisin-like shell.

A spike of adrenaline hits my brain, causing a strange feeling to come over me. I become hyper-aware of my surroundings.

Using my peripheral vision—and maybe seer powers—I can tell exactly what's happening all around me, even places I don't have a good angle on.

Is this something new I can do, thanks to my blindfold/ lottery performances on TV?

Whatever it is, it will be handy—same with faster speed and the rest of the boosts.

"Attack them!" Nostradamus yells from behind his hiding spot. "Don't let them take us out one by one like that."

Right. They may outnumber us, but if we attack all at once, it will prevent the ganging-up scenario we just saw.

"I know that voice," Tartarus mutters, his gaze jumping all over the arcade. "Dirk, be ready to—"

Before Tartarus can finish that sentence, Vlad leaps from behind the *Multipede* and pierces Dirk/Criss Angel's shoulder with his lance.

Dirk grunts in pain, then teleports away—taking Vlad and the lance with him.

The rest of us rush at the energy suckers with a war cry, with me setting my sights on James "the Amazing" Randy.

Besides being a magician and mentalist, James Randy is a debunker of paranormal claims, so it's kind of ironic that he—or someone who looks just like him—is going to fight me, a genuine vampire/seer/trickster. I dodge Randy's swipe with a speed I never managed in my training with Thalia, then break his jaw with a punch.

Wow.

I doubt Thalia will be able to beat me so easily anymore. Or at all.

Getting Randy in the solar plexus, I punch him out, then kick his unmoving body a few times for good measure.

What's impressive is that I'm still hyper-aware of the room and what's happening everywhere, with attention to spare.

This will be extremely useful for my magic performances—assuming I survive this and get to do them.

Dirk reappears near the pinball machines, and as soon as he does, Vlad rips the lance out of his opponent's shoulder and sticks it into Dirk's thigh.

With a yelp, Dirk starts sucking the energy out of Vlad, who begins screaming in a very un-Vlad-like manner.

Uh-oh. How much does the energy suck stuff hurt? I'm not looking forward to finding that out.

Dirk rips the lance from his leg, breaks it in half, and tosses the bits to the side. Vlad leaps at him and wraps his hands around Dirk's throat.

Unable to shake the vampire off, Dirk teleports again.

Throughout the room, the other vampires are attacking the magician-looking Tartarus spawn.

Heph—the bear-like one—waves his hands, and an arc of blue energy surrounds him, causing his skin and clothes to shimmer blue.

"Stop him from casting more shields!" Nostradamus yells.

Nero is already on it.

In a blur, he appears in front of the bear guy—who, in that moment, casts the blue energy on Tartarus himself.

Crap.

With my improved eyesight, I can see where the blue energy went—a stone in the necklace Tartarus is wearing. A stone that looks just like the one that was used as a polygraph machine during the Council meeting.

A stone that can harness a Cognizant's power.

To support my theory, the stone shines and casts the same shimmering blue glow over Tartarus that surrounds Heph.

Nero's claw slices at Heph in a gesture I've seen many times before. This is my dragon's signature attack that usually results in chunks of flesh flying around.

But not this time.

With a nerve-stinging sound of nails on a chalkboard from hell, Nero's claws break.

They regrow instantly, but there isn't even a scratch on Heph's body.

Nero's claws can't penetrate the force field shield.

With a bear-like growl, Heph punches Nero in the face. Nero flies back and slams into the *Punch-Out!!* machine, breaking the machine into little pieces.

Meanwhile, one of our vampires attacks Tartarus and finds the shield there as impenetrable as Heph's.

Tartarus focuses his attention on his attacker by

sucking energy from him, and soon, the vampire is on his knees, screaming.

Double crap.

I was right. That stone in Tartarus's necklace makes him invulnerable.

How are we going to kill him now? Oh, wait. Nostradamus said the gate sword can penetrate these force shields.

I look at Lilith, the person currently wielding the sword.

She's hovering just above the floor and has her goddess glamour in full force.

It doesn't help. Instead of worshipping her, Tartarus's spawn attack my mother en masse, and as they do, she shreds them into bits.

"Help me attack Tartarus!" Lilith yells at me.

Did she just send some of her luck powers my way? Because in that exact moment, Randy gives me an opening—so I punch through his breastplate and puncture his heart with my fist.

Jumping over the dead body, I leap toward Lilith, but a new magician gets in my way.

One I have a sex-toy named after.

David Copperfield himself.

"Give up now, and instead of the breeding pits, you can be mine," faux-Copperfield says in a creepy version of the great man's voice.

"No, thanks," I growl, and head-butt the guy.

Typically, this maneuver causes stars to dance in one's vision, but it does no such thing to me.

I recover instantly and kick Copperfield's leg, breaking it with a loud crunch.

"Bitch," he snarls, pointing his hand at me.

Energy streams from my body into his hand, and I learn why someone as tough as Vlad was screaming from this.

The pain is almost on par with that of the Rite. It's a searing and nauseating sensation that seems to permeate every single cell in my body.

More than anything, I want to curl into a ball and fall on the floor shrieking and crying.

But I don't.

Extending my fangs, I rush forward to rip into Copperfield's neck.

The pleasure of drinking my enemy's blood dulls the pain of the energy suck, and soon, he stops sucking all together—which is when I break his neck.

The insane thing is that I'm still aware of my surroundings through all that.

Dirk teleports again and exchanges some blows with Vlad before jumping to a new location.

Nero recovers and punches Heph in the chest. The bear-man's head slams into the CRT-TV of the *Pac-Man* machine, but not a single shard of glass so much as scratches his skin, thanks to the force-field barrier.

The Tony Corinda lookalike attacks me, and I tear his arm off, then smack him with it, channeling my inner Lilith.

Tartarus, meanwhile, turns another vampire into a raisin at his feet. Just like three of his brethren, the poor wretch was unable to penetrate Tartarus's shield.

And speaking of bodies at people's feet, Lilith has her own macabre pile—mainly of magician body parts.

This doesn't stop more of Tartarus's spawn from attacking her. So Lilith shish-kebobs them too.

I've got to hand it to my mother. In terms of damage to enemy forces and stylishness of the kills, she's the most successful of us by far.

As they agreed before this fight started, Nostradamus and Chester rush at Lug together.

Of course, there are other spawn in their way—so they have to fight through them, and it's interesting how similarly their powers manifest in a fight.

Nostradamus is able to dodge every blow that comes his way thanks to his seer powers, while Chester dodges every blow because, I assume, his luck makes his attackers miss their target.

"Will you come and help me?" Lilith yells at me, her voice tighter.

"Trying!" I yell back, and dodge an attack from yet another David—this time, David Blaine.

The real David Blaine has been stuck into a cube of ice, buried alive, drowned, has stabbed himself with giant needles, and the list goes on. Compared to him, the Tartarus spawn in front of me is a wuss. When I rip out his clavicle bone, he screams in a shrill voice and passes out, which is when I bash his skull in to make sure he never gets up again.

At the same time, Nostradamus and Chester reach

Lug—who grabs the seer and tosses him at the nearby TV wall.

Nostradamus's head slams into a TV, breaking the screen.

He then slides to the floor and lies there unmoving.

What?

That's it?

Then again, Lug must've gimped Nostradamus's seer sight, leaving him truly blind.

Nostradamus's head wound is bleeding profusely, which can't be good for his health.

Damn it. Was this part of his plan?

It's feasible, because dealing with Nostradamus has cost Lug greatly. Chester uses the moment provided by Nostradamus's into-TV flight to pull out a dagger and stab at Lug's chest.

Lug's luck—or martial arts skills—must help, because he manages to take the stab on his forearm.

Before Chester can rip the weapon out, Lug shoots the energy-draining arc at him.

I turn to go help my newfound brother, but Lilith yells, "No! Come here."

Reluctantly, I move toward her—which is when two more of Tartarus's spawn, the ones who look like Penn and Teller, block my way.

"You're so dead," Penn says.

"So dead," echoes Teller.

The real Teller doesn't speak; it's part of his stage/TV persona. However, behind the scenes, as a magician, he speaks just fine—and this guy nails his voice exactly, which makes me almost hesitate before hitting him.

Emphasis on *almost.*

Executing the thrust Thalia had drilled into me, I punch Teller out right away—then break a few of Penn's bones before I put him on the floor as well, permanently.

Dirk and Vlad teleport to where Nostradamus's unconscious body lies.

Dirk redoubles the energy drain, and as he does, Vlad's scream changes.

He doesn't sound like Vlad at all anymore—and in that exact moment, he turns into Kit.

Wait, what?

That was Kit all this time?

But how—

Of course. She wanted to join us, then went to "get Vlad."

The person who came back was Kit herself. She must've told Vlad they were switching roles in the upcoming attacks.

There's a big problem with this. According to Nostradamus's visions, Vlad is a critical piece of the delicate puzzle that *might* lead to our already-unlikely victory.

Does this mean that without Vlad here we have no chance?

It sure looks like it.

Before I can freak out about it further, Kit does

something I've seen her do once before—and it's no less nightmarish this time.

She turns into a drekavac—a xenomorph-meets-dementor creature.

Dirk must be the bravest person in all the Otherlands. Instead of running away or screaming, he grabs a shard of broken TV screen and tosses it at drekavac-Kit.

The shard slices the monster's pustule-infested skin, and the scream that follows is as ugly as the drekavac itself.

Ignoring the pain, Kit reaches out with four horrific limbs.

When they touch Dirk, he screams in a voice that isn't recognizable as coming from a throat.

Twitching spasmodically, he collapses in a heap on the ground.

Injured Kit looms over her victim.

A horrific-looking tongue slowly snakes out of the drekavac's maw, and wherever it licks Dirk's skin, the skin melts away, leaving behind raw meat.

On the second lick, Dirk slumps, probably glad to be dead.

Kit turns into her usual form and clutches her grievous-looking wound.

She then takes one step. Then another. Then falls on the floor.

CHAPTER THIRTY-ONE

NO.

No one I care about is dying today.

"Someone give her blood!" I yell at the vampires in the room.

A tall, slender vampire closest to Kit rushes to do as I ask—only in that moment, Lug tosses a dazed-looking Chester into the air, and Chester flies right at Kit's would-be-savior, accidently slashing his throat with the dagger in his hand.

They collapse together in a heap, seemingly passed out or worse.

"I guess I was luckier," Lug says tauntingly.

"And I guess I'm luckier still," Lilith says as she slices Lug into two equal pieces with the gate sword.

Then, instead of helping Kit, Chester, and the rest, Lilith zooms to where Tartarus and a few vampires are battling it out.

Gritting my teeth, I rip through Siegfried, and then Roy, fighting more fiercely than ever before.

When I reach Kit, I extend my fangs and slice my finger open.

As soon as my blood touches Kit's lips, her wound begins to mend. I try to do the same thing for the vampire entangled with Chester, but nothing happens.

"You can't heal a vampire with vampire blood," Lilith shouts. "He has to recover on his own."

Well, that sucks.

That means if I'm hurt, a vampire won't be able to heal me either.

I untangle the vampire from Chester and prepare to give him some blood.

"Enough of this!" Lilith angrily shouts before I get the chance to do that. "You're not here to play healer. You're here to kill Tartarus. Now do so. As your sire, I *command* you."

I halt mid-gesture as the word "*command*" slams into my mind.

In the heat of all the fighting, I completely forgot to dance on eggshells around Lilith—and now I've gone and acted like a decent person, which has clearly pissed her off enough to activate the stupid sire bond.

"I *command* you to attack Tartarus," Lilith repeats, enunciating every word.

My free will becomes a prisoner somewhere deep inside me as my body begins to move with zombie-like determination.

Though not in control of my limbs, I still perceive what's happening in the room.

Kit stands up on shaky feet, and turns herself into a giant orc.

Lilith kills another magician.

Heph punches Nero yet again, causing Nero to growl furiously as he shakes it off.

Then, Nero does something I've never seen him do. He inhales air, then breathes out fire at Heph—without turning into a dragon.

The problem is that stupid force field.

Even when hit with dragon breath, not a hair on Heph's body is singed.

But still. Wow. Could Nero always do that? No, can't be. He would've utilized this power before now. I bet this is something he discovered thanks to that TV appearance.

A Dunninger lookalike blocks my way to Tartarus.

"Kill him," Lilith orders as she dispatches another attacker of her own.

I didn't need her urging.

I sidestep the guy's kick and break his jaw, then his nose, then smash a fist into his temple to put him down for good.

Orc-Kit rips apart another magician on her way to Tartarus.

Tartarus begins sucking energy from her.

Gritting her huge orc teeth, Kit closes the distance between them and strikes.

Catching her green fist, Tartarus twists her arm, then tosses her at the wall.

She hits her head, turns back into her regular Kit shape and slumps down, unmoving.

Damn it. Getting knocked out so easily must be a side effect of getting one's energy sucked.

I better be careful not to get hit on the head.

Nero and Heph exchange more blows as I leap for Tartarus—who in that moment starts to drain energy from Lilith herself.

"Here," Lilith grits out. "Kill him with this."

She tosses me the gate sword. Catching it, I strike at Tartarus's head.

He dodges, then punches me in the face.

I'm not sure if this is the sire bond's benefit, or if I'm tougher in general, but I not only don't pass out—I don't even feel the pain of the strike.

I do, however, fly back six feet.

Instead of letting myself hit the wall with my back as gravity would demand, I use my newly acquired flying powers to hover in the air.

Then, with my sword extended, I whoosh back at Tartarus.

Only the guy is freaking fast.

He sidesteps my maneuver in the last possible moment, and I end up piercing the floor with the gate sword before I hit the ground with my face.

Grabbing my shoulder, Tartarus tosses me at the nearby *Tetris* game.

This one does hurt, but still not as badly as it

should, considering the shards of glass and wood pieces doing their best to stake me.

"She's too weak," Lilith grunts under her breath as Tartarus resumes draining her energy. "Damned Rasputin made her too weak, and now we're going to lose."

Seeing my mother disarmed and under attack, a bunch of still-alive Tartarus spawn run at Lilith with renewed vigor.

My cuts and scrapes heal—even pushing some glass shards out of my skin in the process, Wolverine-style.

Stumbling to my feet, I rush at Tartarus one more time—but miss him with the sword yet again.

In response, he slams his massive fist into my face with such force I finally see stars.

Nero was right when he wanted to get away to Atlantis to train me. I could've used fencing lessons right about now—and also lessons in how to more gracefully take a punch.

"Touch her again, and you're dead," Nero growls from where he's duking it out with Heph.

Tartarus smiles nastily and punches me so hard I fly back ten feet and slam into the wall before I can activate my flying abilities.

Recovering quickly, I jackknife to my feet and rush at Tartarus again.

Before I reach my target, though, Nero grabs Heph by the torso and tosses him at Tartarus.

For good measure, he also throws a stream of dragon fire at Heph.

Pushed either by the flame or the kinetic energy of Nero's toss, Heph rams into his father like a rocket.

Upon impact, they fly into different directions—Heph toward me and Tartarus toward Nero.

"Slice!" Lilith shouts, and my arm obeys without me even registering it.

The gate sword penetrates Heph's force shield like a soap bubble, then effortlessly continues its course to disembowel the bear-like man.

"No!" Tartarus yells as he watches his most resilient spawn die. His face twists with fury. "You'll pay for that a thousand times over."

His hand angrily lashes out toward Nero, and purple energy arcs from Nero's body into the bastard.

Nero tries to blur forward but the pain—or the energy suck itself—causes him to move much slower than usual.

"Attack!" Lilith shouts at me.

I leap toward Tartarus, happy to follow Lilith's command.

Tartarus dodges my sword strike and kicks me—and I fly at Nero, knocking him off his feet and falling on top, my sword rolling to the side.

"You need to power up," Lilith says to me as she rips the heart out of the chest of yet another magician. "Drink Nero's blood, and you'll be stronger. Then, when I say, you'll attack Tartarus again."

Wait, what did she just say?

Drink Nero's blood?

Hell no.

Except my body isn't listening to my free will right now, so my arms reach out and grab Nero's shoulders.

Either not liking Lilith's plan or taking advantage of an opportunity, two of Tartarus's minions join him in draining Nero's energy.

With his energy sucked three ways, Nero grunts and slackens in my grip.

"Hurry before there's nothing left to drink," Lilith says. "I *command* it."

Feeling sick to my stomach, I lean in, my fangs already extended.

Nero locks eyes with me. "She's right." His voice is a raspy whisper. "This may be the only way."

I want to argue with them both, but I'm still not in control of any of my faculties.

Channeling Dracula, my fangs enter Nero's neck, and I begin to suck.

"Yes," Lilith says from somewhere. "Drink it all. I *command* it."

All?

No, she can't mean that. But of course she does. She said it herself. When she gets the chance to drink from a powerful Cognizant, she always drains them to the last drop to maximize the benefits.

Now she's applying the same logic to me, her weapon.

Just like in the vision where I killed my friends, I want to command my mouth to scream, but nothing passes my lips.

I will my body to halt, or to slow, but nothing works.

Making matters worse is the fact that each gulp of Nero's blood brings with it an unwelcome orgasmic pleasure.

As I drink, Lilith kills the two spawn who were helping Tartarus drain Nero's life force.

Great. Nero will live longer before I kill him.

Realizing that I'm becoming a bigger threat, Tartarus starts to suck energy from *me*.

I almost welcome *that* pain.

The torment is a more suitable sensation for what I'm currently doing.

The weird thing is, instead of weakening from Tartarus's energy suck, I actually feel the beginning of an incredible power growing in me.

Of course.

Nero's blood is potent stuff.

Felled trees and craters kind of potent.

If I could speak, I'd beg Lilith to let me stop. I would tell her I can probably already take on Tartarus, but I can't speak and Lilith doesn't let me stop of my own initiative.

Quite the opposite.

If she so much as suspects any slowness in my drinking, she reissues the command to force me to keep going, and going.

Soon, I have no doubts at all.

Lilith will make me kill the man I love.

CHAPTER THIRTY-TWO

AND I DO. I love Nero. I don't know why it took *this* horror for me to realize how I feel. And now it's too late. There's no way to break the sire bond.

Unless… isn't love supposed to conquer all?

It doesn't hurt to give that a try. Picturing myself in a romantic movie, I visualize a montage of all the reasons I've fallen for my boss and Mentor. The end result is more reminiscent of porn, though. Apparently, our best moments were X-rated and above.

The montage idea isn't working—aside from convincing me about my feelings for my soon-to-die lover.

No matter how I feel, the cursed sire bond keeps making me drink Nero's blood.

Inside the dark hidey-hole in my mind, I'm screaming like a banshee.

If it were possible to strain the brain by wishing something, I'd need a splint for mine because that's how hard I want to pull my stupid face away from his neck.

But it doesn't work.

Clearly, my warm and fuzzy feelings for Nero aren't the way to break the sire bond.

Then I get a desperate idea—one that should've occurred to me earlier.

Lilith controls my body, but not my mind; otherwise, I wouldn't be having all these thoughts.

What that means is I should still be able to utilize my mind-driven powers—like probability manipulation and predicting the future.

Assuming I've regained them, that is.

Which I should have. Or at least I should soon, given that Nostradamus thought we could win because of my triple powers.

Bursting with hope, I try to focus in order to get into Headspace.

The pleasure from Nero's blood and the pain from Tartarus's energy sucking almost cancel each other out, but the panic I can't suppress makes focusing nearly impossible.

What's worse, because I'm not in control of my body, I can't make myself take a deep breath and let it out slowly, as Lucretia had taught me.

Well, I have to do this somehow.

Maybe I can do a mental equivalent of the slow breath.

As impossible as it is, I do my best to forget where I am and what I'm doing, and picture myself sitting on a cloud that's similar to the one from my dream therapy with Bailey.

Nope.

Then I picture myself floating in warm water and petting Fluffster. Then Lucifur when she was a kitten.

Closer.

I picture Nero kissing me and stroking my back as he growls sweet nothings into my ear.

Yes, here we go. Focus reached, I plummet into Headspace.

———

FINALLY!

I never thought I'd be this happy to be floating among the shapes—especially ones that sound *this* disturbing.

It's easy to guess what they will show me—Nero's slow exsanguination.

Still. I'm here. I'll summon better visions—ones where I thwart that horrific future.

Somehow.

But first, I need to acknowledge how different this Headspace session is from all my prior ones.

More accurately, it's not Headspace that's different. It's me.

I understand the shapes better. I can see details in them that I didn't notice before—textures, for lack of a better word.

It's like someone gave me binoculars specifically designed for Headspace.

This must be how the TV-boosted seer powers manifest themselves. It's not merely that my daily seer juice allotment is higher now. Everything to do with Headspace is improved.

If the situation weren't so dire, I'd enthusiastically explore my new state of being, but as is, I must focus on what to do.

Which doesn't take long as there's only one thing I *can* do.

I have to find a way to use my probability manipulation to save Nero's life.

As soon as I concentrate on that thought, the shapes around me disappear, and a slightly different cloud takes their place.

The tune coming off these guys is still disturbing, but with my new awareness, I can tell there might be something useful there anyway.

Reaching out to all the visions at once is effortless to me now—so I sprout my ethereal wisps and dive in.

———

I'M KILLING Nero by drinking his blood.

Lilith is fighting for her life, and Tartarus is sucking energy from all of us.

So, how do I use my probability manipulation to break the sire bond?

Well, if there's even a small chance that someone could rip me away from Nero, I could bring that about.

But who? And again, how?

Until now, I've only tried influencing the probabilities of a deck of cards.

So that's what I start with. I decide to treat the outcome of "rip me away from Nero" as the totally sorted deck, and the people around the room as cards, or shuffles.

Holding everyone in mind, I picture someone running at me, grabbing me by my hair, and pulling me away from Nero with a good jerk.

Something clicks, and the colorful lines—the strands of fate—appear in front of me faster than before.

Thank you, TV performance.

I examine the strands carefully, paying close attention to their thickness.

What I see doesn't bode well for me. Even the thinnest strand is many, many times thicker than the thickest one I was able to control when dealing with a deck of cards.

As before, the thicker strands feel more right, but they require more power expenditure, as they represent lower-frequency events.

I reach for a strand that's as thick as a redwood tree trunk—figuring the rarer the event, the better. Perhaps this represents a possibility that Tartarus himself will change his murderous ways and pull me away from Nero?

I mentally try to grab the tree trunk strand, but it's like a slippery ghost—completely unreachable even with my TV-boosted powers.

Fine.

I look at one of the thinner ones and choose one at random. It feels more elastic and more yielding than the tree trunk one, but less "right."

So be it.

I metaphysically put pressure on the strand in question, and it snaps.

In the distance, Nostradamus slowly rises to his feet.

I guess there was a possibility he'd come to in that moment.

Unlikely as it was, it was possible and I made it so.

The problem is that he looks barely alive.

Gritting his teeth, Nostradamus stumbles toward me.

One step.

Two.

I begin to get hopeful.

Maybe he can pull me away from Nero?

But then what if Lilith makes me use my vampire strength to squash him like a bug?

Well then, perhaps he can pick up the gate sword and kill me, ending this nightmare.

But no. It's all moot anyway.

Tartarus spots Nostradamus, raises his triangular eyebrow, and stops draining me for a moment to point his hand at Nostradamus instead.

With the pain gone, the pleasure of Nero's blood makes it hard for me to think—but on some level, I'm aware of Nostradamus turning into a raisin.

The sire bond forces me to keep drinking. And drinking and drinking—until, a few hellish minutes later, Nero finally dies from the blood loss.

———

I'M TRYING to use my probability manipulation to stop drinking Nero's blood. Specifically, I'm focusing on a chance that someone who's currently unconscious becomes conscious—or anything else useful like that.

After some mental effort, the strands appear in front of me.

I fail to activate a tree-trunk-sized one, but one of the thinner ones yields to my boosted power.

In the distance, Kit scrambles to her feet.

Tartarus stops draining me and focuses on Kit instead.

Kit turns into a white dove and rushes my way.

One of Tartarus's spawn—the one who looks like Lance Burton—stops advancing on Lilith and snatches Kit from the air.

Once she's in his grasp, he tries to snap her neck.

The real Lance Burton is famous for his dove act and would never treat a bird that way.

At least, I hope.

Before Lance can succeed, Kit turns into an angry rhino.

Tartarus leaps toward them.

The rhino-Kit rams her horn into Lance's stomach, killing him instantly.

But she misses when Tartarus catches up with her and lands a devastating blow to the side of the rhino's head.

The beast turns back into Kit's human form, and she slumps to the floor, clearly dead.

A few minutes later, a fully drained Nero joins her.

———

I STRAIN and bring up the probability strands, then chose one I can wield.

Below me, Nero comes to and tries to pull away.

To my horror, I latch on to him, like some stubborn leech.

I wish I didn't force this outcome. Killing Nero as he tries to free himself is worse than when he was just letting me take his blood.

Come on, Nero. At least grab that gate sword.

He doesn't. Instead, he passes out again, already too drained by both me and Tartarus.

He doesn't move again as I suck out his life.

———

A PROBABILITY STRAND makes the Lance Burton lookalike change his goals. At least I assume so, as he stops fighting Lilith and turns my way.

He doesn't get as far as a step, though.

Lilith uses his distraction for a savage attack, and he ends up in a pool of his own blood.

And Nero still dies.

———

IN THE NEXT VISION, another magician/spawn tries to do the same, and Lilith kills him just as viciously. Same for another. Then another.

———

IN ANOTHER STRING OF VISIONS, one of the still-surviving vampires stops attacking Tartarus and tries to come to my aid—but that gives Tartarus the opening he needs, and he breaks the vampire's neck.

The same thing happens to another vampire. And another.

———

I GIVE up on people and use a probability strand to control the environment around me.

A chunk of the ceiling above me breaks, and the debris smacks me on the head.

It's pointless.

I instantly heal—and resume drinking from Nero until the bitter end.

———

I STRAIN to find a strand that would make it so I don't kill Nero.

Wishing with all my being, I grab one that's slightly thicker than what I think I can handle—and it works.

Except the probability manipulation makes my wish come true in a roundabout way.

Tartarus stops draining energy from me, and channels his attention on Nero instead.

A couple of minutes later, Nero's blood flow stops, and he looks like a shriveled raisin.

I guess in the strictest sense of the word, I wasn't the one who killed him—Tartarus did.

Still, that doesn't change the fact that Nero's dead.

———

A SERIES OF VISIONS FOLLOW. In one, I use luck to make myself choke on the blood, but then I recover and resume drinking. In another, an arcade game short-circuits and hits me with a spark of electricity—not really doing much more than tickling my skin.

All the visions end in the same way.

Nero dies.

CHAPTER THIRTY-THREE

THE VISIONS END, and I'm back in the real world.

Instead of futilely using probability manipulation as I did countless times, I jump into Headspace again.

———

FLOATING THERE, I struggle to understand what just happened.

I was able to use probability manipulation, but it didn't help—not when I used the people around me, nor the environment itself.

Though truth be told, I didn't try to use *everyone*.

There was no vision where Chester got up to help, or one where Lilith decided to simply relent.

Is it because they're also probability manipulators?

That's likely true in the case of Lilith, but when it comes to Chester, there's another, darker possibility. Maybe he's not just unconscious, but dead?

I sure hope not.

Having just learned about our blood ties, I'd love to get to know him better—despite what he did to me in the past.

So, what do I do now?

I can't just let myself kill Nero.

If I have to, I'll locate the outcome where my own vampiric heart stops—though I imagine the probability of that happening is low, especially given all the power I'm getting from dragon blood.

Still, there has to be a way.

I just have to think outside the box, as the saying goes.

Wait.

That's exactly it.

Everything I attempted was constrained to objects and people in this one arcade room. But what if there's a way to draw a new variable into this equation?

Someone or something from outside the building?

Like, say, what if there's a drone flying over us at this very moment? Could I cause it to malfunction and smack me in the head?

Wait, no. There are no drones in this world—all the tech here is decades behind. I guess there's a more horrific version of this idea. If I were willing to kill the innocent, I could make a plane crash into me—assuming one were flying above us, that is.

But no.

Given Nero's weakened state, that could kill him as well.

The best thing would be if a person came to save the day.

But who? And how?

I guess I can start by checking on everyone I know to see what they're up to. Maybe one of my friends is just outside this arcade and can be probability-manipulated to come rip me away from Nero?

To that end, I attempt to bring to mind the essence of "everyone I know." I do so by focusing on the sense of familiarity.

Nothing happens. Even with TV-boosted seer powers, "everyone" might be too vague of a target.

An idea occurs to me, and I perform the mental gymnastics necessary for probability manipulation.

To my shock, it works.

Besides the usual shapes, I also "see" strands, right here in Headspace.

Wow.

Can I use trickster powers to assist me as a seer?

Quickly locating a strand thin enough for me to handle, I snap it and wait for an outcome.

A moment later, a huge cloud of shapes appears in front of me.

Of course.

What else did I expect? When in Headspace, all I deal with are the shapes.

Oh, well. Hoping I get lucky when it comes to one of them, I examine the cloud carefully.

Where usually clouds of visions consist of identical-looking shapes, each one in *this* cloud is unique.

Is the one I need among them? Using my improved understanding of Headspace mechanics, I examine the cloud.

Very interesting. Each of these various visions will be of a different person and place, and some will even be set on different worlds.

All right.

Do I just view them all?

Usually, I wouldn't. With so many, I'll be lost in visions for a while. More importantly, these visions will eat most, if not all, of my remaining seer juice—or at least that's what my improved understanding of Headspace makes me think.

Then again, what's the alternative?

I can't do these one by one. After each one, I'll return to the reality of drinking Nero's blood. Even if I can focus in a moment and get back, a moment will be gone. If I go back and forth enough times, Nero will soon run out of moments.

All of them it is then, but can I even sprout this many ethereal wisps?

There's only one way to tell.

I strain for each shape—and begin to reach them, over and over.

If it were possible to faint from exhaustion without a body, I'd be on the verge of that now.

As is, I finally touch my last shape, and the visions begin.

CHAPTER THIRTY-FOUR

I'M bodiless in the kitchen of our apartment.

Fluffster jumps onto the table and leans the bag of Meow Mix into a bowl on the floor.

When the bowl fills up with enough food, Fluffster pushes the bag back into an upright position and looks down, curiosity in his eyes.

The cat stares back at him a look that seems to say, "Our Majesty will spare you again, fancy rodent. Our mercy knows no bounds. Now we shall feast, and you'll be quiet... or else."

Lucifur then walks over to the bowl and starts eating.

As I watch this, I realize I might not have been specific enough when I decided to see a vision about "everyone I know."

On the bright side, if I perish after Nero is drained —which is likely—at least I got to see my pets one last time.

Eventually, the cat-feeding vision stops, but the next one is just as useless. I see Maya shopping for a present for Felix in a videogame store on Earth.

And the useless visions are just getting started.

In the next one, I see my dad having lunch with wife 2.0. It's nice to know they get along so well, and that she loves avocado rolls, but I don't see how that could in any way help break the sire bond.

In another vision, I witness my mom having a video chat with her friend Zamantha, the one she visited in Paris. Mom is explaining to her that she left Paris so suddenly because she's met a man.

Oh yeah. She'd told me the same thing.

Before I can learn any disturbing details about Mom's love life, the vision cuts out again. My luck powers at work, maybe?

The next vision starts out seemingly more promising than the others. It's of my niece, Roxy, walking down the street with her friends/pack/b-hive, Maddie and Ashley.

The street around them is rundown, and there are no cars in sight. It *could* be the one on the world I'm currently at.

Super unlikely, but it could.

How awesome would it be if they just happened to be outside this arcade? Though only teens, these three girls are werewolves and could probably overpower me if they really tried.

Of course, I would win the worst aunt in the world award if I brought Roxy into this mess.

It all turns out to be moot when I see the building they walk up to. It's definitely *not* on this world, as they're going to Orientation. This street in Queens is just in desperate need of modernization.

An elevator ride later, they walk into class, and I glimpse some of the other kids. Then a person I've never seen walks in and says he will be substituting for Dr. Hekima.

The next few visions turn out to be the most useless of them all. I see my old pediatrician working on some paperwork. Then I watch every dentist I've ever been to fixing teeth. Then I learn what every trader and analyst in Nero's fund is doing. Those exciting scenes are followed by those of my college professors grading papers, and countless more that feature every friend and acquaintance from my past doing the most mundane things.

Jeez.

What's next? A vision of my Facebook feed?

But no.

The next vision is more interesting—in a disturbing way. The bannik is pleasuring himself with a picture of Lucretia in his hand. Things get steamy—literally so—because he's going at it in the steam room of the banya.

The next vision is not happening on Earth, but it's also not on the world I need.

It's Gomorrah, or at least I strongly assume so. In this vision, Bailey, the dream walker, is talking to a hologram of Itzel, the gnome who helped me rescue Rasputin.

"The nightmares are still bad," Itzel says. "I was hoping—"

The vision cuts off, and I feel a pang of guilt. Itzel's nightmares are no doubt the result of when she helped me.

The next vision is at least set on the correct world.

I see Pada—the guy who usually cleans up horrific murder scenes for the Cognizant in New York. He's standing in the meadow on the Pac-Man island among the local Cognizant with his clean-up helpers, Jik and Wen, at his side.

"I know that eating the living is gross," Pada tells them solemnly. "But when all the world Councils ask for a favor, we do it. Besides, the New York people said they'll work with us exclusively as a reward—so there's that. We'll be eating like kings and rolling in dough in no time."

Well, that's disturbing in a different way. I know I drink blood now, but still. Doing my best not to gag at the mental images, I focus in on the interesting part: it's not just the Councils that will help in the fight against Tartarus's spawn. It's anyone the Councils could bribe and convince.

That's good.

That means a lot more help.

The Pada vision cuts out, and in the next one, I'm back to the TV studio where we performed the superpower demonstrations.

Vlad, Eric, and Rasputin are standing next to a clock, according to which this is actually happening mere minutes after Eric took us to the cursed arcade room.

In other words, pretty much now.

"No, I'm going with you," Vlad tells Eric. "Kit took my place."

"Oh?" Eric says. "How come?"

"I didn't ask," Vlad says. "Maybe Nostradamus tweaked his vision at the last minute, or maybe it was Sasha's or Nero's call."

"Yeah," Rasputin says. "It's possible Nero is trying that trick again—like the one he pulled during his war campaign on his home world. He had Kit pretend to be him for a while, and now she's pretending to be you."

"She's a more versatile ally," Eric says. "It makes sense."

"Well, I don't care where I fight. And I actually prefer this"— Vlad shows them a katana that was supposed to be Kit's weapon—"to that lance."

So Kit found him and even changed weapons with him before she decided to lie her way into the Tartarus fight.

Thinking about Kit's switcheroo makes me wonder if everything has gone so wrong because of her.

Maybe I wouldn't be in this situation if Vlad was in this fight, as Nostradamus wanted.

"Ready?" Eric asks, reaching for their shoulders.

They nod, and he poofs them out of existence. They then reappear in a giant parking lot. Hiding behind the cars there is an army of superheros, all in costumes— and Eric, Vlad, and Rasputin join them.

"Any minute now," Rasputin says tensely from his hiding place. "A gate will open right there." He points at the spot everyone else is also staring at—the one someone helpfully outlined with chalk.

The vision ends before the gate can actually show up, and in the next moment, I see Pozoj, the dragon Claudia likes to flirt with.

He's hiding on a roof with a group of Cognizant without outfits, and they're also all staring at a chalk outline—presumably where another gate will open any second now.

Does this mean some of the dragons from Nero's world are here, helping? If so, that should improve the chances of the defense greatly—though not help with my situation.

Or could it?

I guess if a dragon was flying above the arcade at just the right moment, I could get "lucky" and have said dragon fall on my head.

The next vision starts.

Felix has his suit on and is hiding behind a corner of what looks eerily like the Kremlin. The rest of the surroundings support this. They remind me of Red Square in Moscow, just bigger and with more purple and less gold.

Next to Felix is the stocky woman who wore a crimson robe at the Earth Council of Councils meeting —the representative from St. Petersburg. The one who might've been Baba Yaga's old Mentor—or her BFF.

"It's starting," Felix says to the woman in Russian.

He's right.

A gate opens up, and Tartarus's spawn scatter out of it like rabid quail.

Hmm. Curious. To my current, bodiless seer "vision," they don't look like magicians anymore. Instead, they just look like regular people off the street.

"Defenders' League, assemble!" Felix rumbles through the speaker in his suit.

The stocky lady rolls her eyes. "How long have you been waiting to say that? I bet the whole superhero crap was your idea."

My friend ignores her as he makes his robot suit leap forward—and Felix isn't alone.

A whole menagerie of Cognizant jumps out of their hiding spots all around the pseudo Red Square.

The St. Petersburg Councilor lady points her hand at the first person who came out of the gate—no doubt the teleporter of the bunch. Black, greasy energy hits her target—and he just rots. Literally rots, maggots and all—except instead of the process taking weeks or months, the degradation happens as if it were taped and replayed at high speed.

Gross. This lady goes on my list of people never to piss off. No wonder Nostradamus said Baba Yaga was the nice one on that Council.

That's the unholiest power I've ever seen.

Tartarus's people must agree with my assessment. They shout something to each other and then jointly point their hands at the lady.

Felix tries to push her out of the way, but he's too late.

In an eyeblink, she turns into a raisin.

Focusing on only one person, no matter how gross her power, was a strategic mistake for Tartarus's peeps, as it gives the other Cognizant time to attack unimpeded.

A tall, vampire-looking dude slashes two of the spawn with his sword.

Another, bulkier vampire kills five the same way.

Felix grabs another spawn with the glove of his suit, then tosses him at his brothers or cousins.

"Yeah!" he shouts when the move knocks them over like bowling pins. "You don't mess with Neo Golem."

To Felix's right, one of the invaders starts to suck his energy—but that doesn't last long. Some round-faced guy I don't know reaches into the spawn's chest with an arm that phases like that of a chort.

No, not "like." Given this guy's traditional Russian shirt, this must *be* a chort. I guess the ones who worked with Woland weren't the only ones of that kind.

In the next instant, the chort's arm solidifies back, killing the invader instantly.

"Thanks," Felix says to the chort, then hits another one of Tartarus's minions in the stomach, causing the guy to fly ten feet into the air.

Itzel did a great job with the suit.

The rest of Tartarus's henchmen must realize the suit is a problem as well, because a bunch of them start sucking energy from Felix together.

Felix screams.

The Golem's chest opens up. In the place where a person's nipples would be, two giant guns show up—and fire at the idiots who conveniently clumped together.

Two explosions later, Felix's opponents are no more.

This is so cool. I bet Felix is controlling the suit using his technomancer power.

The rest of the fight lasts a couple more minutes, and when there are no more of Tartarus's spawn left to kill, Felix and his remaining allies walk up to the gate.

"It should be stable for a while longer," Felix says uncertainly, and then, to my huge surprise, he steps into the gate.

His allies follow.

I wonder why they're doing that, but before I can find out, the vision cuts out.

———

THIS NEXT VISION takes place in a park with an Eiffel Tower clone in the distance.

Are architectural designs stolen from world to world as much as the comic book ideas? Too many patterns seem to repeat themselves.

Here, the gate is already open, and the fighting must've been going on for at least a minute or so.

I only recognize a couple of people from our side: Thalia, who clearly found this fight a good enough reason to break her vow not to leave Earth, and Sparkles—a.k.a. Sir Lightning.

As I watch Thalia, I realize she was holding back during our training. Here, she moves like death personified—every twitch of her thin arms downing at least one, but usually two or three opponents at a time.

In the meantime, Sparkles shoots lightning left and right—which looks very impressive and makes me wonder if he was always able to do that, or if the TV performance boosted his abilities to this degree.

Just like Felix's crew, when Thalia's comrades finish all the spawn, they enter the gate—giving me an inkling as to what they may have in mind.

———

THE NEXT VISION shows me what's happening on a giant beach near a gorgeous ocean.

People wearing tactical gear and holding automatic weapons are standing next to Dr. Hekima and staring at the gate that materialized in front of them.

"I'll make sure they can't see you," Dr. Hekima says. "Fire on my command."

The rest of the vision shows me just how dangerous an illusionist can be.

As Tartarus's spawn pour out of the gate, Hekima hits them with an arc of his energy, and from there, they indeed act as if the armed-to-the-teeth people don't exist.

"Now," Hekima says when a few seconds pass without anyone else coming out of the gate.

The soldiers open fire.

Tartarus's children just stand there and take it. Hekima must block the sound of the shooting, as well as the sight of their fallen brethren.

In a couple of minutes, the battle—or rather, the execution—is over.

If you forget what Tartarus and his gang came to this world to do, that almost seems unsporting.

Stepping over the dead bodies, Hekima walks into the gate alone—which probably means his allies were humans from this world who can't enter Cognizant gates.

————

THE NEXT VISION is almost identical to the previous one, except it's Jaylen who hides a whole army with his illusionist powers.

Only his hatred for this lot makes Jaylen put a macabre twist on the whole process.

He must be showing his enemies some kind of an illusion that makes them fight each other—which they do viciously at the same time as they get riddled with bullets.

————

IN THE NEXT VISION, Lucretia pierces an invader's

heart with her rapier. To her right, a familiar sex-bombshell of a woman beheads another with a sword.

Is that Pamela Anderson's sister? But no. This is Lola, a nymph who was in some sort of sex-addiction-based relationship with Kit.

A howl makes everyone look to the left.

It's a pack of werewolves, their maws foaming and their roaring so loud it makes the nonexistent hair stand up on the nape of my nonexistent neck.

I recognize three of them. The biggest is Obo, the guy who attacked me in the hotel. A slightly smaller specimen is Eduardo, the alpha of the New York pack who helped Nero in the war on the dragon world. And the smallest of the three—but still on par with the rest of the pack—is Marius, Nostradamus's "service animal."

Ignoring pathetic energy-sucking attempts coming from Tartarus's people, the werewolves rip into their ranks and tear them into bite-sized shreds.

Lola, Lucretia, and everyone else watch the massacre in shocked fascination.

When it all stops, all but Marius turn back into naked men and women, then walk determinedly toward the gate.

"You have some serious issues," Lucretia says to Marius when he passes by her. "When all of this is over, maybe I can give you a few therapy sessions?"

Marius bobs his furry head, then steps into the gate—and the rest of them follow.

———

A GROUP of tanks meet Tartarus's minions in the next vision, where a gate opens next to what looks like an old junkyard.

A dozen armor-piercing rounds later, only the tanks remain.

———

IN THE FOLLOWING VISION, the gate opens in a desert, and as soon as Tartarus's people exit, a ballistic missile hits the spot, wiping them all out.

———

SPECIAL FORCES SOLDIERS attack Tartarus's spawn who gated into what looks like a military base. Supporting them is another Cognizant who helped Nero overthrow the usurper, a woman who can control animals—in this case, a huge cloud of crow-like birds.

Once they win, she walks into the gate.

———

ANOTHER GROUP of human soldiers handles a gate that opens in what looks like this world's rip-off of Jerusalem. With them is the elf-like guy who helped Nero the other day.

The soldiers and the elf decimate the startled newcomers gating in, and the elf jumps into the gate.

———

IN THE NEXT VISION, the fighting is done mostly by the members of the New York Council.

I spot Tatum—the succubus who spoke up during a recent meeting—using her "charms" on the invaders. Left dazed and decidedly horny, they're easy pickings for Albina, the Councilor who can dissolve matter with white streams of energy.

Before long, there are no more enemies left, and the Cognizant jump into the gate.

———

IN THE NEXT VISION, I spot Claudia, Nero's sister. She turns into her dragon form, which is almost as huge as that of Nero.

Aww, how cute. Even as a dragon, she has the cloud-shaped birthmark on her cheek.

Claudia's allies know the score. They run away from the gate as she takes to the air and breathes fire at Tartarus's children before they can even think about sucking anyone's energy.

A second later, it's all over. The gate is now surrounded by melted bones and scorched earth.

Landing and turning back into a gorgeous woman, Claudia steps into the gate.

———

THE NEXT FIGHT is happening in the giant train station where Lilith and I stepped out of the hub.

Colton—the "runt" from the tribe of giants—is holding two of Tartarus's henchmen in his enormous hands. Then he slams their heads together, crushing them like pumpkins.

Nearby is Ariel, proudly wearing her sleek and sexy Sugar Glider suit.

She punches one enemy in the eye. The guy flies up three feet, then crash-lands on the ground and doesn't move.

Pulling out a gun, Ariel unloads it into another guy, then throws her army knife into the chest of yet another.

Three more of Tartarus's spawn surround her before she can reload her gun. Two begin to steal her energy, while the third—a huge dude—hits her in the face.

The pain and the energy drain make Ariel stumble, which lets the bigger attacker sweep her legs.

Ariel falls down, hits her head on the granite floor of the station, and passes out.

This makes it official.

The energy suck does make people more prone to getting knocked out. Ariel is too tough to let a few blows impact her like that otherwise.

Seeing her fall, the energy suckers turn their focus

to Colton, but the one who punched Ariel in the face isn't done with her.

He begins kicking Ariel's unconscious body, over and over.

Even with her TV-boosted super-strength, his blows are breaking her bones, I can tell.

Suddenly, a stream of golden energy shoots from the back of the station and into Ariel's unmoving body.

I follow the arc to the caster and recognize her instantly. It's Isis, the healer on Nero's payroll.

The healing energy does its trick right away. Ariel opens her eyes and catches the foot of her attacker before it can deliver the next blow.

With a vicious twist, Ariel breaks the guy's ankle and leaps to her feet.

The guy screams bloody murder, but not for long. Ariel whacks him in the temple so hard his skull visibly cracks, like an eggshell.

That has to be the TV-boost. She was always strong but not *that* strong.

Ariel then gets revenge on the two energy suckers who got her into that precarious situation. After making quick work of them, she helps Colton and the rest kill off the remainder.

Enemies wiped out, my roommate and her allies step into the gate.

Unlike my earlier visions, this one doesn't end here, but follows Ariel to her destination.

Very interesting.

I'm finally going to see what all those people entering the gates are up to.

CHAPTER THIRTY-FIVE

ARIEL EXITS in a world with two suns in the sky, each smaller than normal. Patches of snow and short grass cover the tundra-like landscape, and there's no sign of civilization in sight.

An army greets Ariel, one that consists of pretty much everyone from my other visions but also some players I haven't seen yet, like the squadrons of centaurs, cockatrices, and giants—all of whom look familiar, probably because they'd been Nero's allies in his quest to win back his world.

Ariel looks all of them over. Then her gaze falls on a group of so-called strongmen, who are wearing very little clothing and looking a lot like the cast of *300.*

Ariel smiles appreciatively and yells something to them in what sounds like Greek.

Did she just catcall a bunch of dudes? It wouldn't surprise me if she did.

The cast of *300* collectively flex a bunch of muscles and grin at Ariel, then reply in the same language.

"Hey," Felix says from behind her. "How is life as a superheroine?"

"Dude, stop cockblocking me," Ariel says, turning to him. "I was hoping to get a date, but now they'll think I'm into robots."

"Are these guys the same type of Cognizant as you?" Felix asks as he examines the warriors' perfect abs and other symmetrical attributes.

"That they are," Ariel says, looking back at the group longingly. "They will be very helpful when it comes to killing the rest of Tartarus's people."

Felix raises his suit's faceplate, revealing a serious expression underneath. "We're not going to kill *all* of them," he says. "Some will turn off their glamour—or whatever it's called—and hide among the humans. More importantly, we're not here to commit genocide. At least *I'm* not."

Ariel rips her gaze away from the strongmen eye candy and raises her perfect eyebrow at Felix. "Did you miss the part about breeding pits?" she asks. "Why would we want to leave any of these bastards alive?"

"Look, I'm all for freeing the prisoners from those pits," Felix says. "That's why I'm here. But, if any of Tartarus's people surrender, they get to live. Nero said so himself."

"Sasha is making Nero go soft. Why do this? What will stop these guys from building up forces and attacking us again one day?"

"Maybe Nero knows history," Felix says. "What you suggest was almost done to the dragons at some point. In any case, the earth movers from the eighties' world are with us for a reason. They will cause the ground to swallow the gates leading to and from this world. That way, since all of the Tartarus-bred teleporters are now dead, no one will be causing trouble outside this world ever again."

"Fine," Ariel grumbles. "All I can say is that these assholes are lucky I'm not the one in charge. *I* would've eliminated them completely."

"Well, your bloodthirsty wish might still happen naturally," Felix says. "Without access to other worlds, they'll need to learn how to drain energy from humans in a sustainable manner, like vampires do. If they fail, they'll run out of humans and die out."

"Which would suck for the humans," Ariel says.

"Again, we don't have a way to separate humans from these guys, so we either kill everyone on the planet or just free the Cognizant from the breeding pits and leave. At least under the latter plan, the humans have a chance."

"Maybe the humans will wipe them out," Ariel says. "Genocides are common in their history, so why not do a helpful one this time?"

"Remind me never to get on your bad side." Felix lowers the robot suit's faceplate.

"I don't have a bad side." Ariel makes a tight ponytail and stretches a few times. "Come on, the march is about to begin."

———

A NEW VISION STARTS—STILL on the two-sun planet.

This new location looks a lot like the prior one. I don't think they walked far. The only difference is there's a castle in the far distance.

Oh, and the army.

Two armies, if you count Ariel and her allies.

The forces stand opposite each other on the plateau, with Tartarus's spawn closer to the distant castle.

"That's a whole world worth of energy suckers?" Felix mumbles through his suit visor. "I thought there'd be more."

"I bet most of Tartarus's forces died in the attack on the eighties' world," Ariel says, glaring at the enemy army. "These are probably guards who were left to make sure the poor wretches from the breeding pits don't escape."

"If that's true, feel free to kill them all without regret," Felix says.

"Oh, I plan to." Ariel cracks her knuckles.

With a war cry, Tartarus's army runs at them.

With a much louder and fiercer answering cry, the centaurs, the cockatrices, and the giants rush forward, with the rest of the Cognizant on their heels.

The armies clash.

Tartarus's people suffer horrific casualties and begin to retreat.

For some reason, our guys let them, which turns

out to be a bad idea, as Tartarus's spawn start sucking energy from them from afar.

Very soon, Felix, Ariel, the giants, the centaurs, and the rest are on their knees, grunting in pain.

Which is when I realize why they let the retreat happen.

It wasn't a mistake, after all.

A dragon roar shakes the ground everyone is standing on.

As the bad guys look up, they see Claudia and a whole sky full of dragons.

"Yeah!" Ariel yells excitedly. "This is going to really hurt."

The dragons must've practiced this next maneuver. Before the spawn can switch their energy-sucking attention to the sky, they swoop down as one and cover the ground with dragon breath, leaving behind nothing but ashes.

CHAPTER THIRTY-SIX

THE VISIONS FINALLY STOP.

I'm back in the arcade, killing Nero.

Tartarus is still sucking energy from me and Lilith and is killing the last of our vampire allies.

On her end, Lilith is fighting the last of Tartarus's henchmen.

Damn it.

All those visions, and I still have no idea how I can turn this situation around.

I attempt a return to Headspace, but it doesn't work on the first, second, or third attempt.

That's it. I must be out of seer juice.

Ugh. Why did my luck help me get all those visions?

Initially, I thought it would show me a way out. But now I wonder if the goal of the visions was to let me die knowing that my friends will at least win their part of the fight, and Earth will survive. Nero was right on that score. Even if Tartarus wins here, he won't have an army to rely on and is therefore unlikely to attack Earth anytime soon.

But no.

There had to be a vision in that bunch I could use.

Somehow.

Then I recall something.

Yes. It could work. But what are the chances?

I guess I'm about to find out.

I bring myself into the probability manipulation state of mind, but this time, I focus only on the unlikely scenario that I just thought of.

A single strand shows up. A familiar one—as thick as a redwood tree trunk.

Crap. This proves this idea is unlikely indeed.

But I still have to make it work. There's no other option.

Wishing I could control my body enough to at least grit my teeth, I metaphysically grasp for the strand—only to have it slip through my metaphysical fingers.

Oh no, you don't.

I grab for it again.

The stupid strand eludes me once more.

"I'm the most powerful probability manipulator on this planet," I tell the strand and try to make myself believe it. "If anyone can make this happen, it's me."

Something seems to yield just a fraction, so I renew my efforts along the same lines, mentally yelling at the strand like a banshee.

Given that this battle is not physical, I pretend I'm in Headspace and will the ethereal wisps to sprout out of me, so I can wrap them around the strand like an angry octopus.

I'm not sure if it's this last bit of visualization, or the probability manipulation experience I gained in my visions, but the strand creaks like a cut tree as it snaps.

The probability manipulation part of me now feels sucked dry, like one of the corpses Tartarus leaves behind. No more probability manipulation today. Just to test if I'm right, I attempt to control fate again—and fail miserably.

Everything now depends on that strand doing what I hoped.

And a second later, it happens.

Eric, Vlad, and Rasputin materialize between me and Lilith, with Vlad clutching his katana and Rasputin looking around in shock.

Yes! This is what I was shooting for. I saw them teleport to some parking lot and wondered if I could make Eric come here instead.

"What the hell?" Eric says, looking around. "This isn't where I meant to teleport to."

"A teleporter." Tartarus stops draining energy from me and Lilith, kills the last vampire he was fighting, and advances on Eric. "You will take me out of here."

Crap. This is a flaw in my plan. Nostradamus insisted there be no teleporters at the scene so as not to give Tartarus a chance to escape.

But it's a risk I had to take. Nero has to be saved, even if that leads to Tartarus's freedom.

Eric looks at the oncoming Tartarus like a rabbit would at a snake.

If I could speak, I'd shout for Eric to teleport *me* away from Nero.

"No one is teleporting anywhere," Lilith snarls, locking her mirror-turning eyes on Eric's face. "Don't move. Got that?"

"Yes," Eric says in a glamoured voice.

Before Tartarus can return to draining her, Lilith swiftly dispatches the Lance Burton lookalike and two of the last spawn she's been fighting.

Tartarus is almost on Eric by the time she whooshes in that direction.

"Hold this." Vlad thrusts his katana into Rasputin's hand and bends to pick up the gate sword near my feet.

This is a risk.

If Lilith commands me, I will attack Vlad. The good news is Lilith is too busy going for Eric.

"What's Sasha doing?" Rasputin asks of no one in particular. "Why is she killing Nero?"

"The sire bond," Vlad growls, activating the sword. "She wouldn't be doing this of her own volition. Trust me."

A stone mask seems to drop over Rasputin's face.

Lilith reaches Eric a split second before Tartarus does—and rips into the poor teleporter's throat with her fangs.

Seeing the teleportation opportunity slip through his fingers, Tartarus stops, gives Lilith a deadly stare, and points both of his energy-sucking hands at her.

She convulses in pain but keeps sucking Eric's blood—likely in the hopes it will counteract some of the energy drain.

Rasputin looks at me, then at Lilith, then back at me.

Vlad leaps for Tartarus, gate sword raised.

"Yes, get him," Lilith hisses, lifting her head. "I'll join you in—"

His hands shaking, Rasputin swings the katana.

The sharp blade bites into Lilith's neck, then comes out on the other side, separating her head from her shoulders.

What. Just. Happened?

A fountain of blood gushes from Lilith's neck, covering Rasputin from head to toe. Her headless body turns on its heel and slaps him across the face—so hard that he crashes into the nearby *Donkey Kong* machine.

Seriously, is this a nightmare?

I half-expect Lilith's body to snatch her head from the air and put it back on, but she's not really a goddess. The last movement complete, her headless body collapses.

The head itself rolls across the floor, coming to rest face up, with Lilith's blue eyes staring at unconscious Rasputin accusingly until the last spark of life in them fades.

I wonder if she saw the irony in her last moments. She met Rasputin to birth me in order to avoid dying by Tartarus's hand—and it worked. Thanks to my probability manipulation and Rasputin's resolve, she doesn't need to worry about Tartarus ever again.

I blink of my own volition—and realize the sire bond is gone.

I jerk away from Nero.

Now that my heart is back under my control, it starts beating against my chest as if possessed by an army of hyperactive squirrels.

Underneath me, Nero looks paler than a vampire.

Is it too late?

Oh, please, don't let it be too late.

Hands shaking, I search for the pulse on the unbitten side of his neck.

It's so faint I can barely feel it.

Slicing my thumb with one of my fangs, I squeeze out a droplet of blood and shove the finger into Nero's mouth.

His tongue touches the droplet, and he turns the tiniest shade less pale. Without my improved vision, I doubt I would've even noticed the change.

"Are you okay?" I whisper to him. "Please be okay."

Nero doesn't reply, so I pull out my thumb and see the problem. The wound is already healed. I pierce the finger again, squeeze more blood out, and put it in his mouth.

Nero's pulse strengthens a little.

Yes. I'm on the right track.

"You *have* to be okay," I tell him. "Because I love you too."

I'd like to think this last bit is what really helps.

It certainly would be romantic if that were so.

No matter the reason, Nero manages to open one eye and even minutely lifts an eyebrow.

I suspect that if he was in any condition to talk, he'd say, "This is what I had to suffer through for you to finally admit how you feel?"

Fighting the urge to melt into a relieved puddle, I feed him another droplet of my blood.

"Tartarus," he whispers in a hoarse voice. "Go. I'll survive."

This is when I become aware of what else is happening in the room.

Vlad is slicing at Tartarus's throat with the gate sword, his movements blurringly fast.

Yes! Behead the bastard!

But instead of Tartarus's flesh, the blade bites into the stone that's powering the force field protecting him.

Roaring in anger, Tartarus catches Vlad's wrist and rips the gate sword out of his grasp.

Not good.

I leap for the katana next to Lilith's beheaded body and toss it to Vlad. Then I run toward them.

Tartarus's force field flickers and dies.

Vlad catches the katana and slices for Tartarus's now-exposed stomach.

Tartarus parries with the gate sword—which cuts through the metal of the katana as if it were made of fog. Vlad continues the swing with the remaining shard of the sword, but only scratches Tartarus's skin.

Tartarus's blade doesn't slow.

"No!" I scream, speeding up until I'm almost blurring. But I'm too late.

The gate sword enters Vlad's body, cleaving him from shoulder to groin.

With a grunt, Vlad falls to his knees at Tartarus's feet.

Reaching them, I slam a fist into Tartarus's face.

He flies through the room, destroying two arcade games before he slams into the wall, sheetrock raining down all around him.

Wow. Nero's blood really does make me powerful.

Though I know I should attack Tartarus before he recovers, I kneel next to Vlad instead.

He doesn't look good. The gaping gash doesn't look healable.

"Nothing you can do for me. Just go," he rasps, coughing up blood. A beatific smile lights his pale face as his gaze lifts to the ceiling. "Rose, darling, I'm coming. I'm finally coming to you." And with one last breath, his eyes close, his body slumping to the floor.

I feel numb.

Nero is half-dead.

My biological mother, with all her faults, is gone, killed by my biological father.

Rasputin, Chester, and Kit are all knocked out, or worse.

And now Vlad.

I promised Rose to look after him—and failed in the worst possible way.

My hands turn into fists.

If I couldn't protect Vlad, I will at least avenge him.

I zoom up to the ceiling, then dive to where Tartarus lies in the debris.

It's time for me to fulfill Nostradamus's prophecy once and for all.

CHAPTER THIRTY-SEVEN

TEETH CLENCHED, I fly in a pose Superman would be proud of, my fists outstretched.

Before I get to the debris, Tartarus leaps to his feet and swipes at me with the gate sword.

Moving fast, I dodge the attack and uppercut him in the jaw.

He flies up seven feet, then crash-lands into an *Evel Knievel* pinball machine, glass shards exploding everywhere.

I rush to snatch his sword as he jumps back to his feet.

Seeing my intent, he swings the weapon in a wide arc, and the plasma blade whooshes an inch away from my neck.

I swipe at his legs.

He jumps and thrusts at me with the sword.

I side-step it, then clutch the wrist of his sword-wielding arm in an iron grip.

He hits me in the face with his other fist.

I see stars but manage to stay on my feet, my split lip healing instantly.

He hits me again, in the stomach this time. Something inside me tears, then heals almost as fast as the lip.

I catch his other wrist.

He headbutts me, crashing his forehead into mine. *Ouch.*

My skull cracks, and the skin on my forehead tears from the impact. But these wounds are also as short-lived as the others—thank you, TV performance and Nero's blood.

Tartarus's forehead, on the other hand, is still bleeding. Looks like his attack hurt him more than it did me.

He tries to twist out of my hold, but I'm stronger.

Straining, I push his sword-holding hand toward him.

Panic appears in his eyes, and he deactivates the gate sword.

Jerking hard, I twist his wrist, and the weapon clanks to the floor.

Snarling, Tartarus twists his other hand to point his fingers at me, and I feel the powerful energy drain begin.

His full power is directed solely at me now, and the agony is so dizzying I fight not to pass out from it.

But two can play this game. My fangs punching out, I yank him toward me and rip into his neck.

The taste of his blood should be vile, but instead, it's heaven. Greedily, I start gulping it and feel my energy levels replenish.

He starts writhing like a fish on a hook, but I just suck harder.

The pain of the energy drain dulls to the levels I experienced at the Rite.

Tartarus's struggles intensify. "I'll get your life force out before you can drink me dry," he hisses. "Then I'll kill everyone you—"

Before he can finish the threat, I squeeze his wrists so hard they break, and whoosh upward like a rocket.

We slam into the ceiling, ripping through it, then burst through the roof as we torpedo into the sky.

Through all this, I keep drinking the bastard's blood, and he's draining my energy.

When we're a few hundred feet up, I plummet like a hawk diving after prey, with Tartarus positioned underneath me.

He flails harder as we rocket toward the ground, but I barely feel his struggles.

We slam into the roof of the arcade at supersonic speed, the crash jarring every bone in my body. Tartarus's back takes the brunt of it as we smash through the roof, then the ceiling, then the floor.

Panting, I crawl off him—and realize we've made a crater in the arcade floor.

It's official. Me plus Nero's blood equals craters everywhere.

In the crater, Tartarus's body looks broken beyond repair, but I'm not taking any chances.

Limping to the gate sword, I pick it up, activate the blade, and return to the crater.

Tartarus begins to stir.

So he wasn't dead.

"This is for Vlad," I say grimly as I slice him in half the long way. "And this is for Chester." I slice him across the torso. "And this is for all the billions of people you killed."

I slice again.

And again.

CHAPTER THIRTY-EIGHT

THE THOUGHT of Nero pulls me out of my bloodlust. Stopping my grisly work, I rush over to him and see that he still looks like a wraith.

"Here." Kneeling, I cut my finger and extend it to him.

He shakes his head. "Vampire blood won't heal me further. Go help the others instead."

I'm reluctant to leave him, but he's right. The others do need help.

Jumping to my feet, I quickly scan the room and sprint over to Chester—who may or may not be alive.

When I press my fingers to his pulse, it's there.

Lucky trickster. He's just passed out, after all.

I give him some of my blood, and he opens his eyes right away.

"Did we win?" he asks in a hoarse voice, sitting up.

"Tartarus is no more," I say somberly, glancing over at Vlad's body.

"Oh," Chester mutters when he spots Lilith's headless corpse.

I follow his gaze, my chest tightening.

Despite what she was and what she nearly made me do, this loss still hurts. Does that mean something's wrong with me? Or something's right?

Monster or not, she *was* my biological mother.

Speaking of biological parents, I blur toward still-passed-out Rasputin and give him a droplet of my blood.

He comes to his senses a moment later, then looks at Lilith's corpse. His face twists with pain before smoothing out into an unreadable mask. "Is it finished?" he asks unsteadily. "Did you get him?"

I point at Tartarus tartare in the middle of the room, and Rasputin solemnly nods.

Next, I run over to Kit and give her a drop of blood.

"That's nice," she croons, opening her eyes. "Can I have some more?"

"No," I say sternly. "You don't need yet another addiction."

"Spoilsport," she mumbles, sitting up.

I heal Eric next, then walk over to Nostradamus and hesitantly heal him as well. Coughing, he sits up, rubbing the scars that remain in place of his eyes. "So." His voice is raspy. "You did it."

He says it as a statement, not a question, as if there was no doubt all along.

I want to interrogate him about the whole thing, but now is not the time.

Leaving him, I walk over to Vlad.

His body lies unmoving, his open eyes dull and unseeing.

My chest squeezes painfully as my eyes begin to water.

Vlad is gone.

Really gone.

The last thread connecting me to Rose is broken.

"You can mourn him later." Nostradamus puts a hand on my shoulder. He must've followed me here. "I've seen the futures. Nero needs you. His condition is still—"

He doesn't need to say more.

"Eric, take us to the hub," I say urgently, grabbing the teleporter and whooshing toward still-prone Nero —who's looking rather pale again.

Blinking groggily, Eric nevertheless poofs us next to the exact gate I need to leave this world.

"Thanks," I tell him. "Now go help with the upcoming fight."

Because the visions I had while searching for a way to break the sire bond were of a future that was still to come. All the battles I saw are just about to unfold, if not already in progress.

Eric poofs away, and I pick up Nero in that bridal carry he likes to use on me so much. Though his eyes are closed, a faint smile curves his lips, and he loops a heavy arm over my neck as I fly us both into the gate.

As soon as we come out on the other side, I head straight into the next gate. Then another and another.

It's a good thing I memorized the route Lilith took when she kidnapped me.

I fly from gate to gate in rapid succession until we get to Earth. Here, I have two options: go to our work building, where his local hoard of treasure is, or take him to the dragon world, where the imperial stash resides.

I can't fly openly on Earth, so that means cabs and traffic. And if the traffic is bad enough, it may actually be faster to fly Nero through all those gates and straight to the dragon castle on his world—where the hoard of imperial treasure is much greater.

Decided, I whoosh into another gate and start following the path to Nero's homeland.

When I get to Jaylen's world—the one Tartarus and his kin already sucked dry—I exit the airport and take to the skies, reaching the other hub in record time. The other gates blur until I reach the dragon world; then I fly again, whooshing toward Godiva like a jet.

I wonder if I'll always be able to fly this fast, or if it's just a temporary side effect of gorging on Nero's blood.

Once inside the castle, I rush to the back, whoosh down the staircase that leads into the treasure room, and lay Nero down on a bed of gold coins.

Instantly, his pulse returns to normal, and color comes back to his cheeks. Opening his eyes, he meets my gaze. "Thank you," he says in his growly voice as I brush a lock of hair off his forehead. Then he pulls me to him, presses a hard kiss to my lips, and sits up.

"What are you doing?" I ask, blinking.

"We need to go back to help Claudia and the others."

I frown. "Don't you need healing sleep in dragon form to fully recover?"

"It's fine," he growls, standing up. "I'll be able to fly now. What about you? Are you too tired to fight?"

"Nope. I'm still running on your blood," I say. "Let's go."

He nods, and we blur out of the castle side by side. Then he turns into a dragon, and I float up to perch on his back.

This time around, the ride is almost fun. It really helps to know that if I fall, I'll just fly on my own.

By the time we get back to the eighties world, the fight in the train station is over, but the temporary gate leading to Tartarus's world is still there.

Nero changes into human form so as not to tip them off to the dragon attack that comes later, and we jump in.

Exiting on Tartarus's world, we blur toward the place where the armies are facing each other and, with a war yell, join the fray.

Hands turning into claws, Nero shreds Tartarus's spawn to bits, and in a fittingly grisly tribute to Lilith, I kill each enemy in disturbingly creative ways until I'm covered in blood and gore.

Thanks to our contribution, some of Tartarus's children surrender instead of retreating, and as a result get to live.

The rest follow the script I saw in my vision. They

retreat, only to cowardly suck energy from us from a distance, and then they get incinerated in a coordinated dragon attack.

And just like that, the remnants of Tartarus's forces are gone.

CHAPTER THIRTY-NINE

IN THE AFTERMATH of the battle, Nero and I make sure everyone is fine, then decide against sticking around for the next phase—the release of prisoners from the breeding pits and the destruction of gates that lead to this world.

Our allies are more than capable of handling that themselves.

Instead, Nero orders Eric to teleport us to the yet-intact hub. The three of us go through a few gates before Nero allows Eric to leave. Once we're alone, Nero turns into a dragon and asks me to get on.

We fly through the Otherland that I soon recognize as Atlantis—the world the strongmen are from.

After circling an island for a few minutes, Nero lands on a ridiculously romantic cliff where a majestic, weather-worn mountain faces the blue ocean.

Turning into a naked male, Nero makes the view better still.

"Figured you could use a vacation," he says, his blue-gray eyes gleaming. "Time passes fast here, so you can take as long as you need to recover and no one back home would even notice."

Ah, yes. Finally, this is our chance to talk.

Holding Nero's gaze, I take a breath. "Back home." I cock my head. "Where exactly is that for you?"

He frowns.

"Do you plan to rule the dragon world?" I clarify. "Is that where your home is now? Because mine is on Earth, you see, where my parents—"

He lifts his eyebrows. "Are you making things needlessly complicated?"

At my lack of expression, he sighs and lays his big hands on my shoulders, squeezing my tense muscles lightly. "I never meant to abandon my fund, and all the rest of the life I've built on Earth. You and I can spend part of our time in New York, and part on my world. It was never going to be one or the other."

As he talks, a weight lifts off my chest. How did I not think of this idea? It's literally the best of both worlds. It's perfect.

"As for your parents," he continues. "Just tell them you got a promotion, and you now have to spend part of your time in our Japan office."

"About that." I grin. "I don't think I can work for you anymore. I'm not into sleeping with my boss and all that."

A smile touches his eyes. "In that case, I think I'll finally allow you to quit."

"So generous, thanks."

His smile widens to a grin. "You've earned a retirement, if that's what you want. Alternatively, now that you bullied the Council into letting you perform your illusions, I imagine you could do *that*—and on multiple worlds, if you wish."

"I do wish," I say. "I plan to be a household name on Earth and your court magician on the dragon world. Like Merlin, only hotter."

"No." He curves his palm over my jaw. "On my world, you will be known as my queen."

I nearly choke on my own saliva.

Was that a roundabout proposal?

I stare at Nero's hard-featured face.

He stares back, unblinking.

Yes, it totally was.

Crap. I'm not prepared to even think about that.

We aren't even technically dating yet. There are steps to these things, and saving worlds together doesn't count.

Then again, I don't need my seer power to know that I'll greatly enjoy all the steps, and if all goes well, we'll see. For now, I better change the subject.

"Can we get away from New York in the winter months?" I ask. "How is Godiva at that time of year?"

He raises an eyebrow. "Otherland snow-birding? If you want to get away to good weather, *this* is the place." He gestures at our picturesque surroundings.

I inhale the salty breeze and let my gaze follow the horizon. "You're right. Let's spend a year here. Or two."

"As long as you need," he says seriously. His thumb strokes over my lip. "With your seer power, you'll know if anyone dares to bother us here—and I'll kill them before they even get the idea to come."

"Deal," I say and suddenly feel tired, the events of the day catching up to me all at once.

As if sensing my shift in mood, Nero frames my face with both of his palms and gazes intently into my eyes. "How *are* you, Sasha? Really?"

"I don't know." My voice catches. "Tired. Numb. Glad we're alive. But Lilith and Vlad and—"

"I know," he says gently. "That's why you need time."

"Yeah." I feel a pressure behind my eyes, and my chin begins to quiver.

Damn it. Am I really about to burst into tears like a wimp instead of the superpowered vampire-trickster-seer hybrid I've become?

Yeah, okay. Maybe.

Before I get the chance, though, Nero pulls me against him, enfolding me in his arms, and the worst of the stinging behind my eyes subsides. He holds me like that for what feels like a couple of days, and by the time we pull apart, I feel well enough to fly down into the ocean.

Once there, I promptly lose my clothes, and Nero swiftly joins me in the waves. Before long, we're creating tsunamis, celebrating life in the best possible way.

HOURS LATER, as I lie on the beach in his arms in a state of post-coital bliss, I lazily check if my seer abilities came back—and find that they have.

Good. I'm curious about the future. Specifically, *our* future.

Jumping into Headspace, I expertly summon the needed shapes and dive in.

———

I SEE myself performing in New York's Madison Square Garden, with Nero, Mom, Dad, and Rasputin looking at me proudly from the front row.

It's a show I've polished over hundreds of performances, and it's the best one yet.

It better be, since it's being recorded for a special on Netflix.

———

IN AN ECHO OF the previous vision, I see a giant theater on the dragon world—a theater built specifically for this purpose, with trap doors and other sneaky business I personally designed.

On a world without TV, I'm the best entertainment these humans have ever seen, and even dragons are impressed when they come.

———

IN THE THIRD VISION, Dad and Rasputin—whom I've been calling Papa more often—are leading me down the aisle.

The venue is The Palace, my dad's favorite New York hotel.

All the Cognizant who helped us during the battle with Tartarus are here—at least those who look human enough to be allowed on Earth. The others attended my first wedding on the dragon world.

And speaking of the first wedding, the dragons liked it so much they're attending this one too.

I look at where my family is sitting, and something really odd catches my attention. The person next to Mom is supposed to be the mystery guy she's been dating. Because they "finally got serious," today's the day she's introducing him to us.

Except I already know him. Know him too well.

It's Nostradamus.

I blink at the blind seer as all the pieces fall into place.

Mom met her guy during her visit to Paris, where Nostradamus usually resides. He needed her back in New York as part of the scheme that ended in me becoming a vampire, so he must've contrived a meeting with her, and I guess things escalated from there.

It's tempting to go bridezilla on their asses, but I don't. Still, who pulls a stunt like this on someone's wedding day? It's all about me—and Nero, I guess—but mostly me.

The royal wedding on the dragon world was about His Imperial Majesty.

After the festivities are over, Nostradamus and I are going to have words. Maybe Nero will also contribute—depending on what Mom tells me about their relationship.

"I didn't know how to tell you about that," Rasputin whispers when he follows my gaze. "For what it's worth, she's happy in every future I've checked."

"She better be," I hiss back. "If he hurts her, I'll kill him."

Nostradamus waves at me. He must've foreseen this. Sometimes I can't help the feeling that every single moment in my life was scripted by the guy long before I was born.

Then again, if that's true, maybe I should thank him? It did lead to this.

As we get closer to the altar, I look at the groom himself. Dressed in a million-dollar Stuart Hughes Diamond Edition suit, Nero looks as much a king here on Earth as he does in his traditional royal accoutrements on his home world.

His limbal rings expand as he drinks me in. Ah, yes. He likes my dress, which figures. It's basically my superhero outfit done in white, so there's a lot—and I mean, a lot—of skin exposed.

I pick up the pace until I'm walking as fast as my two fathers can keep up with, and then I'm finally there, joining Nero in front of Chester—who somehow persuaded us to let him be the officiant in this ceremony. He looks mischievous, even though Nero told him not to pull any tricks on penalty of death.

Ariel, Kit, Claudia, Lucretia, Maya, Roxy, and Thalia are wearing bridesmaids' dresses and standing to our right. Ariel is also my maid of honor—an honor she more or less demanded, proving to me that my vampire nature no longer bothers her as much.

Felix, who looks like a pirate with Fluffster sitting on his shoulder, is standing with the rest of the groomsmen to the left. That group also includes Pozoj —who's now officially Claudia's beau—a couple of heads of state, several religious leaders, some famous billionaires, and a few more people that Nero strategically honored.

"I was asked to make this short," Chester says with an evil grin. "So here goes. If anyone has a reason for these two not to wed, speak now and prepare to die."

No one is suicidal enough to make so much as a peep.

Chester's grin widens. "I didn't think so. Now, do you, Nero, take Sasha to be your lawfully wedded wife and queen?"

"I do," Nero growls.

"And do you, Sasha, take Nero to be your lawfully wedded husband and king?" Chester asks with a wink.

I pause for drama, then wait another second, like a good performer should. When I have everyone's absolute and undivided attention, I look Nero over, as if I really need to think this through. And then, when the tension in the room is unbearable, I say ceremoniously, "I do"—and the room bursts into applause.

"You may kiss," Chester says, making a smooching face, and we do.

———

I COME BACK to the present moment on the beach with a smile on my face.

Looks like Nero *will* get me to marry him at some point in the future. And not even once, but twice.

Well, like with any vision, now that I know what the future could hold, it's up to me to allow it to happen… or not.

All will depend on someone's good behavior.

I inhale Nero's warm, ocean-salty scent, stroke his muscular bicep, and sigh contentedly.

Who am I kidding?

The future I just saw is as inevitable as Nostradamus's prophecy was. Like poor Tartarus, Nero has no choice when it comes to his fate.

He's mine.

And we're going to be kicking ass together forever. and ever more.

Thank you for reading! I hope you enjoyed the conclusion to Sasha's story. Her adventures with Nero are over for now, but you can see Felix, Ariel, and many other characters from the Cognizant world in my upcoming series about Bailey Spade, the dream walker. To be notified when her story is out, please visit www.dimazales.com and sign up for my mailing list.

Love audiobooks? This series, and all of my other books, are available in audio.

Want more exciting action and adventure? Check out:

- *Mind Dimensions* - the action-packed urban fantasy adventures of Darren, who can stop time and read minds
- *Upgrade* - the thrilling sci-fi tale of Mike

Cohen, whose new technology will transform our brains *and* the world
- *The Last Humans* - the futuristic sci-fi/dystopian story of Theo, who lives in a world where nothing is as it seems
- *The Sorcery Code* - the epic fantasy adventures of sorcerer Blaise and his creation, the beautiful and powerful Gala

I also collaborate with my wife on sci-fi romance, so if you don't mind erotic material, you can check out *Close Liaisons*. Visit www.annazaires.com for more information and to get your copy.

And now, please turn the page to read the first chapter of *Dream Walker*, the upcoming story of Bailey Spade.

EXCERPT FROM DREAM WALKER

Dream Walker, the story of Bailey Spade, is coming soon! Sign up to my newsletter at www.dimazales.com to be notified when it becomes available.

—————

I swallow a droplet of diluted vampire blood.

"Alarm and surveillance disabled," Felix whispers in my earpiece. "Your breaking and entering may commence."

Before I can reply, the blood kicks in, lifting the weight off my eyelids as my sleep deprivation retreats.

Except the droplet must've been too big, or I drank it too soon after the last dose. I feel an unwelcome side effect—orgasmic pleasure—coming on.

Tightening my grip on the lockpick until it hurts my fingers, I stab myself in the forearm.

"What the hell?" Felix exclaims. "What did you do *that* for?"

The camera on my lapel didn't catch me drinking the drug, so I can see why this would look odd on his end.

"Never mind that." Euphoria quickly annuls my pain, and I thank my lucky stars I took the time to sterilize all my equipment—or else this would end with me getting gangrene.

When I pull the lockpick out of my arm, the wound heals instantly, and best of all, no sign of pleasure remains.

There we go. I didn't enjoy that one bit—other than the boost of alertness that was my goal, and my libido skyrocketing to the levels of a teenage boy in a strip club.

"I thought your weirdness was limited to cleaning rituals," Felix says, his voice sounding bizarrely sexy in the vamp blood afterglow.

I don't reply. Instead, I take a quick internal scan to make sure no part of me is feeling the pull of the highly addictive substance.

With all my current problems, becoming a vampire-blood addict would be like jumping off a cliff after drowning myself in cyanide.

"I'm going in," I whisper and grasp the doorknob.

"What you're about to do is illegal on this world," Felix reminds me, as if I didn't already know that.

"What about hacking all those banks?" I hiss back. "You wouldn't like it if I lectured you about that."

Felix calls himself a technomancer. He can make silicone-based technology do his bidding, a power he wastes on feats that a regular—albeit very talented—human could pull off.

"Dream walking will not help you escape human prison," he replies. "Or survive it, for that matter."

"That's arguable." I decide against telling him about the time I gleaned one of his wet dreams, specifically the one where he fancied himself a guard getting attacked by suspiciously attractive female convicts. "If you've done your job properly, I shouldn't end up in prison."

"I can only take care of the smart alarm," he whispers. "If this Bernard guy is paranoid enough, he might have the older, dumb alarm set up as well, and it will blare as soon as you get inside. Or he might have a dog. Or he might even be awake."

I sneak a guilty peek at my wrist, where most people would see a furry bracelet. But it's actually a creature called a *looft*. Pom, as my looft likes to call himself, is sleeping as usual, but his pitch-black fur shows my inner turmoil. If I die, Pomsie dies with me—that's how our relationship works.

So I'll just have to not die.

Simple.

Turning my attention back to the heavy wooden door, I stroke Pom to calm myself down. When my hands have steadied and his fur has turned a more neutral shade of blue, I go ahead and pick the lock.

"Seriously, Bailey," Felix says right as I touch the

doorknob. "There's got to be better ways to make money. With your—"

I mute the earpiece. Obviously, there are more legit ways to earn the money I need—except those ways don't pay nearly as well as what my current employer is offering. I'm already a month behind on Mom's medical bills, and if I don't come up with two million cc—Gomorrahn crypto cash—in the next two weeks, they'll turn off her life support. There are no honest jobs that would let me make that kind of cash in the little time I have left. As is, I've had to forgo sleep in order to make ends meet. In fact, I haven't slept at all since Mom's accident four months ago—staying up naturally at first, then using pharmacological stimulants, then eventually resorting to vampire blood.

Reaching into my pocket, I grab one of my last two sleep grenades and twist the knob.

No alarm blares.

No dog barks.

No one shoots me dead with a gun.

Pressing the button on the grenade, I toss it into the apartment.

The sleeping gas hisses as it spreads throughout the place.

"That gas will go inert in two minutes," I whisper for Felix's benefit. "If there's a dog in there, or if Bernard was awake, they're asleep *now*."

I unmute the earpiece in time to hear Felix grumble something about "decent plan."

What he doesn't realize is the most dangerous part of this job might well be coming up.

I tiptoe inside the penthouse.

Alistair—the guy who hired me to do this—must pay Bernard well. The place is spacious, especially for New York, where real estate is nearly as pricey as on my home world of Gomorrah.

Locating the bedroom, I step inside and look at the bed.

Phew.

Bernard is in there, covered by a heavy blanket.

"Doesn't he look like Mario?" Felix whispers as I creep toward the bed.

When I first met Felix, we bonded over our love of video games, which makes his comparing a man to a digital plumber not as crazy as it sounds.

"To me, he looks more like Wario," I say, looking over the pudgy man's mustachioed face. "That's Mario's archrival."

"I know that," Felix says. "But neither of them has a scar like that."

He's right. The scar on Bernard's forehead belongs on the face of an interdimensional warrior, not a guy who's Head of Engineering at a VR company on Earth.

"So what now?" Felix asks.

"I have to touch him," I whisper. "But not in a dirty way."

Felix chuckles humorlessly as I examine my victim's eyelids for rapid eye movement and find none.

Crap.

I pull off my gloves and do my best to prepare for the unpleasantness that is to come. Specifically, the least risky part of what I'm about to attempt.

Skin-to-skin contact.

The bead of sweat trapped by the scar on Bernard's forehead doesn't help, nor does the stench of night breath emanating from my target's mouth.

"What are you waiting for?" Felix asks. "Is it your OCD again?"

"Caring about hygiene doesn't mean I have OCD." I touch the bottle of hand sanitizer in my pocket—my lifesaver in these types of situations. "Besides," I lie. "I mostly hesitate because he's not in REM sleep."

"Which means you'll have to do that dangerous subdream battle thing when you enter him?" Felix asks.

I huff. "That sounds way too rapey. I'm not going to 'enter him.' I'm just visiting his dreams. But yes, if the subdream battle thing kills dream-me, real-me will go insane."

Actually, that's an understatement. Not long before her accident, as a way to discourage me from using my powers, Mom showed me footage of what happened to one dream walker who died in the dream world. He went on a killing rampage, like a rabid puck, and even cannibalized his victims. I checked on this, and even years later, he has to be kept in a padded cell, in restraints.

"So you're going to wait until he goes into REM sleep?" Felix asks.

"Ideally."

"How long is that going to take?"

I sigh and look at my Earth phone. "Ninety minutes, if it was my gas that knocked him out."

I hear Felix clicking away on his keyboard. Then he says, "I see that he takes Ambien. I doubt it was your gas that put him under."

"Damn it." I resist the urge to kick the leg of the bed. "That drug suppresses REM sleep. I might have to come back later or—"

"Oh, crap," Felix says. "I think you're about to have company."

I spin around to face the door, my heart rate spiking as Pom's fur darkens on my wrist.

"It's vampires," Felix rattles out. "Enforcers. They have every exit covered. Running would be pointless."

Pucking puck. Why couldn't it be any other type of Cognizant? Vampires only sleep if they want to, so my remaining grenade won't knock them out—and I don't have any other weapons at my disposal.

"Can I hide?" I say, mostly to myself, as my gaze falls on the walk-in closet in the corner of the bedroom.

"They probably have your DNA," Felix says. "How else did they zero in on you with such laser precision?"

He's right. Even *I* didn't know I'd be here until I read my encrypted email an hour ago.

This is bad.

Armed with my DNA, a vampire could find me even if I ran to another world.

"What do they want?" I stroke Pom, trying not to panic.

"No idea," Felix says. "But I doubt they care about your breaking and entering."

"Arguable." I turn back toward Bernard. "Sounds like I have no choice. If I want to keep Mom's life support running, I go in, REM sleep or not."

"And I'll do my best to stall the Enforcers," Felix says. "I think I can make the elevator run slower, and maybe even—"

"Thanks." Ignoring the shaking of my hands, I pull out the hand sanitizer and judiciously apply it to Bernard's hairy forearm.

"Here goes nothing." I start reaching for the (hopefully) decontaminated patch of skin.

In a way, there are silver linings to this clusterpuck.

Firstly, if the subdream kills me and I go homicidally crazy in the real world, at least the vampires will put me down before I can cannibalize anyone.

Secondly, all this adrenaline is short-circuiting my usual thoughts of getting *Staphylococcus aureus* and other cooties as I touch my target.

I make connection with the sleeper, and the world of wakefulness goes away.

———

Dream Walker, the story of Bailey Spade, is coming soon! Sign up to my newsletter at www.dimazales.com to be notified when it becomes available.

ABOUT THE AUTHOR

Dima Zales is a *New York Times* and *USA Today* bestselling author of science fiction and fantasy. Prior to becoming a writer, he worked in the software development industry in New York as both a programmer and an executive. From high-frequency trading software for big banks to mobile apps for popular magazines, Dima has done it all. In 2013, he left the software industry in order to concentrate on his writing career and moved to Palm Coast, Florida, where he currently resides.

Please visit www.dimazales.com to learn more.